［美］潘维廉（William N. Brown）◎著　李晶◎译

老潘写给青少年的18封信

中英双语

CIPG
China Foreign Languages Publishing Administration
中国外文出版发行事业局

外文出版社
FOREIGN LANGUAGES PRESS

Contents
目 录

Chapter 2 Stories of China

第二章 中国故事

Chapter 3 Family Education

第三章 家庭教育

Chapter 4 Lessons from Prevention and Control of COVID-19

第四章 抗疫经验

Appendixes

Preface

I had no interest in China as a youth because my history and geography classes ignored Asia. My earliest dream was to live in remote, exotic Australia, but the Australian embassy replied to my immigration request, “We welcome men of vision like you but you must wait 10 years and reapply because the minimum age is 18 and you are only 8.”

Even at 20, when the U.S. Air Force sent me to Taiwan, I’d never met a Chinese, eaten Chinese food or used chopsticks, and still had no interest in Asia. But within my first month in Taiwan I had fallen for the people and culture, and when I left in 1978, I vowed to someday see the rest of China and learn Chinese. That dream took ten years.

In 1981, I met Susan Marie, a blond, blue-eyed American girl born and raised in Taiwan who also wanted to go to China. China quite literally was our matchmaker. That “made in Taiwan” American girl became my best friend and we were married in Taiwan that Christmas, though it was 1988 before we made it to Xiamen.

When we disembarked the 18 hour boat from Hong Kong to Xiamen in 1988, we found that Xiamen was a very beautiful island but living conditions weren't what we were used to in Southern California. It was not easy with two kids to cope with daily water and power outages and cycle all over the island for staples like toothpaste and toilet paper. But we loved the people, who embraced us so warmly that they even invited us to their homes on holidays. They had very little – even eggs were a luxury – but they shared generously. The people were happy and optimistic because, in spite of problems, life had never been better and they fully believed things would only get better. I too was optimistic, but I suspected we were planting trees so the next generation could enjoy the shade. I never imagined my own generation would see such sweeping changes.

My Personal China Story

As soon as I arrived in Xiamen in 1988, I began writing letters to family and friends to help them see the side of China ignored by foreign media. I avoided politics and talked about how Chinese lived, and how they shared with us the same hopes and dreams – peace, stability, and a better life for their descendants. By personalizing China, my friends also came to better appreciate the government because China's government, after all, is composed of China's people.

I also used humor and cartoons because, as Lin Yutang discovered, humor breaks barriers. Lin Yutang, a native of a village not far from Xiamen, invented the Chinese word for humor, yōumò, and he used cartoons in his stories and books to bridge the gap between East and

West. As Lin wrote so brilliantly on his 40th birthday:

> "One mind seeks the learning of ancients and moderns;
> Two legs straddle the cultures of East and West."[1]

No one bridged East and West better than Lin Yutang – at least according to the *New York Times*, which wrote in Lin's 1976 obituary:

> "Lin Yutang, poet, novelist, historian and philosopher, had no peer as an interpreter to Western minds of the customs, aspirations, fears and thoughts of his people and their country, China, the great and tragic land."

Mickey Mouse in "With Love and Irony"
Lin Yutang

My letters about life in China were only for family and friends, but within months they were being copied and read by hundreds of people. Even children wrote to ask such questions as how Chinese children played or studied, or what we ate. But not everyone liked my letters. An American professor wrote, "You should not write lightly (joke) about what you do not understand."

I replied, "If I only write about what I *do* understand, I'll have nothing to write about."

He wrote again one year later, "I just received your latest 'Off the

① Lin Yutang, *On the Wisdom of America*, The John Day Co., 1950.

Wall' letter. I look forward to them each month because you have a way of making China real..."

But the hardest reader to reach was my own father because he had spent 11 years in the U.S. Army fighting in Asia and was not keen on me living in a Communist country. But in August, 2004, the last time I saw him, he hugged me and said, "I finally understand why you moved to China, and I'm proud of you. It was the right thing."

It was worth writing hundreds of letters just to hear my dad's parting words.

In January, 2019, I was surprised and honored to receive a letter from President Xi Jinping about my book *Off the Wall* ②, a compilation of 47 of my letters. President Xi said he was confident I'd write even better stories in the future and I agree – but not because I'm a good writer. I agree only because China is such a great subject – but my stories are not enough. The world needs "your personal China Story" far more than mine.

Over the years I've told China's story in many ways – letters, books, TV programs, and programs encouraging foreigners to study or work in China. My best idea however, in my eyes at least, was a book of bilingual dialogues on Fujian history and culture that Chinese could practice on foreigners. But that book only covered Fujian, so I was delighted when Prof. Hu Min, CEO and founder of New Channel Education Group, asked me to help edit his 3-volume series, *Stories of China Retold in English*.

② *Off the Wall*: Short for *Off the Wall – How We Fell for China* published in 2018.

I could never have chosen better stories myself – from ancient tales of Chinese philosophers, artists, heroes and inventions to inspiring tales of New China's highways and hi-speed railways, space exploration, and the fight to end poverty. Prof. Hu Min then produced new translations of classics such as *The Analects of Confucius, Sunzi: The Art of War,* and *Tao Te Ching*. These beautifully illustrated books are not only bilingual but also have *Pinyin* with tones – which showed me, to my chagrin, that I've mispronounced some words for decades.

Since 2019, I've been honored to serve as the Ambassador for New Channel's Stories of China Retold in English. If you supplement your personal China Story with this series' carefully selected stories, you will never lack an audience of foreigners eager to learn firsthand about China, and you'll improve your English even as you help the world, and yourself, better understand China's rich heritage, its vast changes, and its hope for the future.

Telling Your Personal China Story in English

Yet in spite of China's vast changes, the world still knows little about China.

There are two reasons that China knows the world better than the world knows China. First, the Western media's portrayal of China is as politically biased today as it was when I was in Taiwan in the 1970s. Second, millions of Chinese have gone into the world but far fewer foreigners are coming to China.

Over 1/3 of the U.S.' 1 million international college students are Chinese, and over 30,000 Chinese study in American high schools (compared with 369 Chinese in 2005). But only 11,000 Americans studied in China during the 2017-2018 school year.

In 2015, President Xi Jinping and former U.S. President Obama announced the "One Million Strong" Initiative with its goal of one million K-12 American students learning Mandarin by 2020. Thanks in part to that program, more Americans than ever now study Chinese, yet in spite of China's importance in the world, the most popular foreign languages in the U.S. are still Spanish, French, German, Japanese and Italian, with Chinese way down the rung at No.7.

Since the world is not coming to China, we must take China's Story to the world – and not just through official channels. Foreigners distrust "official" propaganda but they are far more open to your personal China Story – both what you have experienced and also your own knowledge and perspective of China's rich past and present.

Telling your China Story in English is helpful in at least three ways:

1. It helps the world better understand China.

2. It helps you better understand your own history and culture. (I've been surprised to learn that many Chinese don't know that much about their own homeland's rich history and culture, or modern achievements.)

3. It helps you master oral English by guaranteeing you an audience of native English speakers, because any foreigner would love to hear about China firsthand from an English-speaking Chinese who is not only passionate about his homeland but also about its contributions to the global community.

Global Chinese Youth

For three decades, what has most impressed me about Chinese youth is their passion for learning and improving themselves, and their keen sense of patriotism while at the same time having the most global mindset of any young people I've met. Foreigners have long had the idea that China has been isolated from the world but history shows that this has never been true – especially with New China.

Chinese youth's most outstanding attribute is their confidence in the future – and they have two reasons for this. One, they trust their leadership, which has proven repeatedly that its priority is its people. Two – they are extremely diligent in preparing for the opportunities they expect China to provide. As the old saying goes, "The harder I work, the luckier I get."

When I first started teaching, I was amazed that my Chinese students knew more about American history than many Americans! They knew the dates of major events, and could even quote parts of Presidential speeches, the *Declaration of Independence* or the Constitution. I doubt I could find many American students who could quote from Chinese writings or speeches. And even before the internet, my students had a far better understanding of world affairs than the world had of Chinese affairs.

And over the years I've been encouraged to see that once Chinese do succeed, they use their wealth and experience to not only help their own homeland but also other nations – even as Chinese have done for centuries.

Two other traits of Chinese youth are gratefulness and loyalty – to family, friends, country – even teachers! Chinese say that if you teach someone, you're their teacher for life, and it seems true. Students I've not seen in 30 years write to me as if I taught them only yesterday. Chinese are grateful – and I too am grateful because I honestly believe that I've learned far more from Chinese youth than they have learned from me.

If the world can come to see Chinese youth as I have, it will have much more confidence in China because tomorrow's China is today's youth. So share your experiences as a Chinese youth who loves his homeland but also embraces China's positive role in the world. Share with foreign friends stories that they can readily identify with and relate to – stories of childhood and the values you learned from family (and, if you can, the cultural or historical stories behind them). Share your challenges in school – what you liked and what you were not so fond of but learned from anyway. Share your hobbies and your passions. Above all, share your dreams. We speak of the China Dream and the American Dream but in the end we all have the same dreams, though as a father and teacher in China for decades I've seen that East and West often pursue the same dreams in different ways, and each has its pros and cons.

As well as providing some insights on the pros and cons of Eastern and Western education, and on language learning, much of which I learned from watching my sons learn both Chinese and English, I would also like, in these 18 letters, to share my views on China's fight against COVID-19 and the importance of telling your China's stories. The four themes are:

1. How to improve your English. I love languages, and I'm happy that teens and adults can learn a second language at least as easily as children. The key is how you learn.

2. East vs. West Education. Raising two sons in China helped me see the strengths and weaknesses of both Eastern and Western education, and why we need to adopt the best of both worlds – though if I had to choose one over the other, I'd choose East over West.

3. COVID-19. I was not surprised at how quickly and efficiently the Chinese government and people worked together to bring this virus under control and to help other nations. If the world's most populous nation can use Precision Poverty Alleviation to eliminate absolute poverty in 2020, I'm not surprised it can also use precision to resolve any other problem it faces. And history shows us that Chinese ingenuity and industriousness is nothing new.

4. Telling Your personal China Story. Personalizing China through our own stories helps overcome foreigners' naive stereotypes and prejudices, but we must know not only the stories foreigners want to hear but also the stories they need to hear (even if they don't know it yet) – stories about China's rich past and present.

China knows the world, and if you can help the world to know China, perhaps the China Dream can become the World's Dream as well.

Dream!

Dr. Bill Brown

序言

年少时我对中国并没有兴趣，因为历史地理课没教给我多少有关亚洲的知识。我最初的梦想是到遥远且充满异国情调的澳大利亚去生活。但对于我的移民申请，澳大利亚大使馆却回复：“我们欢迎像你这样有远见卓识的人，但你必须等10年再来，因为申请者必须年满18岁，而你才8岁。”

直到20岁被美国空军派去台湾前，我还从未见过中国人，吃过中国菜，用过筷子，对亚洲了无兴趣。但来台湾不到1个月，我就爱上了那里的人和文化。1978年离开台湾时，我立下誓言，日后一定要去中国其他地方看看，并学习中文。那个梦10年之后实现了。

1981年，我遇到了金发碧眼的美国女孩——苏珊·玛丽。她在台湾出生长大，也梦想着去中国大陆。中国这片土地简直就是我们的媒人！这个“台湾制造”的美国女孩成了我最好的朋友，同年圣诞我们走进了婚姻殿堂，而我们动身去厦门却是1988年的事了。

从香港乘船辗转18个小时在厦门靠岸时，我们发现厦门是个风景优美的地方，但它的生活条件却“令人担忧”，没法和我们在南加州时相比。我们带着两个年幼的孩子不仅要应付日常的停水断电，还要应付牙膏、卫生纸等主要生活物品的稀缺，不时得骑着自行车在岛上四处搜寻，可真不容易。但我们喜欢那里的人们，他们待我们也非常热情，到了节假日还会邀请我们去他们家里做客。他们的经济并不宽裕，连鸡蛋都算奢侈品，但他们不吝与我们分享。他们幸福、乐观——尽管生活仍面临着诸多问题，但当时的日子比从前好多了，并且他们坚信一切只会更好。我也很乐观，相信我们这一代“种好树”下一代就能够“乘凉”，但从未想到仅在我们这一代就见证了如此巨大的发展成就。

我的中国故事

1988年一到厦门，我就开始给亲朋写信，向他们展示一个不同于外国媒体视角下的中国。我不谈政治，谈论的是中国人怎样过日子，谈论的是中国人和美国人有着相同的期望和梦想——和平、稳定，让子孙过上更好的生活。透过我眼中的中国，我的朋友们也变得更加理解中国政府，归根结底这个政府是由那里的人民组成的。

林语堂曾说，“幽默可以打破障碍”，于是我也在信中采用幽默的笔调，配上一些漫画。林语堂出生在厦门附近的一个村庄，创造了“幽默”这一中文用法，为了消除东西方隔阂，他喜欢在自己撰写的故事或书籍中添上几笔漫画。以下是他40岁生日时写下的妙言佳句：

“两脚踏东西文化，一心评宇宙文章。”[①]

他消弭了东西方文化的鸿沟，此举无人可与之比肩——至少在 1976 年《纽约时报》为林语堂刊登的讣告中可见一斑：

“林语堂，诗人、小说家、历史学家和哲学家，在向西方介绍其同胞的习俗、梦想、所思、所惧，以及他伟大而悲情的祖国时，无人能出其右。”

我在信中写的是我们在中国的生活，原本只是用来问候亲朋，但不到几个月，它们就被广泛复制，在众人间传开了。甚至有美国孩子会写信给我，问中国孩子是怎样玩耍、学习的，或者好奇我们吃什么。但也有人不喜欢我的来信。一位美国教授就写道：“你不该为了娱乐他人，对你不甚了解的事物信口雌黄。”

我答复道：“如果只写我了解的事物，我就无事可写了。”

一年后他又给我寄了一封信：“我刚收到你最近一封‘即兴而作’的信。我每个月都会期待你的来信，在你的笔下，中国变得真实起来……”

但最苛刻的读者是我的父亲。他曾随美军驻亚洲 11 年，对于我到一个社会主义国家生活一直心有不悦。但在 2004 年 8 月我们最后一次见面时，他拥抱着我说：“我终于明白你为什么会搬去

① 林语堂 . 美国的智慧【M】. 纽约：庄台公司，1950.

中国，我为你感到骄傲。你的选择是对的！”

仅是父亲的这番临别之言，就值得我写上几百封信了。

2019年1月，习近平主席就我的新书《我不见外》②寄来回信，让我倍感荣幸。这本书是从我写给亲朋的信中挑选47封编撰而成。在习主席的回信里，他说道：“我相信，你将会见证一个更加繁荣进步、幸福美好的中国，一个更多造福世界和人类的中国，你笔下的中国故事也一定会更精彩。” 我十分认同习主席的看法，但这无关乎我的写作水平，只是因为中国本就是一个伟大的话题，但我的故事还远远不够。世界更加需要你们每个人的中国故事。

这些年，我用过许多方式讲中国故事，包括写信、出书、拍电视节目、写外国人“在中国生活指南”等。我最好的创意，至少在我自己看来是如此，是以双语对话的形式写了一本介绍福建历史文化的书，方便中国人和外国人练习英语。但那本书仅介绍了福建，所以当新航道国际教育集团的首席执行官兼创始人胡敏教授邀请我编辑三大本《用英语讲中国故事》时，我感到非常高兴。

这些是我见过的最好的中国故事——不仅有对古代哲人、艺术家、英雄人物、创造发明的介绍，还传播了当代中国公路高铁建设、太空探索、消灭贫困等激动人心的事迹。

2019年我开始荣任新航道“用英语讲中国故事”活动形象大使。在我看来，如果你的中国故事里能增添一些这样精心挑选的元素，你将永远不乏渴望直接了解中国的外国听众。此外，在帮助世界以及自身更加了解中国的过去、现在以及将来的同时，还能提升自己的英语水平。

② 《我不见外》：潘维廉于2018年出版的图书《我不见外——老潘的中国来信》。

用英语讲述你的中国故事

尽管中国社会日新月异，但世界对她仍知之甚少。

中国和世界彼此了解不对等，原因有二：其一，今天西方媒体对中国的刻画和我70年代在台湾时听到的西方报道带有同样的政治偏见；其二，大批中国人走出了国门看世界，但来中国看看的外国人却远少于此。

目前，在美就读的100万国际大学生中，中国学生占比三分之一以上；中学阶段，中国留学生超过3万名（2005年仅为369名）。但2017—2018学年，来华留学的美国学生却只有1.1万名。

2015年，习近平主席和美国前总统奥巴马宣布了“百万强计划”，提出到2020年美国中小学生学习普通话的人数达到百万。某种程度上正是得益于该计划，美国学习汉语的人数达到了历史最高峰。但和中国瞩目的国际地位形成反差的是，汉语课在美国仅为第七大语言课程，位列最受欢迎的外语课程——西班牙语、法语、德语、日语和意大利语之后。

既然世界还没主动走向中国，我们就必须将中国故事讲给世界听——不仅仅是通过官方渠道。外国人对“官方”宣传缺乏信任，对你个人的中国故事却大为欢迎，比如你个人的经历、你对自己国家丰富历史的了解、对今天日新月异的中国社会的看法等。

用英语讲述你的中国故事至少能起到以下三个作用：

1. 帮助世界更好地了解中国。

2. 帮助你更好地了解自己国家的历史、文化。（我就惊讶地发现不少中国人对自己国家丰富的历史文化、伟大的现代成就鲜有了解。）

3. 确保你能吸引母语为英语的听众，从而帮助你掌握英语口语。任何外国人都拒绝不了那些热爱自己国家并对它的世界贡献感到骄傲的中国人用英语介绍自己的祖国。

世界的中国青年

30 年来，中国青年给我留下最为深刻印象是，他们不仅对掌握新知识、提升自己充满热情，还具有深厚的爱国主义情怀；同时，在我所见过的年轻人中，他们拥有最全球化的思维模式。长期以来，外国人一直认为中国是孤立于世界之外的，但历史告诉我们，从来就不是如此——尤其是新中国成立以后。

中国青年最为突出的特点是，他们对未来充满信心。这有两个原因：第一，他们相信自己的领导人，这也再次证明这个国家将人民的利益放在首位；第二，他们非常努力，时刻为渴望的时代机遇做准备。正如俗话所说："越努力，越幸运。"

刚走上讲台时，我就惊讶地发现，我的中国学生竟然比许多美国人更了解美国历史！他们不仅对美国重大历史事件的发生时间了如指掌，甚至对总统演讲、《独立宣言》或宪法也能加以引用。但我无法确保能找到许多可引用中文著作或演讲的美国学生。早在互联网兴起前，我的那批中国学生对世界的了解就远超世界对中国的了解。

这些年来，令我深受鼓舞的是，中国人一旦获得成功，不仅会利用自己的财富、经验帮助同胞，还会帮助其他国家和民族——就像几个世纪以来中国人所做的那样。

中国青年的另外两个特点是，对家人、朋友、国家，甚至老师都心怀感激、持有忠诚！中国人说“一日为师终身为师”，看来这是真的。比如30年未见面的学生会用信件给我捎来问候，就像他们昨天才毕业一样。中国人懂感恩——我也如此，我打心底认为，中国青年教给我的远比我教给他们的多得多。

如果对中国青年持有与我相同的看法，世界将增加它对中国的信心，因为这些青年就是这个国家的未来。因此，热爱自己国家、为它在世界发挥的积极作用深感自豪的中国青年，向世界分享你们的故事吧；让外国朋友听一听那些让他们感同身受、与之共鸣的故事，如童年生活、家庭价值观（如果可以，还可以分享它们折射出的历史、文化）；分享你们在学校遇见的挑战，无论是令人欣然接受的，还是令人“排斥”但具有启发性的；分享你们爱好和热衷的事物。最重要的是，分享你的梦想。我们谈论中国梦，谈论美国梦，但最终谈论的是同样的梦。作为一名在中国生活了几十年的美国爸爸和老师，我发现东西方的梦想常殊途同归，方式各有利弊。

在这18封信中，我将提供自己对东西方教育利弊以及语言学习的看法，这些看法多基于我对两个儿子双语学习的观察，此外，我还想分享我对中国抗击新冠病毒以及讲述你的中国故事重要性的看法。这四个主题如下：

1. 提高英语水平的方法。我喜欢语言，欣慰于青少年、成年人能像儿童一样轻松地学习第二语言。学习方法是关键。

2. 东西方教育。在中国抚养两个儿子让我看到了东西方教育的利弊，以及需要互补的原因——如果只能二选一，我会选择前者而不是后者。

3. 新冠病毒。我一点也不惊讶中国政府和中国人民能携手迅速有效地将新冠病毒控制，并向其他国家提供帮助。这个人口最多的国家如果能在 2020 年精准扶贫消除绝对贫困，我便不再惊讶它用精准的方式解决其他任何问题！历史上，中华民族历来就以聪明勤奋著称于世。

4. 讲述你的中国故事。讲述我们自己的故事，让中国个性化起来，这将有助于外国人消除心中无知的成见和偏见。为此，不仅要清楚他们想听的，还要了解他们需要听的（哪怕他们还未意识到这一点），如中国丰富的历史、日新月异的今天。

中国了解世界，而如果你能帮助世界了解中国，那么中国梦也许就成了世界梦。

坚持梦想！

潘维廉博士

Chapter 1
English Learning

第一章
英语学习

扫一扫

看老潘读信视频

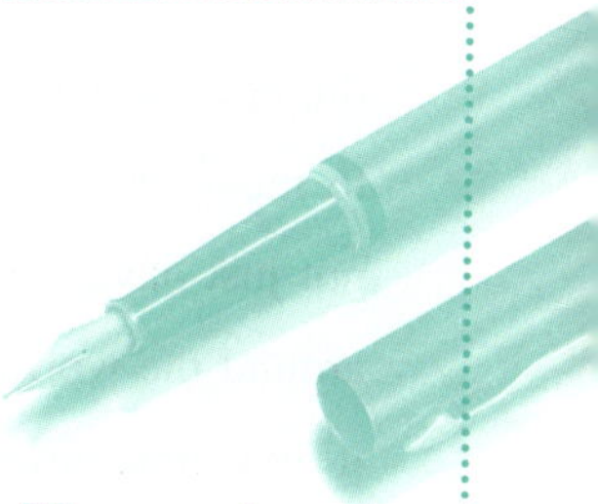

Three Secrets to Mastering Spoken English!

March 13, 2020

Dear Chinese friends,

We hope you are safe and well – and using this time fruitfully to hone your English with many of the online programs. English is important to you, and your career, but it's also important to help you tell China's story to the world.

And speaking of English, today I want to tell you 3 No Fail Secrets to Improving Oral English!

First of all – are you motivated to improve your Spoken English? If yes, hold your hand up until I ask the next question. Is your hand up? Now, keep your hand up if you spend at least 20 minutes a day practicing, aloud, your spoken English.

Wow – even from here I can see hands go down! If your hand went down, you are not motivated!

"But I am motivated," some students complain. "I just have no time or environment."

Nonsense! If you were motivated, you would find time or create the environment. What exactly is motivation? We cheapen the word to mean "hope" or "desire," but that is only part of it. Motivation is not just daydreaming. The world is full of daydreamers – like people around the world who talk about ending poverty but do nothing about it. In China, however, a core belief has been that a modestly prosperous Socialist society cannot coexist with poverty – so China has fought poverty since Liberation in 1949; now that is motivation.

So motivation is the internal and external forces that arouse enthusiasm and persistence to pursue a goal.

Desire is important, but if you do not persist it is not motivation, just wishing, or daydreaming.

MBA students told me, "We really have no time!" So I encouraged them to speak to each other in only English during the 20-minute walk to the dorm, or during a 20-minute break. "We'll do it!" they said. But after a few minutes, they were back to using Chinese. "We're tired," they said. "We need the rest."

"I do understand," I said. "But if you were truly motivated, this would be a priority and you'd make the time daily for it. And not a lot of time!" Many people start out with a couple hours a day and quickly burn out. Better to set a smaller, reachable goal that you can stick to. Learn a little but use it a lot.

Marathons teach a lot about motivation. Every year, the day after the Xiamen marathon, many people are out running because they watched the race and want to run it themselves next year. A week later, fewer people are running. After a month, the only ones running each morning are those who run the marathon every year anyway because they have motivation. So, they have persistence.

Xiamen Int'l Marathon 2004!

But I have met some Chinese language learners who did have motivation. In 1988, I met Professor Ji Yuhua, who is now famous even outside China. His English was as good as mine.

Professor Ji had never been overseas and he had few foreign friends, but every day he listened to audio tapes and radio and repeated it. He was busy but he practiced his English, aloud, while doing other things – walking, cycling, cooking or cleaning (he was henpecked like me). Today, if you see someone talking to themselves, you assume they aren't crazy; they're just talking on a phone. Back then, we didn't have cell phones. We barely even had landline phones. So when people saw Ji walking down the road talking aloud to himself, they probably thought he was crazy – especially when he answered himself!

Ji was very busy but he creatively made time, and made an environment. Today, he has taught on CCTV and has traveled to many countries to tell China's story in English – even singing Chinese opera in English!

I remember MBA Professors who spoke good English asking me how to get their children to learn English. I think they just hoped I'd teach them, but I asked, "Do you speak to your children in English?"

"Oh, no!" they'd say. "They don't want to talk in English to their parents!"

They weren't really motivated, just wishful. But Prof. Ji was so motivated for his 3-year-old daughter to learn English that he only spoke to her in English, even if she cried.

"How cruel!" Chinese neighbors said. "How will she ever learn Chinese?"

"Nonsense!" he'd say. "Her mom and grandparents speak Chinese; other children speak Chinese. I'm the only one who only speaks English to her!"

Now that is motivation!

So the first secret to improving spoken English is motivation – which is desire plus persistence. But there is another very important secret!

Many students ask me, "Professor Brown, how can I improve my spoken English?" They're looking for some trick or secret – so I tell them the secret.

"Do you really want to know the secret?" I asked.

"Yes, I do! Please tell me!"

I lower my voice, look around, and say softly: "The secret to improving your Spoken English is to... SPEAK ENGLISH!"

Chinese students, like language students around the world, have two problems. One, they lack motivation to persist long-term. Two, they spend most of their time reading and writing; they don't speak aloud. If you'd learned Chinese that way, you would not be speaking Chinese today!

Ten hours a day of reading and writing will not improve your spoken English one bit because Spoken English is a physical activity. You have to speak aloud, move your mouth and tongue to get used to the motions. That's why Prof. Ji's English was perfect – he listened to English all day, regardless of what he was doing, and repeated everything aloud!

Of course, Prof. Ji is a smart guy – but if you learned a first language, you can learn a second one. But you have to learn the second spoken language the same way you learned your first – by speaking it aloud, unafraid of making mistakes. Do this and you will improve. 100% guaranteed. The best proof is my granddaughter.

When my granddaughter Kate was only 3, she spoke Chinese, English and Spanish because my son Matthew only spoke Chinese to her, his wife, who studied medical Spanish, only spoke Spanish to her, and other children spoke English. Of course, she did make mistakes. I remember her using all 3 languages in one sentence: I want to chuān *zapatos*① – I want to wear shoes. But who cares about mistakes? That's how you learn, and if someone laughs at your mistakes, that's their problem, not yours.

When I drove 40,000 km around China in 1994, in remote Gansu and Sichuan, I met two young men who both spoke great English, better than university students, even though neither had finished high school

① It is spanish for shoes.

and neither had ever met a foreigner! Their secret?

They dreamed of learning English, even though they never thought they'd be able to use it, so they learned it exactly the same way as Prof. Ji – listening to audio all day and repeating, aloud, what they heard.

I was so impressed by these youth. I think China should scour the countryside for such talented youth and give them opportunities.

In conclusion, those are two Secrets to learning any spoken language. You need motivation – which isn't just wishing or hoping – and motivation includes persistence. And you need to get your nose out of the books and learn to speak English by SPEAKING English.

But there is one last secret. Unless you are extremely disciplined (do you spend at least 20 minutes a day on English?), then you, like most people, need some external accountability.

It is hard to stick to a goal alone, just as it is easier for a marathon runner to finish the race if he runs with a friend who will encourage him to keep up the pace. In the same way, it is good to have someone who will ask, "How have you done today? This week?" This can be your teacher or classmates, or friends and family with whom you've shared your goals.

If you really want to consistently improve your English, I dare you to make yourself accountable to someone.

Motivation, method (improve spoken English by speaking English!), and accountability. These three, and being consistent – learn a little and use it a lot – and you too will master English like Prof. Ji, the youth in Gansu or Sichuan, or my 3-year-old granddaughter.

And improving English will not only help you with your career, regardless of what field you pursue, but also help you to better tell China's story to the world!

Stay healthy and safe.

Àipīn cáihuì yíng!

Bill Brown

Quotes from Lao Pan:

老潘金句:

Desire is important, but if you do not persist it is not motivation, just wishing, or daydreaming.

渴望很重要,但没有坚持就不叫动力,那只是愿望,或者是白日梦。

That's how you learn, and if someone laughs at your mistakes, that's their problem, not yours.

这就是你学习的方式。如果有人为此嘲笑你,那是他们的问题,而不是你的。

掌握英语口语的三大秘诀！

亲爱的中国朋友们：

希望你们一切安好，并在疫情期间通过丰富的线上教学卓有成效地提高英语水平。英语对你们来说非常重要，不仅在今后的事业上，对于你们向世界讲述中国故事也是大有帮助。

说到英语，今天我想跟大家分享三大屡试不爽的提升英语口语水平的秘诀！

首先，你有动力提高你的英语口语吗？如果有，请举手，在我提下一个问题前，别放下。你举手了吗？现在，每天至少花 20 分钟大声练习英语口语的请举手。

哇，仅在这，我就能发现举手的同学变少了！如果手放下去了，就说明你没有动力！

“我很有动力呀，只是没有时间和练习环境罢了。”一些学生抱怨道。

这完全没道理！如果你有动力，你就会挤出时间，创造环境。动力到底是什么？我们习惯把它等同于“希望”或“渴望”，但后两者仅是它的一部分。它也不是白日梦。到处都有做白日梦的人，例如世上那些要求消除贫困对此却毫无作为的人。而在中国，消除贫困、建设社会主义小康社会是人们的核心信仰，所以自 1949 年新中国成立以来他们就一直与贫困做斗争。这就是有动力！

动力激发人们追求目标的热情和毅力，这是源自内部或外部的力量。

渴望很重要，但没有坚持就不叫动力，那只是愿望，或者是白日梦。

我 MBA 的一些学生告诉我，他们真的很忙！所以，我鼓励他们在步行回宿舍的那 20 分钟，或者在一段 20 分钟的休息时间里，只用英语交谈。他们对此信誓旦旦。但没一会，他们就切回了汉语，理由是累了需要休息。

我说："我当然明白，但如果你真有动力，就会优先考虑它，每天腾出时间练习。但我不建议花太多时间练习！"不少人起初斗志高昂，每天练上几小时，但如此以来倦怠感也来得快。最好是设定一个你能坚持且易实现的小目标。学到一点，就反复练习。

对比马拉松赛事，我们对动力就会有更深刻的认识。每年厦门马拉松比赛结束后，第二天会涌现出许多跑步的人。他们因为观看了比赛，便萌生来年参赛的想法。但一周后，跑步的人就变少了。一个月后，每天晨跑的又只剩下那些年年参赛的人——他们心中有动力，所以能坚持行动。

我在中国确实也遇到了动力十足的英语学习者，如我在 1988 年认识的纪教授，他现已享誉海外。那时他的英语就和我的一样好了。

纪教授尽管从未去过海外，也没有几个外国朋友，但他每天坚持听磁带录音、听收音机，并进行跟读。他工作虽然繁忙，但他会利用散步、骑自行车、做饭或打扫卫生等空闲时间大声练习英语（他和我一样是个妻管严）。今天，你如果看到有人在自言自语，你不会认为他是疯子，知道他是在打电话。但我们那时，不仅没有手机，就连座机也是个稀罕物。所以那时纪教授走在路上大声自言自语时，可能会有人认为他疯了，尤其是听到他自问自答的时候！

他不以忙作为借口，反而想办法腾出时间，给自己制造好的练习环境。因此，他不仅在央视开过讲，还到许多国家用英语讲过中国故事，甚至还能用英语演唱中国戏剧呢！

我记得一些说着流利英语的 MBA 教授，也曾问我让孩子学习英语的方法。我想他们只是希望我给出答案，但我却提出了问题："你们会用英语和孩子说话吗？"

他们往往会说："哦，不会！他们不愿和父母用英语交流！"

其实，这些教授（在孩子学习英语上）没有强劲的动力，只是一厢情愿罢了。但说到纪教授对于他 3 岁女儿的英语学习，可以说积极性很高，即使小女孩为此哭闹不愿配合，他仍旧坚持只用英语和她交流。

我的一些中国邻居抱怨道："真残酷！这样她怎么会愿意学习汉语呢？"

他反驳道："这完全没道理！她的妈妈、祖父母都对她说汉语，其他孩子也对她说汉语。我是唯一一个只跟她说英语的人！"

这就是动力！

所以，提高英语口语水平的第一大秘诀就是找到动力——既渴望又能坚持。但这只是其一！

不少学生问我："潘教授，怎样才能提高英语口语水平呢？"他们在找窍门、秘诀，所以我如实相告。

"你真想知道？"我问。

"是的！请教给我吧！"

于是我环顾四周，轻声说道："提高英语口语水平的秘诀就是……开口说英语！"

和其他国家的语言学习者一样，中国的语言学习者也有两大问题：第一，缺乏长期坚持的动力；第二，大部分时间都在读写，缺乏大声练习。如果你这样学习汉语，你的汉语口语能力肯定也不行！

每天读写 10 小时却不见英语口语水平有丁点提高，是因为英语口语是一项体力活，你必须大声练习，让嘴舌适应这些发音动作。这也是纪教授能讲一口流利英语的原因——不管是否事务缠身，他都坚持听英语，并且大声跟读！

当然，这和纪教授天资聪颖不无关系。但如果你学会了第一语言，你就可以学习第二语言。并且，学习第二口语时就该像学第一口语那样，大声地说出来，不要害怕犯错。这样，你就会得到进步。这种方法绝对是有效的。我孙女凯特就是很好的例子。

她 3 岁时就会说汉语、英语和西班牙语，因为我儿子马修只跟她说汉语，我那学习医用西班牙语的媳妇只跟她说西班牙语，别的小孩同她说英语。当然，她会犯错。我记得她曾在"我想穿（chuān）鞋（*zapatos*[①]）"这句话里就使用了 3 种语言。但谁会

① 西班牙语的"鞋"。

在乎呢？这就是你学习的方式。如果有人为此嘲笑你，那是他们的问题，不是你的。

1994 年，我驱车 4 万公里环游中国，在内陆省份甘肃四川地区时，我遇到两位英语说得很棒的年轻人，他们的英语水平甚至高过许多大学生，但他们连高中都没有上完，之前也没见过外国人！那他们的秘诀是什么呢？

尽管他们未曾想过能用上英语，但他们一直怀揣学好英语的梦想。于是，他们采用了和纪教授相同的方式学英语——整天听录音，并大声跟读。

这些年轻人给我留下了深刻的印象。我认为中国应该在农村地区挖掘这类优秀人才，并给他们提供施展才能的机会。

总之，这两大秘诀放之四海而皆准。你需要找到自身动力，了解这不仅是愿望或希望，还需要坚持。别只顾埋头书本，大声开口练习吧！

接下就讲到最后一个秘诀了。除非有着强大的自制力（看看自己能坚持每天至少花 20 分钟学习英语吗？），否则你就和大多数人一样，需要外部督促。

独自一人坚持目标并不容易，就像马拉松运动员有朋友在身旁鼓劲时，相对而言，他们能更容易完成比赛。同样，如果有人关注你每天、每周的学习状况，对你也是有利的。这些关注你的人，可能是你的老师、同学，也可能是与你有共同目标的朋友和家人。

如果真想不断提高英语水平，就问问自己敢不敢接受外部督促。

挖掘动力，找到方法（通过说英语来提高英语口语水平），接受外部督促。记住这三大秘诀，并且坚持采用“学会一点就反复练习"的方式，你们也会像纪教授一样，像我在甘肃四川遇到的那两位年轻人一样，或者像我3岁的孙女那样，把英语学得很好。

无论你梦想的领域是什么，良好的英语水平不仅会促进你事业的发展，还能帮助你更好地向世界讲述中国故事！

多多保重！

爱拼才会赢！

潘维廉

2020年3月13日

Quote from Lao Pan:

老潘金句：

If 25 was old, I was positively ancient when I came to China as a 32-year-old to pursue my China Dream of learning Chinese, and I was disappointed to find that my oldest classmate was only 20.

如果25岁就算老，32岁到中国追寻汉语梦的我，实在是太老了。当时班上年纪最大的同学也只不过20岁，令我这名"高龄"学生再次受挫。

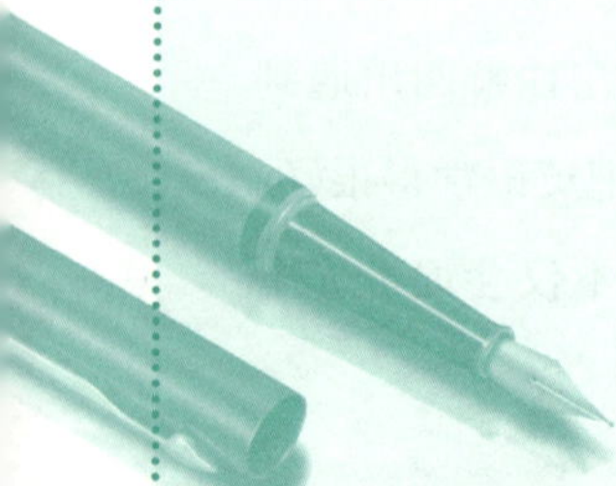

扫一扫
看老潘读信视频

Why Adults Can Learn Languages Faster than Children

May 5, 2020

Dear Chinese friends,

I had hoped that studying linguistics in graduate school would help me learn new languages faster, but I still struggled. I was disappointed when a respected linguist told me, "At 25, you're too old to learn a second language. Children's brains are hardwired for language learning but adults outgrow that ability."

If 25 was old, I was positively ancient when I came to China as a 32-year-old to pursue my China Dream of learning Chinese, and I was disappointed to find that my oldest classmate was only 20.

But my experience in China, which has been confirmed by much research, is that adult failure at learning a second language is rooted not in biology but in method. MIT scientists' research of almost 700,000 Americans showed that language learning ability does not decline until age 17 to 18[①] – well after the brain has fully developed. This suggests

① Hartshome, Tenenbaum, Pinker, "A Critical Period for Second Language Acquisition: Evidence from 2/3 Million English Speakers," *Cognition*, Vol. 177, August 2018, pp. 263-277.

the decline is rooted not in biology but in factors such as lifestyle and study method. For one thing, at age 18, life's pace and pressures ramp up as we enter college or the workforce, leaving us less time for learning a language.

But even in the 1960s, as experts like Lenneberg argued that children's brains were more "plastic," other experts argued that adults could learn languages even better than children. In 1964, Dr. Ausubel of the University of Illinois, wrote that "adults can acquire new languages more readily than can children." He also disputed the notion that children learn languages easily:

> "To begin with, we must appreciate the fact that the child does not learn his native language with phenomenal ease and rapidity. Quite the contrary! His acquisition of his native tongue is a long, slow, and arduous process, and despite exceeding strong motivation to learn so that he can communicate with adults and peers."②

Children only appear to improve rapidly and easily because they learn without being taught, but they are immersed in the environment morning to night and focus entirely on oral language because they can't yet read or write. Even so, it usually takes a child 5 to 6 years to obtain a child's vocabulary, whereas adults only studying part-time often

② Ausubel, David, "Adults Versus Children in Second-Language Learning: Psychological Considerations," *The Modern Language Journal*, Vol. 48, No. 7, November 1964, pp. 420-424.

master a language in a year or two.

Although there is probably no biological basis for children learning faster than teens or adults, there is, unfortunately, a social factor – the "fear of failure" that hits all of us at about age 7.

Research on 16,000 American children showed that 98% ages 3 to 5 are "creative geniuses."③ At that age, my sons reminded me of kittens. I doubt there's a sane kitten on the planet that can resist a rolling ball or a dangling piece of string. In the same way, children are born with an insatiable curiosity about their new world and need no prodding whatsoever from adults to eagerly learn new words, phrases and sentences about anything that interests them – at least until they enter school and learn to fear failure.

A five-year-old doesn't fear looking foolish by repeating the same "stupid question." By age 7, however, we've all felt embarrassed after giving the teacher a wrong answer, or being laughed at by other children, and over time we repress our outward expressions of that glorious creativity that sets us apart from all other species.

By age 8-10, the percentage of "creative geniuses" has plummeted from 98% to 32%; by age 13 to 15, it has fallen to 10%; by age 25 it is less than 2% and we've joined the herd, content to chew our cud until we're 65 and put out to pasture.

This repression of creativity and outward expression explains why teenage and adult language learners the world over face the same problem. We excel at reading and writing because we can read and write

③ Land and Jarmen, *Breakpoint and Beyond*, 1993.

safely, in silence, but we fare poorly at oral skills because we're afraid to open our mouths. Many Chinese have told me, "I'm afraid foreigners will laugh if I make a mistake."

"Who cares?" I ask. "I'm not fluent but I'm fluid; I let it flow until I get it right!"

Chinese often say, "Your Chinese is so good!" but I don't get a swelled head over it because Chinese are so polite that they'll compliment me even after I've greeted them with "Your horse is good!" instead of "How are you?" (A common mistake my first year.) But then they ask me, "How can I improve my spoken English?"

I peer left and right, then lean close to my questioner and whisper, "You want the secret to mastering spoken English?"

"Oh, yes!" they reply, eyes alight as they lean towards me conspiratorially.

I reply, "The secret to improving spoken English is to SPEAK ENGLISH!"

I'm not joking. Even a child could not improve their oral language by sticking their noses in a book for 10 hours a day because a spoken language is physical as well as mental. Our mouths, lips and tongues move in unfamiliar ways, and until we've practiced aloud so much that the movements become second nature, speaking a second language can tie up our tongues faster than a tongue-twister in our native language.

But fortunately for us adults, research increasingly reinforces the fact that if we do invest the time and energy and use proper methods, we can learn a new language as easily as a child can – or even outperform children!

"Research comparing children to adults has consistently demonstrated that adolescents and adults perform better than young children under controlled conditions."④

But I learned this myself in 1988 when I watched my two-year-old and six-month old sons learn both Chinese and English at home while I struggled in the classroom.

Learning was easier for my sons in part because they chose to learn words and sentences about their own interests. My youngest son Matthew's first word was "Mom!" and I waited with baited breath for "Dad!" but his second word was "ball!" Matt was passionate about balls and sports even before his first birthday, and passion is motivational. With no prompting from his parents, Matthew rapidly learned everything he wanted to say in both English and Chinese about sports, and sports was the springboard to fluency in other subjects. I marveled as I watched Matt learn words and string them together in different ways. He made amusing mistakes but he wasn't yet old enough to be embarrassed so he pressed on.

He once asked at dinner, "Dad, how do you say 'cài' in Chinese?"

"Matthew, 'cài' is Chinese."

"Well, then how do you say 'cài' in English?"

My sons took to Chinese like ducks to water but my own experience was far different. I rose at 4 AM every morning to memorize that day's 15 to 20 new characters. I then helped Sue with the boys' breakfasts, cycled to XMU and spent all morning and afternoon in

④ https://effectivelanguagelearning.com/language-learning-tips/language-learning-myths.

classes, then fixed my bike (it broke daily), cycled home to help Sue with dinner, did homework until 10 or 11 PM, and crashed into bed. Exhausting.

No wonder my sons learned Chinese faster than me, but I eventually surpassed them both when I changed both motivation and methods.

My dream of learning Chinese language and culture began when I was in the U.S. Air Force in Taiwan in the 1970s but my only motivation was curiosity about China's rich history and culture. I had no plans to actually use Chinese in a career, so after struggling in an XMU classroom for 3 months, I jumped at the opportunity to put my studies on hold for a year or two to help start XMU's MBA program – and my motivation for learning Chinese grew rapidly.

My students spoke English but everyone else spoke only Chinese, so my motivation was pure survival – the same motivation as a child's. Young Shannon and Matt were forced to learn English and Chinese to communicate with those around them, and I was forced to learn Chinese to survive. I kept a journal in which I jotted down useful words or phrases on how to mail a letter, use ration coupons at the cafeteria, get my salary from the bank, pay to board the bus. Each day, I "learned a little but used it a lot" on everyone I met, friends and strangers alike. And the more I learned, the more curious I became about Chinese history, culture, humor, legends.

To many people's surprise, including my own, my Chinese surpassed my sons' – at least for a few years. But as MIT reported 30 years later, adults have several advantages over children when it comes to learning languages or anything else.

In Scott Chacon's, "MIT Scientists prove adults learn language to fluency nearly as well as children," he quoted an excerpt from the MIT paper, "A Critical Period":

> "Studies that compare children and adults exposed to comparable material in the lab or during the initial months of an immersion program show that adults perform better, not worse, than children (Huang, 2015; Krashen, Long, & Scarcella, 1979; Snow & Hoefnagel-Höhle, 1978), perhaps because they deploy conscious strategies and transfer what they know about their first language.
>
> "...What is remarkable about language is that we are (nearly) all extremely good at it, including adult learners."

Unlike children, who are easily distracted and may forget tomorrow what excites them today, adults usually have a purpose for learning a new language, and purpose, like passion, can be a powerful motivation that leads to a focus, self-discipline and determination that most children lack.

Another advantage for adults is that over time our brains become even more skilled at complex thought, and adults can compare and contrast the new language with their mother tongue. Children, however, are working with a blank slate – which is why it takes them 4 or 5 years, 24/7, to gain the language proficiency of a kindergartner.

In a language learning experiment by Ferman and Avi Karni from the University of Haifa, Israel, "The adults were consistently better in everything we measured."⑤

If children do surpass adults at learning, it's largely because adults' lives are busier with many distractions and competing priorities, but we can alter our environment to help us focus.

At XMU, I transformed a corner of our bathroom into a tiny learning cubicle with books, photos of China and a flag. That small sanctum helped me shut out the world and focus. Another advantage of my WC Office was that, given my frequent intestinal bouts during that first year, it was handy having a desk only one meter from the toilet.

Three decades in China have proven to me what scientists are increasingly recognizing – that I wasn't too old at 32 to learn a new language, and I'm still learning even at twice that age because I know that our learning ability actually improves with age – but only if we choose our approach wisely and strategically. And one of the most powerful language learning methods that I've found, especially in China, is the ancient art of storytelling – which I'll share about next time.

Good evening from Amoy (Xiamen)!

Bill Brown

⑤ De Lange, Catherine, "Age No Excuse for Failing to Learn a New Language," *New Scientist*, 20 July 2011.

Young Bill on a campus of Xiamen University, 2002
年轻的老潘在厦门大学校园（2002 年）

Bill singing with his students, 1989
老潘和学生们一起唱歌（1989 年）

Bill discussing with his MBA students, 1989
老潘与厦门大学 MBA 班学生（1989 年）

成年人比儿童
能更快掌握一门语言的原因

亲爱的中国朋友们：

研究生阶段，我曾希望通过研究语言学帮助自己学习新语言，但我学起来仍十分吃力。一位受人敬重的语言学家告诉我："你25岁太大了，不适合学第二语言。儿童在学习语言方面更出色，成年人随着年纪增长逐渐失去这项能力。"这番话真令我气馁。

如果25岁就算老，32岁到中国追寻汉语梦的我，实在是太老了。当时班上年纪最大的同学也只不过20岁，令我这名"高龄"学生再次受挫。

但我学习汉语的经验表明，成年人学不好第二语言不在于年龄而是方法，这在许多研究中已得到证实。麻省理工的科学家对近70万美国人进行了一项研究，表明人的语言学习能力直到十七八岁才会下降[①]，即在大脑充分发育后。该研究认为，能力下降的原因不在于生理状况，在于生活方式、学习方法等因素。原因之

① 哈茨霍恩，特南鲍姆，平克．二语习得的关键期：基于近67万英语使用者的调查【J】．认知，2018-8（177）：263-277.

一是，18岁后我们开始上大学或工作，这时生活节奏变快，生活压力变大，语言学习时间就变少了。

到了20世纪60年代，尽管勒纳伯格（Lenneberg）等专家仍旧认为儿童的大脑更具“可塑性”，但已有专家指出成年人比儿童能更出色地学习语言。1964年，伊利诺伊大学的奥苏贝尔（Ausubel）博士写道：“成年人比儿童更容易掌握新语言。”他还反驳了儿童能轻松学好语言的观点：

> “首先，我们必须认识到，儿童学习母语的过程并不是惊人地轻松和快速。恰恰相反！他们习得母语的过程实则是漫长、缓慢、艰辛的，这还是在他们为了和大人、同龄人进行交流、学习动力超强的前提下。”②

儿童的进步只是看似快速轻松，这仅仅是因为他们不是被教会的，而是通过整天沉浸在语言环境中，并且由于他们还不具备读写能力，可以专注口语能力发展。即便如此，他们通常需要5到6年才能掌握儿童交际词汇，而成年人只利用业余时间就能在一两年内掌握一门语言。

儿童学习语言更具优势的说法，在生物学上可能站不住脚，但不幸的是，有一种社会因素在推波助澜——大约7岁时，我们开始受制于“害怕失败”的困扰。

一份对1.6万名美国儿童的研究表明，98%的3到5岁儿童是

② 戴维·奥苏贝尔.成人和儿童的二语习得比较：心理因素【J】.现代语言杂志，1964-11，48（7）：420-424.

“创意天才”。[③] 我的儿子在那个年龄就像只小猫。我相信这个星球上任何健全的小猫都抵挡不住滚球或悬绳的诱惑。同样，儿童对新事物有着天然的好奇，永不满足，无须大人督促就会急切地学习新的单词语句，表达一切令他们感兴趣的东西——至少在学校学会害怕失败前，他们是如此。

5 岁的孩子不会担心重复“笨问题”而显得愚蠢。然而，到了 7 岁，在课堂上回答错误，或者被其他孩子嘲笑，都会令我们感到尴尬。久而久之，将人与其他物种区别开、值得称道的创造力在向外展现时就会受到我们自身的抑制。

8 至 10 岁，“创意天才”的比例从 98% 骤降到 32%；13 至 15 岁，这一比例只有 10%；到了 25 岁，已不足 2%。因为我们随大流，甘于反复纠结，到了 65 岁就接受退休。

创造力和外在表现受到抑制，解释了世界各地青少年和成年人在语言学习时面临同样问题的原因。我们擅长阅读和写作是因为阅读、写作无需发声，是一种安全的状态；我们口语水平不佳是因为不敢开口。我就听到许多中国人说：“我怕（口语）犯错遭到外国人嘲笑。”

“谁在乎呢？”我说道，“我的汉语不流利，但我会说到流利为止！”

中国人常说：“你的中文真好！”这并没有让我沾沾自喜，我知道即使我问候“你的马很好！”而不是“你好吗？”（我第一年常犯的错），他们也会出于礼貌这样恭维我。但他们转而就问我：“怎样才能提高英语口语水平呢？”

③ 兰德和贾曼 . 极限和超越【M】. 1993.

我左右张望一下，凑近低声说：“想知道掌握英语口语的秘诀？”

“哦，正是！”他们眼睛闪闪发亮，心照不宣地朝我靠近。

我的回答是，秘诀就是开口说英语！

我没在开玩笑。一个孩子即使每天花10个小时埋头苦读，也未必能提高口语水平，因为它不仅需要智力，更需要身体机能的投入。嘴、唇、舌彼此生疏，多次大声练习后，它们之间才变得默契协调，我们才能说一口比用母语说绕口令更流利的外语。

对成年人来说幸运的是，越来越多的研究证实：如果我们投入时间和精力，且方法适当，我们可以像儿童一样学习新语言，甚至比他们更出色！

“基于儿童、成年人比较的研究不断表明，青少年和成年人在受控条件下表现优于儿童。”④

我意识到这一点是在1988年。当时我观察到，我的两个儿子（一个两岁，一个半岁）在家就能学汉语和英语，我自己在课堂上却学得十分吃力。

他们学起来轻松，部分原因是他们所学的是自己感兴趣的词句。我小儿子马修说的第一个单词是“妈妈”，当我屏住呼吸等着他叫“爸爸”时，第二个单词却是“球”！不到1岁时，他就对球类和运动充满激情，这种激情成了他的动力。即便我和他妈妈没有给予鼓励督促，马修也能很快学会用汉语和英语谈论运动方面所有他感兴趣的事情——运动是他流利谈论其他话题的跳板。

④ https://effectivelanguagelearning.com/language-learning-tips/language-learning-myths.

通过对马修学习单词的观察，我惊讶地发现他会用不同的方式将它们组织在一块。尽管会犯一些有趣的错误，但他还没到会尴尬的年纪，所以他坚持了下来。

两个儿子喜欢中文，就像鸭子喜欢水一样，但我的经历却大不相同。我每早 4 点起床背 15 到 20 个新汉字，然后帮苏给孩子们准备早餐，接着是骑车去厦门大学；上了一整天课后，再修好我的自行车（每天都坏）骑车回家；到家后就帮苏准备晚饭，再是写作业到晚上十、十一点，最后累瘫在床上。筋疲力尽呀！

难怪儿子们学汉语比我快，但后来我改变学习动机和方法，最终超过了他们。

学习汉语和中国文化的想法在上世纪 70 年代就在我心里萌芽了，那时我在美国空军驻台湾的部队服役。这些想法仅出于我对中国丰富历史文化的好奇，我并没有计划将汉语纳入我的职业生涯。于是在厦大的课堂上苦苦挣扎 3 个月后，我趁机把汉语学习搁置了一两年，投入到协助厦门大学开办工商管理硕士课程的项目中，但我学习汉语的动力却迅速增长。

我的学生说英语，但其他人只会说汉语，所以我学汉语纯粹是为了生存——这和孩子们一样。为了与周围人交流，年幼的山农和马修不得不学习英语和汉语，而我为了生存不得不学习汉语。我有一本日记，上面简单地记了一些实用的单词短语，包括邮寄信件、在自助餐厅使用配给券、从银行领取工资、支付乘车费等。每天，我都能学会“一点点，但会反复使用它们”，无论是遇到朋友还是陌生人时，我都会如此。因此，学得越多，我对中国历史、文化、幽默、传说就越加好奇。

令许多人惊讶的是，包括我自己，我的汉语水平竟然超过了我两个儿子——至少有几年是这样。麻省理工2018年的那份报告就佐证了，成年人在学习语言或其他事物上比起儿童具有一定优势。

斯科特·查康（Scott Chacon）在他的《MIT科学家证实成年人能和儿童一样流利地掌握新语言》中，从麻省理工一篇名叫《关键时期》的论文中摘录如下：

> “在实验室或在一个沉浸式项目最初的几个月，对接触可比材料的儿童和成人进行比较表明，成人比儿童表现更加出色，而不是相较逊色（Huang，2015；Krashen，Long，& Scarcella，1979；Snow & Hoefnagel-Höhle，1978），也许是因为成年学习者有意识地采取策略，免受母语的干扰。
>
> “……语言的神奇之处在于（几乎）所有人都可以非常擅长它，包括成年学习者。”

儿童容易分心，第二天可能就忘了前一天让他们兴奋的事情，不同的是，成年人在语言学习上通常目标明确，而目标和激情一样，是一种强大的驱动力，激发专注、自律、决心，这是大多儿童缺乏的。

成年人的另一个优势是，随着时间的推移，我们的大脑能进行更复杂的思考，将新语言与母语进行对比。然而，儿童却是在白板上学习——这就是为什么他们需要长达四五年整天泡在语言环境里，才能达到幼儿园的语言水平。

一项由以色列海法大学费曼（Ferman）和艾维·卡尔尼（Avi Karni）发起的语言学习实验表明，“成年人在我们的每一项指标中都表现得更出色。”⑤

如果儿童在学习上确实超过成年人，很大程度上是因为成年人的生活更加忙碌，有很多干扰因素和着急处理的事项，但我们可以改变环境，帮助自己集中精力学习。

在厦大的家里，我把浴室的一角改成了一个小小的学习间，摆放着书籍、在中国拍摄的照片和一面旗子。那一方净土把世界的喧嚣挡在门外，让我保持专注。在这办公的另一个好处是，让来中国大陆第一年肠胃经常不适的我离厕所很近，生活更便捷。

我在中国三十几年的经历证实了科学家们日益认同的观点——我32岁开始学新语言也不晚，即使现在我64了还是坚持语言学习，因为我知道学习能力实际上和年龄成正比，当然前提是你得明智、战略性地挑选学习方法。我认为学习语言最有效的方法，尤其在中国，就是借助古老的讲故事艺术。关于这个方法，以后我将与大家进一步分享。

来自厦门的晚安！

潘维廉

2020年5月5日

⑤ 凯瑟琳·德·兰格. 年龄不是新语言学习失败的借口【J】. 新科学家，2011-7-20.

扫一扫

看老潘读信视频

Why Acting Is Learning at Its Best

May 18, 2020

Dear Chinese friends,

I remember very little from my 20 plus years of education – little of what I read, or of what teachers and professors told me. But I remember quite vividly the things they had me do – arts and crafts, field trips to Mrs Rhodes' sheep farm when I was 7, and so many plays and musicals that I can chart my life by which songs were popular in which year.

I was only six when I played the lead role of *Jack Frost* but to this day I can sing the song about Jack Frost nipping at the window pane.

The next year, 1963, we learned songs from *The Music Man*, my favorite being "O-ho the Wells Fargo Wagon is a-comin' down the street, Oh please let it be for me!"

In 1964, when I was eight, I sang "Feed the birds, tuppence a bag," from *Mary Poppins*.

In 1965, we sang songs from *The Sound of Music*, and in 1966 I learned "Try to Remember" from the off-broadway play *The Fantastiks*.

In 1970 we sang "I don't know how to love him," from the rock musical *Jesus Christ Superstar*.

When I was 17, I played Romeo in high school (praying that Juliet would really kiss me).

While I remember little from my first 12 years of school, those songs and plays are still vivid.

But the biggest reason that I prize plays and music for learning is that all of us are actors!

I often ask my MBA students, "Have any of you ever been an actor?" No one ever raises their hand so I then ask, "Do any of you have a boss? Do you speak to your boss the same way you do to a subordinate or peer? No! You all play many roles, and naturally act quite differently in each role that you play."

One of my most vivid memories is of a book that taught me how to draw Australian animals. I was only 8, but 55 years later I can still quote the poem because the book had me draw while I read the poetry. I will never forget:

> "Now you have seen within these pages,
> birds and beasts of bygone ages,
> and you can draw a kangaroo,
> a wombat and a black swan too."

And that's why I think Shakespeare was not being poetic but quite literal when he said, "All the world's a stage." We are all actors, and we all have our parts, and we'd best play them well because that's the entire point to our three score and ten years on this little blue ball – to experience life, and to learn from it.

And on that note – I look forward to seeing what part I will play tomorrow.

Bill Brown

Quotes from Lao Pan:

老潘金句：

If children do surpass adults at learning, it's largely because adults' lives are busier with many distractions and competing priorities, but we can alter our environment to help us focus.

如果儿童在学习上确实超过成年人，很大程度上是因为成年人的生活更加忙碌，有很多干扰因素和着急处理的事项，但我们可以改变环境，帮助自己集中精力学习。

We are all actors, and we all have our parts, and we'd best play them well because that's the entire point to our three score and ten years on this little blue ball – to experience life, and to learn from it.

我们都是演员，都有自己的角色。我们最好把它们演好，因为这就是我们在这个蓝色小星球生活一辈子的全部意义——体验生活并从中获得成长。

Bill (left) playing Coyett in the TV drama *Koxinga*, 1997
老潘（左）出演电视剧《郑成功》（1997 年）

Bill (right) playing Elliott in the film *Lin Zexu*, 1995
老潘（右）出演电影《林则徐》（1995 年）

Bill with kids in costume and makeup, 2020
老潘和身穿戏服的孩子们（2020 年）

为什么表演是最好的学习方式

亲爱的中国朋友们：

回顾20余年的学生生涯，我能记起的事情很少，读过什么、老师和教授说过什么，都已记得不太清楚，但他们指导我做的一些事情，我至今记忆犹新，如制作手工艺产品，7岁时去罗德夫人的牧羊场实地观察，观看大量戏剧和音乐剧——这些戏剧和音乐剧多到可以用它们带红的歌曲作为我人生的时间轴。

扮演杰克冻人时我只有6岁，但至今我仍记得唱那首杰克冻人吹打玻璃窗时的歌曲。

第二年，也就是1963年，我们学唱《音乐人》里的新歌，我最喜欢的一句是“哦哦，富国银行的马车在街上开下来，哦，请让它为我而来！”

1964年，我8岁，唱着《欢乐满人间》的“喂鸟，一袋一便士”。

1965年，我们学唱《音乐之声》里的歌曲；1966年，我从外百老汇戏剧《异想天开》中学会了那句“试着记住”。

1970年，我们从摇滚音乐剧《耶稣基督万世巨星》中学会演唱《我不知如何爱他》。

17岁时，我在高中扮演罗密欧（祈祷着真能得到朱丽叶的吻）。

对在学校的前12年，我的记忆已十分模糊，但这些歌曲戏剧在我心头鲜活如初。

我十分重视戏剧、音乐对学习的作用，主要是因为我们本就是演员！

我经常问我 MBA 的学生："你们有人当过演员吗？"从不见有人举手。然后我接着问："你们受雇于谁吗？你们对上级说话的方式和对下属或同事时相同吗？不！你们都身兼多角，每个角色扮演得自然也大不相同。"

一本澳大利亚动物的绘本也给我留下了十分生动的记忆。那时我才 8 岁，但 55 年后我仍记得书中的那首诗，它是在我学画画时从这本书里读到的。太令人难忘了！

"翻动书页，
你可以看到远古的飞禽走兽，
你也可以画出，
袋鼠、袋熊、黑天鹅。"

这也是我为什么认为莎士比亚说"整个世界都是一个舞台"时，并不是在制造诗意而是在陈述事实的原因。我们都是演员，都有自己的角色。我们最好把它们演好，因为这就是我们在这个蓝色小星球生活一辈子的全部意义——体验生活并从中获得成长。

在这一点上——我满心期待自己明天将扮演的角色。

潘维廉

2020 年 5 月 18 日

Chapter 2
Stories of China

第二章
中国故事

扫一扫

看老潘读信视频

Selling China's Story in English

March 13, 2020

Dear Chinese friends,

I hope you are all well, and are continuing to take advantage of the time you spend at home by doing things you don't usually have time for – like working on your English so you too can Tell China's Story in English to the world.

We often talk about "telling China's story in English" but if we are to be effective, we have to do more than just tell China's story, we must sell China's story. When I was with a Xiamen University OneMBA class in Washington, D.C. recently, a female Chinese student was so hurt and angry by American students' judgmental and critical questions about China that she cried as she complained to me, "We should not have to prove ourselves to them."

"You are right," I said. "In a perfect world, we should not have to prove ourselves, but in real life we all must prove ourselves in some way if we are to accomplish our purpose, be it doing business or helping people understand China." As the Scottish novelist Robert Louis

Stevenson (1850-1894) wrote in 1892 in *Across the Plains*, "Everyone lives by selling something."

Salesmen don't try to force a product on a customer because the customer will simply refuse it. Even if it is the best product in the world and will save them money, and is something they really need, they will reject the product if they don't understand its value – or if they don't trust the person selling it.

So a salesman must educate the buyer, which may entail overcoming in only minutes or hours their months or years of ignorance.

The same goes for telling China's story.

It may take time and patience to "sell" foreigners on a perspective of China that is different from the one that they've been spoon-fed by Western media for years or decades. So we must plan carefully not just what we say but how we say it.

As we sell China's story, we must choose our words carefully because the meanings of words evolve over time.

The word "propaganda," for example, is the same in both English and German, and 80 years ago it was a neutral term, like xuānchuán (宣传) in Chinese, but since World War II it has had only one meaning: enemy brainwashing. Yet some Chinese still insist on using the word propaganda because they got it from a dictionary that is half a century behind the times.

I laugh when someone shows a foreigner an English business card that says Propaganda Department. They're quite literally saying, "Hi! Please remove your hat so I can wash your brain!"

"Regime" is another word that was neutral 50 years ago but today always refers to an "evil" government.

English, like Chinese, is a living language, and changes with the historic and political context.

In ordinary, daily conversation, of course, if we're too cautious about every word, we won't dare open our mouth! We can't be paranoid about this. But when we "tell China's story" in English or any other language, we must also "sell" that story by crafting it carefully and trying to put ourselves in our listeners' shoes because they probably have not had the good fortune to have experienced China as you and I have.

Like my Chinese student in Washington, D.C., I sometimes am frustrated by foreigners' prejudices and snide remarks, but most of these are rooted in ignorance. If we can help them see China as we do, chances are that they too will come to love both the place and the people. For example, over the years I helped a dozen Chinese cities compete in competitions for livable international communities, and in Germany in 2002, I was shocked when a highly educated and well-traveled European mayor said to me, "I did not know that China had tall buildings." Another was surprised that China had modern medicine. And the so-called "objective" judges had their own biases.

Fortunately, I understand foreigners' ignorance and prejudice so I prepared in advance. First, I chose to see them not as judges but as customers. I'd have been nervous as a competitor in front of judges, competing against professional, well-funded foreign teams. But I was not at all nervous about selling my Chinese city because I teach business and I know how to sell!

Second, I did not confront them or argue. I know I can't win an argument with a customer, or a judge. It's even hard to win an argument with my own wife. Besides, some of their criticisms had a little truth, but that is simply because all countries have the same problems!

And that is how I opened their eyes and hearts. I helped them see that Chinese have the same hopes and fears, and the same problems, but they could learn from how Chinese have used their creativity and wisdom to solve those problems.

Perhaps most importantly, I personalized my China story. I showed them a China they'd never seen – my China.

And I used humor, which can help break barriers. I showed police riding bicycles to promote a healthy lifestyle. And I said, "It would be hard for bicycle cops to catch criminals in cars, so the criminals also ride bikes to give the cops a fair chance."

And I used images foreigners could understand – such as the Taoist Yinyang symbol. Foreigners know that it implies balance, so I showed how even the ancients emphasize balance between Man and Nature, and modern China tries to emphasize balance between growing and greening. It was very visual.

I also told them that one ancient city was famous for miniature landscapes, and then I showed them how the modern city also balances manmade and nature, buildings and parks and roads, like a giant miniature landscape.

All but one of my presentations won the gold, and 3 cities got double gold.

A European judge said, "We had no idea China had cities like this. Your city was not only number one but far better than number two!" A Canadian mayor said, "We need to teach Canadian citizens to work together like Chinese do." A European leader said, "We can learn from how Chinese cities creatively solve the same problems we face."

I sold my China story – and they bought it because my story was personal and I told it from perspectives they could understand. And it may have also helped that, unlike the presenters from the dozens of other cities, I was not a professional. I was simply sharing my own home, and I believed wholeheartedly in what I was selling.

During my decades in China, Chinese have come to know the world but the world still does not know China. But as my grandfather used to say, "We can either get bitter or better."

Let's get better, and sell China's story as if our very life depends upon it – because our very life does depend upon it.

All people are dreamers.

We dream of peace and prosperity for our family and descendants. So my dream is that the China Dream can become the world's dream!

But the greatest threat to this dream is fear bred by ignorance between nations. Let's help dispel that ignorance by not just telling China's story but selling China's story.

For as Robert Louis Stevenson also wrote (*Lay Morals*, published in 1911), "All speech, written or spoken, is a dead language, until it finds a willing and prepared hearer."

Our China story, regardless of what language we use, or how well we use it, is dead unless our hearers are willing and prepared to hear it – and it is our job to prepare them. So join us all in Selling China's Story in English, selling your China story in English!

Dream!

Stay safe and healthy!

Bill Brown

Applying for the International Awards for Livable International Communities in London, 2007

老潘在伦敦参与申请“国际花园城市”（2007 年）

TV host, 2012

老潘在电视台主持（2012 年）

Bill with Prof. Hu Min on a Fujian TV programme, 2019

老潘和胡敏教授做客东南卫视（2019 年）

用英语讲中国故事，为中国做“推销”

亲爱的中国朋友们：

你们好！希望大家一切安好，继续利用这段时光，在家涉猎一些平时没时间做的事情，如学习英语用来向世界讲中国故事。

我们经常谈论“用英语讲中国故事”，但想要取得成效，仅仅依靠讲述是不够的，我们必须推销中国故事。

不久前，我带领厦门大学 OneMBA 的学生去了美国华盛顿，面对美国学生对中国品头论足、质疑批判的情形，一位女同学深感受伤愤怒，向我抱怨时不禁潸然泪下：“我们真没必要向他们证明什么。”

我回道：“你说的对。在一个完美的世界里，我们无须证明自己是谁，但现实生活中，如果要实现自身目标，无论是做生意还是帮助人们了解中国，我们都必须采用某种方式证明自己。”1892 年，苏格兰小说家罗伯特·路易斯·史蒂文森（Robert Louis Stevenson）在他的作品《穿越平原》中就写道：“人生来就需要推销自己。”

但推销员不要试图强行推销，这样只会招致客户拒绝。即使产品质量绝佳，能为客户节约开支，还正是他们所需，但如果客户对产品价值不了解，或者对推销员不信任，他们还是会拒绝。

因此，推销员必须教育顾客，这可能需要花点时间帮助客户消除经年累月所积累的“无知”。

讲中国故事也是如此。

让外国人“接受”一个不同于西方媒体长期以来所灌输的中国形象，可能需要时间和耐心。我们不仅要慎重规划要说的话，还要慎重规划怎样去说。

词汇的含义会随时间而变化，鉴于此，在推销中国故事时我们必须谨慎措辞。

例如，和德语写法相同的英语词 propaganda，80 年前是一个中性词，中文意思为“宣传”，但二战以来，意思窄化为敌方的洗脑。但一些中国人仍坚持用该词去翻译汉语的“宣传”，这是因为他们用的是 50 年前的辞典。

当看到涉外的英文名片上写着“洗脑部”[①]时，我不禁哑然失笑。它们的字面意思就是：嗨！请摘下你的帽子，我好帮你洗洗脑！

另一个词语是“政权”。50 年前，它也是一个中性词，但今天它总跟“邪恶”政府相关。

和汉语一样，英语是一门鲜活的语言，受制于历史、政治语境的变迁。

当然，日常会话如果过于谨慎，我们就不敢开口了！对此，我们不能过于偏执。但我们用英语或其他语言“讲中国故事”时，推销我们的故事时，我们必须精心准备，设身处地为听众着想，

① 汉语旨在表达“宣传部”，但英译选词不当，闹出笑话。

因为他们可能没有你我这般幸运，有在中国生活的经历。

正如我那位之前在华盛顿抱怨生气的学生一样，我有时也会因为外国人的偏见和尖刻评论感到沮丧，但我知道很多时候是源于对方的无知。如果能帮他们像我们一样看待中国，他们可能也会爱上这片土地和这里的人民。

这些年，我帮助十几个中国城市参加“国际花园城市”竞选。2002 年在德国时，一位受过高等教育、游历丰富的欧洲市长对我说“过去我不知道中国有高楼大厦”，这令我十分震惊。中国拥有现代医学同样也出乎一些人的意料。此外，所谓 “客观”的评审员们也有自身的偏见。

幸运的是，我理解他们，所以我未雨绸缪。首先，我把他们看作顾客而不是评审。因此，站在评委团前与一群专业、资金雄厚的外国团队竞争时，本该十分紧张的我却丝毫不受这些影响！这当然归功于我在学校教授商科的经历，让我对推销方法熟谙于心。

第二，我不和他们产生冲突或争吵。我深知无法在与客户或评审的争论中取胜。我甚至都争不赢我的妻子。有时他们的批评也不无道理，但那仅是因为所有国家都面临着同样的一些问题！

也是在认清这点后，我打开了评委的心扉。我帮他们意识到中国人怀有同样的希望和恐惧，面临着同样的问题，并且他们解决这些问题所用的创意及智慧可为世界借鉴。

也许最重要的是，我把我的中国故事个人化，给他们展示一个他们从未见过的中国。

我用幽默打破障碍。我展示了中国警察为提倡健康的生活方式骑自行车工作的图片。我解释道："自行车警察很难抓到汽车里的罪犯，公平起见，罪犯也骑自行车。"

我用的图像也是外国人能理解的，比如道教的阴阳符号。他们知道这意味着平衡，借此我展示出甚至在中国古代人们就强调人与自然关系平衡，以及现代中国平衡发展和环保所做的努力。这种方式非常直观。

我还同他们展示了一座以盆景闻名于世的中国古城，借此介绍现代城市平衡人与自然关系的做法，如大楼、公园、道路之间的平衡，就像在打造一个巨型盆景。

在我助选的"国际花园城市"竞赛中，除一个城市，其余都获得金奖，还有 3 个城市获得双金奖。

一位欧洲评审说："我们不知道中国竟有这样的城市。你的城市不仅获得了第一，还让第二名难望项背！"一位加拿大市长说："我们需要让加拿大人学习中国人的团结合作。"一位欧洲领导人说："了解中国城市创造性地解决我们自身也面临的问题，真是受益匪浅。"

我推销我的中国故事并得到接受，是因为我的故事是个人的，我选取听众能理解的角度讲述。而我不像其他几十个城市的主持人出身科班，也许是有所裨益。我仅仅是在分享自己的家，我全心全意地相信我要让别人接受的东西。

在中国生活的几十年里，我发现中国对世界的了解日益加深，但世界对中国仍是知之甚少。但正如我祖父过去常说的，我们要么变得痛苦，要么变得更好。

让我们变得更好，推销中国故事吧，好像我们的生活就依赖于此——而我们的生活确实有赖于它。

人人都是梦想家。

我们都梦想家人和子孙后代安享和平、繁荣。所以我的梦想是中国梦成为世界梦！

但这一梦想面临的最大威胁仍是来自各国间对彼此不甚了解所滋生的恐惧。因此，我们不仅要讲中国故事，还要推销中国故事，推动这种无知的消除。

罗伯特·路易斯·史蒂文森在1911年出版的《世俗道德》中曾写道："所有的言语，无论是书面还是口头的，直到它找到一个愿意聆听的听众才获得了生命。"

因此，不管我们使用何种语言，不管我们多么精通它，只有听众愿意聆听，我们的中国故事才具有生命力——这就是我们的任务，用你的中国故事打动世界。请加入我们，一起用英语推销中国故事！

逐梦吧！

祝愿大家平安、健康！

潘维廉

2020年3月13日

扫一扫

看老潘读信视频

The Three Kinds of China Stories Foreigners Need to Know

May 13, 2020

Dear Chinese friends,

Chinese often ask, "Is America hot or cold?" and I ask in turn, "Is China hot or cold?"

"It depends!" they say, "on whether it's summer or winter, north or south."

"Same with America."

Generalizations are dangerous because they lead to ignorant stereotypes and dangerous misperceptions. A century ago, for example, Westerners feared China as the Yellow Peril, which was ironic, given that half a dozen Western nations were occupying China but Chinese had never conquered far-off lands.

Another false stereotype of China is that it has always been isolationist and avoided contact with the rest of the world, but even 3,000 years ago, Chinese were trading with ancient Egypt, and in 43 AD, the Roman geographer Pomponius Mela wrote, "The Seres [Chinese] are 'a race eminent for integrity and well known for the trade..."

Dr. Arthur H. Smith (1845-1932), who authored many books on China, knew how difficult it was to understand China. He wrote that the only ones who dared claim to really understand China were newspaper reporters (who think they know everything) and globetrotters, but, Smith, who lived in China and explored it for 54 years, admitted, "As for myself, I am continually discovering a continental area still unexplored."

China varies greatly not only from province to province but even county to county. My own Fujian Province differs between North and South, East and West, with each county, town and village boasting a dazzling diversity of dialects, foods, arts, crafts and customs.

Even the foreigner's naive notion that all Chinese eat rice is wrong! Many Chinese eat wheat or millet, often as *jiaozis* or noodles – though thanks to modern infrastructure and markets, you can now eat any kind of food you can imagine anywhere in China.

I was not surprised when Philip Le Gall, a Frenchman who was the Seychelles' first ambassador to China, said, "We say if you come to China for one week, you feel you can write a book; for one month, an article; but for more than six months, you can pen nothing."①

Le Gall was fascinated with China even during childhood in France, but "had limited access as a young and eager reader." Today, Le Gall lives in a Beijing hutong and, like Dr. Arthur Smith a century ago, is finding that China is endlessly fascinating – but how do we open the eyes of the vast majority of people who will never visit China or live in

① Mei Jia, "Beyond Diplomatic Language," *China Daily*, 2012-10-09.

a hutong?

The key to sharing China's Story is using carefully selected stories to show that China is indeed unique – an entire nation worthy of being a UNESCO World-Heritage Site – but also a nation that from antiquity has embraced the same universal values and dreams as the rest of humanity – love of family, patriotism, a passion for peace and justice – along with the indomitable spirit of determination and persistence that has made the China Dream a reality. But whether the China Dream instills hope or fear in foreigners depends on who is telling the story.

A century ago, Western media wrote of China as a Yellow Peril. Today, China's BRI, which is already raising nations from poverty, is being called a tool of "Chinese economic colonialism"② even by supposedly objective media such as the *Financial Times*. The lesson is obvious: if we don't tell China's Story, others will, so let's shatter the prejudices and open people's eyes and hearts with stories that focus on the true China of past, present and future:

1. Past: Ancient tales show that Chinese, like all peoples, love family, peace, prosperity and morality – in other words, the same dreams as everyone else.

2. Present: Modern tales can show how China freed 1/5 of the world from poverty – a miracle that wealthy nations have

② Anderlini, Jamil, "China Is at Risk of Becoming a Colonialist Power," *Financial Times*, September 19, 2018; Symon, Fiona, "China's BRI – a New Colonialism?" *Financial Times*, May 7, 2019.

not even attempted.

3. Future: China's BRI is already not only helping to lift other nations from economic poverty but also, as Xi Jinping has said, "fighting poverty of spirit" (a notion rooted in Confucian and Taoist ethics).

But with so much to share, how do we begin? I try to capture foreigners' imagination with a story that they can relate to, otherwise the story is too alien to interest them. "Aladdin" is a great eye-opener.

Foreigners, and even Chinese, are surprised to learn that "Aladdin," one of the world's most popular "rags-to-riches" stories, took place in China, not the Middle East! Although the story originated in Syria, it was about a Chinese boy named Aladdin. The story begins with, "Aladdin was the son of a poor widow who lived in a city in China." The Syrian storyteller chose China because, for centuries, the rest of the world viewed China as the richest and most magical place upon the planet. I have many 19th century Aladdin books and every volume is richly illustrated with Chinese people in Chinese clothes in Chinese cities. Only after Disney's Aladdin cartoon did the world come to associate the tale with the Middle East.

I also show foreigners why Sinbad, the mythical explorer, was actually China's Admiral Zheng He, who made 7 great voyages like Sinbad.

A few years ago I shocked an audience of 450 American businessmen and a couple of U.S. government representatives by telling them that had it not been for Xiamen there would have been no USA!

The tea in the Boston Tea Party of 1773, which sparked the War of Independence, was from Fujian, and the 3 ships were from Xiamen, so if no Fujian tea and Xiamen ships, there would have been no war and no USA. Everyone laughed, but the humor helped break the political tension and piqued their interest in Xiamen investment, as well as its history and culture.

I also like to share how ancient China excelled in things that the West has explored only in recent decades. For example, over 2,000 years ago, Chinese emphasized good diet, exercise and stress relief, but Western medicine began stressing "healthy lifestyle" only in the past couple of decades because curing people is far more lucrative than keeping them healthy. This focus on prevention rather than cure is deeply rooted in Chinese philosophy, psychology and morality, and influences everything from medicine to politics and war. While discussing medicine with foreigners, I also shock them with facts such as Chinese inoculating against deadly smallpox over 1,000 years ago, or Tu Youyou winning the Nobel Prize for medicine for a malaria cure based on ancient Chinese medicine.

Such stories as these surprise foreigners with how little they really know about China and help whet their appetites to learn more.

Most foreigners won't read ancient Chinese classics, so for years I've pieced together my own collections of stories. This is why I was excited and relieved to learn of the publication of *Stories of China Retold in English*. These carefully selected tales of both old and new China reveal the ancient, unchanging spirit of the nation, and each tale ends with a relevant insight on Chinese' values or beliefs that shed light on where China is headed tomorrow.

Some of my favorite stories of China retold in English are about inventions such as brush, paper and ink, gunpowder, or the compass. I also appreciate the insights on Chinese character by stories about the "Four Gentlemen": plum, orchid, bamboo and chrysanthemum. The bamboo, for example, is hollow, so modest, but strives upward, dauntless in the face of adversity; the chrysanthemum symbolizes upright character.

Other stories show how today's China is already well on the path to tomorrow, and offering hope for other nations as well, with its mastery of graphene, or its Beidou satellite system that helps even remote Mongolian herdsmen track their cattle with their mobile phones. The South-North Water Diversion Project is even more ambitious than the Dujiangyan Irrigation Project, which for 2,300 years has fed more people than any other engineering feat in history.

I also marvel at stories such as China's development of hybrid rice, which is helping to end hunger around the world, and how China's space exploits are so rapidly surpassing those of other nations thanks to the dedication of scientists and bravery of astronauts. And the story of the bullet trains is special to me because I remember the steam locomotives that belched black smoke 30 years ago, but today our family can ride modern bullet trains from Xiamen to anywhere in the country.

My favorite stories, however, are about China's intangible treasures – the Chinese philosophy and morality that unify past, present and future. We can understand Chinese ancient passion for peaceful coexistence, for example, when we read of how Confucius warned Zi Lu against relying upon the sword – that the lifelong goal of ancient kings was virtue, and that they treated even rebels with benevolence. When Zi Lu argued that benevolence was useless on a battlefield, Confucius replied that force could conquer only temporarily, whereas benevolence could improve mutual understanding and lead to world-wide peace.

Another bedrock of Chinese civilization is righteousness. Mencius claimed he loved both life and righteousness, but if forced to choose, he'd opt for righteousness over life. Throughout history, Chinese have tried to appeal to righteousness and reason rather than force – though as *Art of War* warns, if they have no alternative, they will fight, but even then, Chinese seek peace and rapid restoration after victory.

But in addition to stories such as those in Prof. Hu Min's collection, it is also important to tell stories of how ordinary, common people's lives have changed because these are the stories that people all over the world can relate to, and gain hope from.

I've written about "common" Chinese lives since I moved to Xiamen – people like the man who repaired my bike and refused payment, even though he and his wife lived in a tiny shack. He was poor but proud and had high hopes. I wrote of Anxi tea farmers who toiled dawn to dusk but were so poor that they could not afford to drink their own tea, so brewed weeds. Today, many of those farmers have new homes and cars, some of their children are at university – and they can afford to drink tea!

I came to know Fujian like the back of my hand but I was curious –

was reform and opening up helping people even in the remotest regions? In 1994, I drove with my family over 40,000 km around China, even to remote Inner Mongolia and Tibet and through the Gobi desert, and was amazed at how lives were changing in every corner of China. But with 2020 approaching, I was curious just how close China was to reaching Xi Jinping's goal of ending absolute poverty, so in 2019, I drove over 20,000 km around China, this time with friends and colleagues, to see how China had changed in 25 years. We were all absolutely astonished and delighted that every corner of China had benefited from change. Even villages in remote Tibet, Ningxia and Gansu had concrete roads and new homes, and remote villagers used mobile phones to buy and sell online.

And of course I fell in love with the children, who throughout China showed a pride and confidence in their homeland. I now have many grandchildren!

Although I've also shared many "rags to riches" stories such as the XMU professor's maid who is now a multimillionaire and philanthropist, it is the stories of common people that really touch hearts because we can relate to them, and they give us hope. If they can do it, so can I – if I persist, and never quit.

And that is the greatest lesson of all effective China stories. Chinese, past and present, have succeeded because they follow moral, peaceable pursuits to make a better life for themselves, and they persist until they succeed. And now, through the BRI, China is using its hard-won experience to lift other nations from poverty.

That is the China Dream in a nutshell – and if we can tell China's

Story well, we can help the China Dream to become the World Dream.

And they are the stories about China that foreigners need to know.

Bill Brown

Quotes from Lao Pan:

老潘金句：

When we "tell China's story" in English or any other language, we must also "sell" that story by crafting it carefully and trying to put ourselves in our listeners' shoes because they probably have not had the good fortune to have experienced China as you and I have.

当我们用英语或其他语言"讲中国故事"时，推销我们的故事时，我们必须精心准备，设身处地为听众着想，因为他们可能没有你我这般幸运，有在中国生活的经历。

Generalizations are dangerous because they lead to ignorant stereotypes and dangerous misperceptions.

一概而论是危险的，会招致无知的成见、危险的误解。

Bill hosting a Fujian Straits satellite TV programme, 2015
老潘在海峡卫视主持节目（2015 年）

Bill loves playing the guitar to express his love for China, 2019
老潘喜欢用弹吉他的方式表达对中国的热爱（2019 年）

Bill reading *The Analects of Confucius*, 2019
老潘阅读《论语》（2019 年）

外国人不可不知的三类中国故事

亲爱的中国朋友们：

中国人喜欢问："美国热还是冷？"我反过来喜欢问："中国热还是冷？"

"看情况！"他们回答道，"分冬夏，分南北。"

"美国也一样。"

一概而论是危险的，会招致无知的成见、危险的误解。例如，一个世纪前，西方人担心中国人是"黄祸"，这很讽刺，因为不下6个西方国家曾侵略中国，而中国却从未占领遥远的异邦。

对中国的另一错误刻板印象是，中国一直奉行孤立主义，不与其他国家接触，但早在3000年前，中国与古埃及就有贸易往来。公元43年，罗马地理学家庞波尼乌斯·梅拉（Pomponius Mela）写道："丝国人（古代西方对中国人的称呼）是一个以诚信著称的民族，它因贸易而闻名……"

亚瑟·H·史密斯（Arthur H. Smith）博士（1845–1932）著有许多有关中国的书籍，十分清楚了解中国的难度。他认为唯一敢宣称真正了解中国的是报社记者（他们认为自己无所不知）和环球旅行者，但在中国生活探索了54年后史密斯承认："在我看来，我仍旧是在探索一个未知的大陆。”

在中国，不仅各省份之间差异明显，就连县与县之间也是如此。以我所在的福建省为例，南北东西各不相同，县与县之间、镇与镇之间、村与村之间，都有着各自的方言、特色食物、工艺品、风俗习惯等，令人眼花缭乱。

外国人甚至天真地认为所有中国人都吃米饭，但事实并非如此！不少中国人的主食是小麦或谷子做成的饺子面条，不过现代的基础设施和市场物流，让你在中国任何地方都能吃到任何你能想象的食物。

所以我一点都不惊讶塞舌尔第一任驻华大使法国人菲利普·勒加尔（Philip Le Gall）会说：“如果你来中国一周，你会觉得自己可以写本书；待上 1 个月，能写一篇文章；但 6 个月后，就写不出什么了。”①

早在童年时代，生活在法国的勒加尔就对中国心驰神往，但“作为一名如饥似渴的年轻读者，当时他能接触中国的机会十分有限”。今天，勒加尔住在北京的一个胡同里，和一个世纪前的亚瑟·史密斯博士一样，发现中国有着无穷的魅力——但我们如何才能让绝大多数永远不会到访中国或住进胡同的人们感受到呢？

讲好中国故事，关键是要精挑细选出实实在在反映中国独特性的故事，因为这是一个可以被整个列入联合国教科文组织世界遗产名单的国家；同时，这些故事还要反映中国历史悠久的、为其他民族共有的普世价值观和梦想，如对家国的热爱，对和平与正义的向往，以及反映实践中国梦所展现的不屈不挠、持之以恒

① 梅贾（音译）. 外交辞令之外【N】. 中国日报，2012-10-9.

的精神。但中国梦给外国人带来希望还是恐慌，取决于讲中国故事的人。

一个世纪前，西方媒体将中国视为“黄祸”。今天，中国的“一带一路”倡议使沿线一些国家摆脱贫困，却又因此被一些西方所谓的客观媒体称为“中国经济殖民主义”② 工具。教训是显而易见的：如果我们不讲中国故事，其他人会讲，因此让我们用贯穿古今、展望未来的真实的中国故事让人们摒弃偏见、敞开心扉吧：

1. 过去：古代传说表明，中华民族和所有其他民族一样，热爱家庭、和平、繁荣，重视道德。换言之，中国人和其他国家的人们有着相同的梦想。

2. 现在：现代的故事向我们展示中国如何使世界五分之一的人口摆脱贫困，这是发达国家都未曾尝试的奇迹。

3. 未来：中国的“一带一路”倡议不仅帮助沿线国家摆脱经济贫困，而且，正如习近平主席所说，是“与精神贫困做斗争”（一种根植于儒家和道家伦理的观念）。

但可分享的故事太多，我们从哪入手呢？我的方法是讲述能引起外国人共鸣的故事，否则会令他们感到太陌生，令他们索然无味。《阿拉丁》的效果就令人眼前一亮。

② 吉密欧·安代利尼．中国正冒险成为殖民帝国【N】．金融时报，2018-9-19.
菲奥娜·西蒙．中国“一带一路”倡议——新殖民主义？【N】．金融时报，2019-5-7.

外国人，甚至中国人，都十分惊讶世界最知名的“白手起家”的故事《阿拉丁》竟然发生在中国而不是中东！这个故事起源于叙利亚，但讲的是一个叫阿拉丁的中国男孩。故事的开头是这样的，“阿拉丁是一个贫穷寡妇的儿子，生活在中国的一座城市里”。叙利亚人将故事背景放在中国，是因为很长一段时间中国被视为地球上最富有、最神奇的国家。我有好些19世纪出版的《阿拉丁》，每一卷都配有大量插图，画着身着中国服饰的中国城市居民。人们把这个故事与中东联系起来，是在迪士尼推出阿拉丁的卡通片之后。

我还向外国人介绍了虚构的探险家辛巴达（Sinbad）的原型为中国的郑和的原因。像辛巴达一样，郑和七下西洋。

在几年前的一次演讲上，我提到没有厦门就没有美国，让在座的450名美国商人和几位美国政府代表感到震惊。1773年波士顿倾茶事件是独立战争的导火索，而这些茶叶来自福建，那3艘船来自厦门，所以说，没有福建茶和厦门船，就不会有独立战争和美国。这引来了哄堂大笑，但这种幽默有助于打破紧张的政治气氛，还激起他们投资厦门、了解厦门历史文化的兴趣。

我还想分享，早在古代，中国就在西方近几十年才着手探索的事物上做得十分出色。例如，2000多年前中国人就强调均衡饮食、坚持锻炼和释放压力，但西医开始强调“健康生活方式”只是几十年前的事，因为治愈病人远比使病人保持健康有利可图。这种注重预防而非治疗的理念深植于中国哲学、心理学和道德层面，影响着从医学到政治到战争的方方面面。在我与外国人谈论中药时，中国人1000多年前就接种预防致命天花的疫苗，或屠呦呦因青蒿素对疟疾的疗效获得诺贝尔医学奖等事实也会令他们震惊。

这类故事让外国人惊讶于自己对中国了解之少，从而有助于激发他们了解的欲望。

大多数外国人不读中国经典，所以多年来我一直在整理自己的故事集。这就是为什么得知《用英语讲中国故事》的出版时，我感到兴奋和欣慰。这些精心挑选的新老中国故事揭示了古老、永恒的民族精神，每个故事结尾都附有对中华民族价值观或信仰的深刻见解，为我们阐明中国未来的走向。

在这套书中讲述中国发明的故事是我的最爱，如毛笔、纸墨、火药、指南针等的发明。我也十分欣赏故事作者借用梅兰竹菊“花中四君子”阐述对中国品格的感悟。比如，竹子空心代表谦虚，但又代表奋发向上、面对逆境不屈不挠的精神；又如，菊花象征正直的品格。

还有一些故事展示了今天中国的良好发展，如它不仅掌握了开发石墨烯的技术，它的北斗卫星系统甚至可以帮助偏远的内蒙古牧民用手机远程牧牛。这些成果为其他国家带来希望。而比起建于2300年前、历史上辐射人口最多的水利工程都江堰，南水北调工程更显雄心与抱负。

我还惊叹于中国杂交水稻的研发，它正在世界范围内帮助人们消除饥饿；惊叹于在无私奉献的中国科学家和勇敢卓绝的中国宇航员的努力下，中国太空开发事业如此迅速跻身世界前列。而高铁的故事对我来说很特别，30年前冒着滚滚黑烟的蒸汽机火车让我记忆犹新，但今天我们全家从厦门乘坐高铁可以去往中国各地。

然而，我最喜欢的是关于中国无形宝藏的故事——中国的哲学和道德准则，它们把中国的过去、现在和未来有机地统一起来。从中，我们可以理解中国人自古对和平共处的渴望。例如，孔子告诫子路不要诉诸武力，因为古代君王一生致力于追求美德，他们甚至会对叛乱者施以仁德；子路声称仁政在战场上无用，孔子声称军事力量只能暂时征服，而仁德可以增进相互了解，促进世界和平。

中华文明的另一座基石是正义。孟子宣扬对生命和正义的热爱，但面临取舍时，他选择正义而非生命。纵观历史，中华民族一直呼吁正义和理性，而非武力。《孙子兵法》警告世人，战争是不得已才使用的手段，即使深陷战争，中国人还是渴望和平，希冀胜利后秩序迅速恢复。

但除了这些故事，讲述普通百姓生活变化也很重要，这可以引起世界的共鸣，给予他们希望。

搬到厦门后，我就开始写“普通”中国人的生活——包括那个和他妻子住在小棚屋里但为我修自行车拒绝收钱的人。他很穷，但很有自尊，且满怀希望。我写过从早到晚辛勤劳作的安溪茶农。他们穷得连自己种的茶都喝不起，只能冲泡杂草喝。但现在，许多茶农不仅购置了新家、新汽车，还有些茶农送孩子去上了大学——并且喝得起茶了！

我对福建十分熟悉，但我还不清楚中国最偏远地区的人民是否也受益于改革开放。在 1994 年，我和家人驱车 4 万多公里环游中国，甚至抵达偏远的内蒙古和西藏，穿越戈壁沙漠，一路上中国各地居民生活的变化让我惊讶不已。这次临近 2020 年，因好奇由习近平主席提出的消除绝对贫困的目标在中国的实现情况，我和朋友、同事驱车2万多公里，一睹中国25年的发展。我们非常惊讶也非常高兴地看到中国各地都从中国的发展中受益。甚至在偏远省份西藏、宁夏和甘肃，那里的村庄也铺上了水泥路、盖起了新房，偏远地区的村民也用上了手机网购、做买卖。

当然，我也爱上了中国的孩子们，他们向我展现出对自己祖国的自豪和信心。现在我有很多孙子孙女了呢！

我的分享中不乏“白手起家”的故事，比如一位昔日厦门大学教授的保姆现在已是一名千万富翁和慈善家，但真正触动人心的是普通百姓的故事，他们给了我们共鸣，给了我们希望。如果他们能做到，我也能做到——只要坚持，永不放弃。

这是所有打动人心的中国故事都推崇的经验。无论过去还是现在，中国人的成功离不开他们遵循道德、和平的方式为自己谋求美好生活，以及坚持不懈的精神。现在，通过“一带一路”倡议，中国正利用来之不易的经验帮助其他国家摆脱贫困。

简而言之，这就是中国梦。如果能把中国故事讲好，我们就能帮助中国梦成为世界梦。而这些关于中国的故事正是需要讲给外国人听的。

潘维廉

2020年5月13日

扫一扫

看老潘读信视频

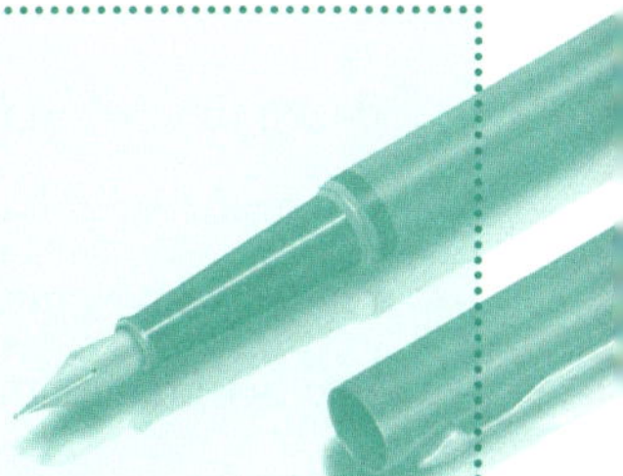

Stories – A Powerful Language Learning Tool

May 13, 2020

Dear Chinese friends,

> "The human species thinks in metaphors and learns through stories."
>
> Mary Catherine Bateson

I was only 7 when my parents gave me the best gift of my childhood – Olive Beaupre Miller's (1883-1968) 12-volume set of stories called *My Book House*. The first thing that captivated me was the beautiful color and monochrome illustrations much like those in New Channel's Chinese classics of *Tao Te Ching* , *Analects of Confucius* and *Art of War*. The drawings and paintings were so intriguing that I could not wait to read the stories to see what they were about and finished all 12 volumes within the year.

Some stories were fantasies, others had historical or adventure plots, and others were about science, or biographies, but every story was a door to another world or life. I reread the entire set at least half a dozen times, and last year I gave a 50-year-old set of *My Book House* to my granddaughter Kate. She too was captivated, and is now a diehard reader who wants to learn about everything she comes across – just like her granddad, who still doesn't know what he wants to be when he grows up.

I've known from childhood that stories can be powerful and life-changing, but only after moving to China did I learn that stories are also a powerful language learning tool, as well as a means for overcoming cultural misunderstandings and prejudices.

Storytelling is a primal art that predates writing, and perhaps even language itself. Over 40,000 years ago, Borneo islanders told stories with simple cave drawings, and no sooner had people begun to speak than they huddled around dancing fires by night to enthrall each other with tales of real life that over time were embellished until they evolved into folktales and mythology.

The veneration for storytelling is seen in India's *Mahabharata* epic, which has been passed down orally for 2,000 years even though each generation of storytellers had to memorize over 100,000 verses. But that ancient tale pales beside the Tibetan's *Life of King Gesar*, which has been passed down orally for 800 years even though it is the world's longest poem, with some 120 volumes and over one million verses.

The allure of storytelling is evident even in the modern age. Americans average 4 hours a day on TVs and the internet viewing everything from movies and documentaries to "reality shows" about people whose situations are very similar to their own. It seems people are addicted to stories – any stories at all.

But stories are not just entertainment but also powerful tools for teaching all ages, from kindergartners to graduate students. Even Harvard Business School (HBS) teaches everything from statistics and strategy to accounting and economics with "business cases," which are simply stories in formal attire. Since I took HBS' course in case-centered teaching, I too have taught my own students not only with business cases but I also throw in skits, demonstrations and competitions, or have them do role plays where they solve economic, social or cultural challenges in my fictional country of Indolaysia or Chinese province of Funan (福南).

Oral stories are powerful because in the absence of visual content, which the TV and internet spoon feed us, listeners are forced to actively personalize and internalize what they hear according to their own imagination, experience and interests. This is why 100 people can hear the exact same tale and come away with widely disparate impressions and conclusions.

Stories make language learning more fun and effective for many reasons. It is much easier, for example, to expand my vocabulary through a good story than through rote memorization of new words. I used to hate memorizing 20 Chinese characters a day, 100 a week, because characters memorized out of context had little meaning or use, and by Friday I'd often forgotten everything I'd memorized between Monday and Wednesday. But I discovered, to my delight, that I could easily master 100 new characters in a week if I learned them together, organically, in the context of a story – especially if it was a story that I liked or related to.

Grammar is also easier to learn through stories than by memorizing rules. I skipped 3 years of high school English and went straight to Honors English, which focused on writing, because they assumed from my essays that I knew grammar. Actually, I heartily disliked grammar and had skirted my way around it for so long that I barely knew the difference between a gerund and a gerbil. But after reading at least 3 or 4 books a week since the 2nd grade, I had read so much that my usage of English was as correct as those who had memorized such guidelines as why "an" is used not before words with vowels but before words with vowel sounds. To this day I'm not sure why words like cough, enough, plough, and though all end the same but are pronounced differently, but I've no problem pronouncing them correctly after reading them in thousands of stories.

Stories also engage us emotionally, evoking joy, anger, fear, nostalgia, wonder – and psychology has shown that emotional experiences create the most vivid and lasting memories. So stories with universal themes – bravery, patriotism, overcoming obstacles, sacrifice for family – not only help us learn a language but also help impart unforgettable lessons about a land's history or culture.

Lastly, stories help us overcome misconceptions about other countries – and they are a great way to get a foreigner to practice the language with us!

In the early 1990s, I wrote the book *Magic Fujian* with dialogues and recordings to help foreigners better understand Fujian and give Chinese a way to interest foreigners in practicing English with them.

Foreigners get tired of Chinese asking the same questions. "How are you?" "Where are you from?" "Where do you work?" But any sane foreigner in China would delight in speaking with a Chinese who can share about his homeland's rich history and culture.

Storytellers are the best teachers, whether in kindergarten, Harvard Business School, or XMU, but the stories are most vivid when not just voiced but also acted out. Better yet, lessons can be absolutely unforgettable when students themselves act out the stories.

So I encourage you to transform your own language learning from mere lessons into unforgettable experiences that you'll never forget. Learn stories, and then share your stories by acting them out. You'll not only learn but you'll also teach others – and that, after all, is the point of life.

Bill Brown

Quote from Lao Pan:

老潘金句:

While I remember little from my first 12 years of school, those songs and plays are still vivid.

对在学校的前 12 年，我的记忆已十分模糊，但这些歌曲戏剧在我心头鲜活如初。

Bill interviewed by CCTV, 2004
老潘做客中央电视台（2004年）

Bill reading to his granddaughter Kate, 2016
老潘给孙女凯特讲故事（2016年）

Bill telling “stories” in an MBA classroom, 2016
老潘在MBA课上讲述“故事”(2016年）

故事——强大的语言学习工具

亲爱的中国朋友们：

> “人类用隐喻思考，用故事学习。”
>
> ——玛丽·凯瑟琳·贝特森

7岁时，我从父母那收到童年时代最好的礼物——奥利弗·博普雷·米勒（Olive Beaupre Miller, 1883–1968）的12卷故事集《我的书屋》。首先吸引我的是它绚丽的色彩和单色的释例，就像新航道推出的《道德经》《论语》《孙子兵法》的风格那样。这些图画非常有趣，让我迫不及待地想了解这套书讲了什么，于是一年内我就读完了全部的12卷。

无论是奇幻历史、冒险还是科学、传记故事，书中的每个故事都是通向另一个世界或另一种生活的大门。我至少读了6遍。去年我把一套有着50年历史的《我的书屋》送给了孙女凯特。她也被迷住了，俨然一名“执着”的读者，读到任何内容她都想了解——就像她的对于未来仍充满好奇的爷爷一样。

从小我就领略到故事有着强大力量，能够影响人生，但只有搬到中国后，我才知道故事也是一种强大的语言学习工具，消除文化误解和偏见的重要手段。

讲故事是一种原始的艺术，它早于文字出现，甚至可能早于语言本身。4万多年前，婆罗洲岛民用简单的洞穴图画讲述故事；人类刚学会说话时，就在夜晚围着舞动的火焰挤成一团，分享各自生活吸引彼此。随着时间推移，这些生活中的经历被美化，演变成民间故事和神话。

人类对讲故事的追崇在印度史诗《摩诃婆罗多》中可见一斑。该史诗已口头流传了2000年，这意味着每一代故事的讲述人都要背诵超过10万节的诗句。但比起藏族史诗《格萨尔王传》，是小巫见大巫。流传800年的《格萨尔王传》是世上最长的诗歌，约120卷，包含100多万诗节。

在现代，故事的魅力也是显而易见的。美国人平均每天花4小时在电视和互联网上，观看电影、纪录片以及与自己处境非常相似的人们出演的“真人秀”节目。似乎故事总让人沉迷——不管什么故事。

故事不仅可用于娱乐，还是有效的教育方式，从幼儿园到大学都是如此。就连在哈佛商学院，“商业案例”也是包括统计、战略、会计到经济学的所有课程都会采用的授课方式，而这些案例不过是穿上正装的故事罢了。在哈佛商学院参加以案例为中心的课程后，我也在自己的课堂上给学生分享商业案例，还奉送一些幽默小品、示范表演和竞赛，或者让他们在我虚构的国家或虚构的中国省份里进行角色扮演，解决那里的经济、社会或文化问题。

口述故事的作用强大，是因为没了电视、互联网提供视觉内容，听众只能根据自身想象力、经验和兴趣，积极地个人化和内化听到的内容。这就是为什么一个故事一百个听众有一百种感想和结论。

故事让语言学习更加有趣、有效的原因是多方面的。例如，通过一个好故事扩充词汇量远比死记硬背容易得多。以前我讨厌一天背20个汉字，也就是一周背100个，因为干巴巴地背汉字意义不大，每到周五，周一到周三背的东西我是一点印象也没有。令我高兴的是，通过故事将汉字有机地结合起来，一周内我就能轻松掌握100个单词，尤其是用我喜欢或熟悉的故事。

用故事学语法也比死记规则强。高中3年我不用上基础英语课，因为当时我的老师从我的作文水平断定我熟悉语法，让我直接去了专教写作的英语荣誉课。事实上，我打心底不喜欢语法，对它一直是避而远之，我几乎不知道动名词和沙鼠这两个词的区别。但从高中2年级开始，我每周至少读三到四本书，读得多以后，我使用语言的正确程度和那些背过“在元音音素而不是元音字母前加‘an’”等准则的人不相上下。直到今天，我还不知道“咳嗽、够了、犁、尽管”这些词为什么结尾的字母拼写相同发音却不同，但读了成千上万的故事后，我能做到发音正确。

故事还能调动我们的情感，唤起心中的欢喜、愤怒、恐惧、怀旧、惊奇，心理学表明情感体验能创造最生动持久的记忆。因此，具有无畏精神、爱国精神、直面困难、为家庭自我牺牲等普世主题的故事，不仅有助于我们学习一门语言，还有助于了解一个国家历史文化中令人难忘的教训。

最后，故事有助于消除人们对其他国家的误解——和外国人讲故事也是让他们陪练英语的好方法！

上世纪90年代初，我用对话形式写了一本《魅力福建》，并为它配有录音，不仅帮助外国人更好地了解福建，也给中国人提供素材，激发外国人“陪”他们练习英语的兴趣。外国人已厌倦重复回答这样的问题：“你好吗？“你是哪里人？”“你在哪工作？”但任何一个精神健全的外国人来中国时，都乐于同能够分享中国丰富历史文化的中国人交谈。

故事的讲述者是最好的老师，无论在幼儿园、哈佛商学院、还是厦门大学，都是如此。但要让故事十分生动不仅需要口述还需要表演。更好的是，学生如果能将课堂上的故事演出来，一定会对所学留有深刻记忆。

所以，我鼓励你们把自己的语言学习，从仅仅依靠课堂转变成通过难以忘怀的经历的方式掌握。学习故事，然后用表演分享它们。那么你不仅是在学习，也是在传授知识，而这才是人生的意义。

潘维廉

2020年5月13日

扫一扫
看老潘读信视频

Chinese and Americans – We're All Dreamers

May 14, 2020

Dear Chinese friends,

"No matter what happens, it needs no prophetic gift to know that the 20th century will see at the forefront of the nations of the world, – China in the East and America in the West. Well may we pray that, for the welfare of humanity, their purposes will be as peaceful and upright as to-day."

Fujian Governor's Independence Day toast to Americans in Xiamen, July 4th, 1891.

In 1994, I taught my sons (and myself) about the history and culture of China as we drove 40,000 km around the country from Xiamen on the coast to Mongolia in the North and on to the Gobi Desert, Tibet and back. But I also wanted my sons to know their homeland as well as China, so in 1995 we drove 40,000 miles (65,000 km) around the U.S. and Canada.

The more I get to know about both China and the U.S., the more fortunate I feel to be a resident of both countries. As a very prescient Fujian governor said in 1891, both are great nations – and I hope that both will work together in the 21st century to achieve the peaceful world we failed to achieve in the last century.

I am only too familiar with the U.S.' many shortcomings, but I deeply admire the principles and values upon which the U.S. was founded, and I respect that my homeland has at least tried to achieve ideals that few other nations have even attempted. The U.S., for example, is truly an ethnic melting pot, with more people speaking Spanish than Spain, and at least 53 languages spoken in Los Angeles schools. I grew up in the South so I'm well aware of the racism, and it is easier to enact equal opportunity laws than to change people's hearts – but in spite of ongoing problems, I'm thankful there has also been vast improvement since my childhood. The U.S. has other serious issues as well, but overall our country has made a positive impact on the planet – and if the U.S. and China can resolve their differences and work together, the synergy could bring unparalleled peace and prosperity.

The world has never had two great nations as powerful and unique as 5,000-year-old China and the 250-year-old U.S., and though they are vastly different on the surface, they are both inhabited by people who share the same values and dreams; we differ mainly in how we seek to accomplish those dreams. If my two homes can set aside differences – agree to disagree – and work together, they can not only be a force for good but also a healthy check and balance for each other (as we've seen, it's dangerous to allow one "little emperor" to police the planet).

Sadly, I had naively hoped that the internet, which seems to instantly inform everyone on everything, would help raise awareness and responsibility to the point where the peoples of the world could pressure their leaders to make transparent, moral and just decisions and policies. That hasn't happened yet. The growing unrest and anger that fueled "road rage" seems to have now given rise to "net rage," with people uncritically influenced and infuriated by fake news even as they ignore the real problems of endemic poverty and endless proxy wars needed to fuel the $100 billion a year arms industry, of which the U.S. accounts for 34%.

These wars are ostensibly fought over democracy or human rights but in reality the battle is over cheaper bananas, sugar, coffee, chocolate or copper. But Chinese of all people know this is nothing new. America's first complaint about China's human rights was ex-President Adams complaint in 1841 about China's refusal to accept opium:

> "The fundamental principle of the Chinese Empire is anti-commercial. It admits no obligation to hold commercial intercourse... it is time that this outrage upon the rights of human nature, and upon the first principles of the rights of nations, should cease."[①]

What Adams did not tell Americans was that the Emperor himself had said China welcomed all trade, opposing only the illegal smuggling

① "Adam's Lecture on the War with China," delivered before the Massachusetts Historical Society, December 1841, *The Chinese Repository*, Vol. XI, January to December, Canton, 1842, p. 281.

of opium.

China is the most ancient trading nation on the planet, with at least 3,000 years of rich international commerce under her belt. In the 1700s, China accounted for 1/3 of the world's GDP, and in March, 2014, Harvard Business Review noted,

> "Until the early 19th century, China's economy was more open and market driven than the economies of Europe."

Adams' war was over opium, not human rights, but he was able to sway policy and public opinion because he spoke for powerful opium merchants whose wealth influenced the media. Little has changed in 180 years. To this day, our warmongering media has fostered such fear and distrust that a 2017 BBC poll found only 33% of Chinese viewed the U.S.' influence favorably and only 22% of Americans viewed China's influence positively. History shows, however, that of all great nations, the U.S. and China have great reason to work together.

I'm well aware of America's injustices in the 19th century, but overall, it made more attempts to help China than other Western countries. The U.S. tried to protect China's sovereignty from the Europeans and Japanese, invested heavily in China's modern education and fought the twin evils of the West's "pigs 'n poison"② trades (coolies and opium).

In 1867, the U.S. Consul in Amoy helped put in motion the events that would halt the evil trade in Chinese coolies, who were treated

② Pigs here refers to coolies; poison refers to opium.

worse than the black slaves of Africa. They were called "piggies" because their destinations – British, French, Dutch and Spanish colonies – were painted on their backs, and they were packed so tightly in ships that it was common for 1/4 or 1/3 to die on the voyage. In October, 1865, 388 of 550 coolies on the ship Dea del Mare perished. Although many Westerners cried crocodile tears for the human loss, it was the U.S. that took action to end it.

The U.S. was also the first Western nation to demand that its citizens cease from the lucrative trafficking of opium in China. Powerful American opium merchants fought the U.S. government for decades but America's leaders finally forced the issue, agreeing with China that no amount of profits justified such an immoral trade. A Chinese official in Beijing ruefully observed that it was the first time he'd seen a so-called Christian country actually act like a Christian country.

The U.S. also opposed Britain, France, Russia, Germany and Japan dividing China into colonial spheres of influence. In 1899, U.S. Secretary of State John Hay urged these nations to respect China's territorial and administrative integrity and he created the Open Door Policy (which Japan and Russia ignored; they both invaded the Northeast of China and then fought each other). I know the U.S.' motivation, in part, was to ensure they had equal footing in China with other nations, but they also had China's interests at heart – as they proved when they abandoned the incredibly lucrative opium trade.

The U.S. was dragged into WW II precisely because of its defense of China. America had opposed Japan's 1931 invasion of the Northeast of China and in 1937 most Americans sided with China in the Sino-Japanese War[3] and many volunteered for the Flying Tigers (1st American Volunteer Group, or AVG), which attacked Japanese planes with American planes painted with Chinese flags. China today has Flying Tiger memorials or museums in Hunan, Sichuan, Yunnan and Guangxi.

In 1941, the U.S. tried to stop Japan's attacks on China by cutting off its major oil supplies, which led to Japan's attack on Pearl Harbor. From that point on, the U.S. fought openly side-by-side with the Chinese.

In 1943, the U.S. passed the "Sino-American Treaty for the Relinquishment of Extraterritorial Rights in China," which ended American and British unequal treaty rights and made them subject to Chinese law while in China.

After the war, in 1948, Secretary of State Marshall told a secret session of congress that the Kuomintang could never defeat the Communists in battle, and he urged the U.S. to conduct negotiations. His advice was ignored, and U.S.-China relations were severed until 1979, the year after I served two years in the Air Force in Taiwan.

Sino-U.S. relations have continued to improve since 1979 in spite of powerful special interest groups and the fear and mistrust incited by manipulative media. The only way to counter this fear is by ending the ignorance – and that is best done by increasing exchanges – especially the educational exchanges which the U.S. and China have engaged in for most of the past 170 years.

③ Quincy Wright and Carl J. Nelson, "American Attitudes Toward Japan and China, 1937-38." *Public Opinion Quarterly* 3#1 (1939): 46-62.

Yung Wing (容闳, 1828-1912), who graduated from Yale in 1854, was the first Chinese to graduate from a North American university. Yale conferred upon Yung an honorary Doctorate of Laws in 1876, and the 1,200 volume collection that he donated to Yale in 1878 became the core of Yale's famous East Asian Library. Yung Wing wrote in 1854:

> "... the rising generation of China should enjoy the same educational advantage that I had enjoyed; that through western education China may be regenerated."

Many Chinese followed in Yung Wing's footsteps thanks to the Burlingame-Seward Treaty of 1868. The first equal treaty between China and a Western power, it stated, "Chinese subjects shall enjoy all the privileges of the public educational institutions under the control of the government of the United States." In 1872, the Qing government launched its first study abroad project by sending 30 teenage Chinese students to study in the U.S.

American missionaries, diplomats and officials founded or cofounded quality education institutions throughout China, the most famous being Tsinghua University, which produced brilliant students like Qian Xuesen. In the 1940s, Qian became a prominent rocket scientist at the California Institute of Technology. After groundless accusations during the "Red Scare" of the 1950s, he returned to China to become "Father of China's Rocketry" and helped develop the first atomic bomb of China.

My own home of Xiamen is proof of American influence on

China's education. From 1900 to 1920, Gulangyu Islet was said to be the richest square mile on earth but it was also probably the most talented square mile on earth. The tiny islet's 20 educational institutes included the Tong-Wen Institute, which was founded by U.S. Amoy Consul A. Burlingame Johnson (subsequent Presidents were all U.S. Consuls). Tiny Gulangyu was home to an astonishing number of great talents like John Ma, Father of Modern Chinese Sports; Dr. Lin Qiaozhi, Mother of Modern Women's Medicine; Lu Zhuangzhang, Father of Pinyin and punctuation; Yu Qingsong, famed astronomer; Zuohuang Chen, famed conductor; Lin Yutang, twice nominated for the Nobel Prize in Literature; Yin Chengzong, China's greatest Chinese pianist, and several hundred other famous Chinese musicians, and many more.

Sino-U.S. Academic cooperation and exchanges ceased after Liberation but in 1978, when Deng Xiaoping asked about sending 300 Chinese to study in the U.S., President Carter replied that China could even send 100,000. By 1981, over 8,000 Chinese were in the U.S. and hundreds of Americans were in China, with over 80 sister-school agreements.[④]

In 2019, the 369,548 Chinese studying in the U.S. (mainly business, followed by engineering, math and computer science) accounted for 1/3 of America's 1.09 million international students. And China is now a top ten destination for American students – though if Americans knew China half as well as Chinese knew the U.S., China

④ https://www.chinadaily.com.cn/a/201911/22/WS5dd6c738a310cf3e355791e1.html.

would be American students' 1st destination – at least for a Gap Year.

Since the 1960s, thousands of students around the world have taken a "Gap Year" before college to travel abroad, play sports, volunteer, join cultural exchanges, etc. This break allows them to catch their breath and rethink their sense of identity, vision, and purpose. Although few Americans take a gap year, perhaps because of the high cost of U.S. education and pressure to enter the workforce, I encourage as many as I can to spend a year in China after high school. It is fun, eye-opening, and relatively inexpensive, and in today's world, a year of Mandarin study in China looks good on any resume, regardless of one's career. And as I know from experience, once China is in a student's blood, their career plans are quite likely to change.

In 1999, I helped arrange for Xiamen University to host the one-semester U.S.-based China Studies Program, and over the years fully 25% of participants returned to China after college for further study or work. I was not surprised that these young Americans fell for China just as I had. I doubt that many Americans can visit China or Chinese visit America without their hearts being touched by the people – as Xi Jinping himself saw with farmers in Muscatine (population 22,000) Iowa in 1985 and 2012.

When Xi Jinping revisited Iowa in 2012, the Muscatine Mayor said, "We've displayed to this world leader our work ethic, No. 1, and our value for friendship; that's No. 2."

Xi Jinping said of the people of Muscatine, "To me, you are America!"

I agree with President Xi.

Americans put in more work hours per week than any other developed nation because, like Chinese, we work hard to achieve our dreams. And Americans are friendly, inclusive and welcoming, except when fearful or ignorant – but that is true of all people, Chinese included. Fear and ignorance are the greatest threats to peace and prosperity, and the only cure is to learn more about each other.

As a child, I cherished the American Dream. As an adult, I've witnessed fulfillment of the China Dream. My dream now is that China and the U.S. can work together for a World Dream – but that won't happen unless we do a better job of telling China's Story to the world. So master your English and tell China's Story – and visit the U.S.

Bill Brown

Quote from Lao Pan:

老潘金句：

Our China story, regardless of what language we use, or how well we use it, is dead unless our hearers are willing and prepared to hear it – and it is our job to prepare them.

不管我们使用何种语言，不管我们多么精通它，只有听众愿意聆听，我们的中国故事才具有生命力——这就是我们的任务，用你的中国故事打动世界。

The Browns' first wheels in Amoy,
1988
初到厦门（1988 年）

Bill's family visiting
in Shaoshan, 1994
老潘一家游览韶山（1994 年）

Bill with his wife and sons visiting the
Great Wall, 1994
老潘带着妻儿自驾游长城（1994 年）

Bill exploring China again, 2019
老潘“重走中国”团队（2019 年）

中国人和美国人——我们都是梦想家

亲爱的中国朋友们：

“不管发生什么，可预见的是20世纪站在世界前列的是东方的中国和西方的美国，这并不需要什么先见之明。让我们祈祷，他们将为了人类的福祉，像今天一样追求和平与正直。”

——1891年7月4日，福建地方官在美国独立日活动上的祝辞

1994年，我们一家驱车4万公里环行中国，从东部沿海城市厦门出发，途经北部省份内蒙古，再向西途经戈壁沙漠抵达西藏，最后再返回厦门。一路上，我向儿子们教授着中国的历史和文化（我自己也从中不断学习）。但除了了解中国，我希望他们也能了解自己的故乡，所以1995年时，我们绕北美4万英里（6.5万公里）。

对中国、美国了解愈深，我就愈加觉得能在这两个国家都生活过是非常幸运的事。正如一位很有先见之明的福建地方官在1891年说的那样，这是两个伟大的国家——我希望他们在21世纪携手努力，实现在上个世纪缺失的世界和平与正义。

深知美国有许多缺点，但我仍深深钦佩我的祖国——美国所推崇的原则和价值，和它至少敢为人先实践鲜有国家敢于尝试的理想，让人尊敬。美国是一个真正的民族大熔炉，说西班牙语的人比西班牙本土的还多，在洛杉矶的学校至少能听到53种语言。我在南方长大，很清楚种族主义是怎么回事，但比起颁布平等机会的法律，改变人们的想法就没那么容易。尽管问题重重，我还是很欣慰地看到，从我童年开始那里的情况也有了巨大的改善。当然，美国的问题不止这一点。但总的说来，无论是中国还是美国，对全球的发展都产生了积极的影响——如果中美可以化解分歧，携手合作，将创造出前所未有的和平与繁荣。

世界上从未有两个国家像有着5000年历史的中国和250年历史的美国这样强大和独特，这两个国家表面看上去有着天壤之别，但这两片土地上的人们却分享着共同的价值观和梦想；我们的主要分歧是在于如何实现这些梦想。如果我的两个家能够求同存异，携手合作，它们不仅可以成为一股向善的力量，还可以形成健康的制衡关系。

令人遗憾的是，我竟天真地寄希望于网络，因为它看似可让人们立即了解到发生的一切；我希望它能够帮助人们增强意识和责任，对其领导人施加压力，促使后者做出透明、道德和正义的决策。但这至今还没实现。反倒是日益增长的不安和愤怒所助长的“公路暴行”现在似乎已催生了“网络暴行”。就像在假新闻的推波助澜下，人们毫无批判力，情绪易被左右，区域性贫困和无休止的代理战争等实质问题却被他们忽视，正是这些刺激着每年1000亿美元的军工产业的发展，其中美国的军费占全球的34%。

表面上是为民主或人权而战，实际上是为了低价获取香蕉、糖、咖啡、巧克力或铜。这种套路对中国而言已不是什么新鲜事。美国对中国第一次进行人权控诉是在1841年，当时美国总统亚当斯（Adams）对中国拒绝接受鸦片进行控诉：

> "中华帝国的基本原则是反对商业。它不承认任何商业交往义务……现在是停止这种践踏人性权利和各国权利第一原则的暴行的时候了。"①

亚当斯没有告诉美国人，清朝皇帝本人说过中国欢迎一切贸易，反对的只是非法走私鸦片。

中国是地球上最古老的贸易国，有着至少3000年丰富的国际贸易历史。《哈佛商业评论》在2014年3月份的报道中指出，18世纪中国国内生产总值占全世界的1/3。

> "直到19世纪初，中国经济的开放和市场化程度还是领先于欧洲。"

亚当斯的战争是为了鸦片，而不是人权，但他能够左右政策和舆论，因为他代表可左右媒体的鸦片大亨的利益。往后的180年依旧如此。时至今日，鼓吹战争的媒体助长了这种恐慌和不信任情绪。英国广播公司2017年的一项民意调查发现，只有33%的

① 亚当斯就第一次鸦片战争发表的演说【R】. 发表于马萨诸塞州历史协会，1841-12，广东：《中国丛报》，1842（11）：281.

中国人认为美国的影响是正面的，只有 22% 的美国人对中国的影响持肯定看法。然而，历史表明，所有像中美这样伟大的国家有充分理由开展合作。

我很清楚美国在 19 世纪的做法不道义，但总的来说，它比其他西方国家做过更多尝试来帮助中国。美国试图保护中国主权不受欧洲和日本侵犯，大力投资中国现代教育，并与西方苦力和鸦片贸易的双重邪恶做斗争。

1867 年，美国驻厦门领事协助发起行动，阻止贩卖中国苦力的邪恶贸易活动。这些苦力的待遇比非洲黑奴还要糟糕。他们被称为“猪仔”，背上漆有目的地英国、法国、荷兰或西班牙等殖民地字样。他们被密集地装在船上，在航行中通常会有 1/3 或 1/4 的人死亡。1865 年 10 月，“德尔玛”号 550 名苦力中有 388 人丧生。尽管许多西方人为这些人的死亡流下了“鳄鱼眼泪”，但是美国采取行动结束了这一损失。

美国也是第一个要求其公民停止在中国进行利润丰厚的鸦片贩运的西方国家。实力雄厚的美国鸦片商贩与美国政府就此分庭抗礼了几十年，但美国领导人最终敦促这一问题解决，同意中国的观点，即再多的利润也不能证明这种不道德的贸易是正当的。当时北京的一位中国官员不无沮丧地说，他终于有幸见到一个所谓的基督教国家像个真正的基督教国家了。

美国还反对英国、法国、俄罗斯、德国和日本将中国划入本国的殖民势力范围。1899 年，美国国务卿约翰·海伊（John Hay）敦促这些国家尊重中国的领土和行政完整，并制定了门户开放政策（日本和俄罗斯对此置之不理；他们都侵略了中国东北三省，然后又相互争斗）。我知道美国的动机，在某种程度上，是为了确保他们在中国享有与其他国家平等的地位，但他们也关切中国的利益——正如他们放弃了利润惊人的鸦片贸易所证明的那样。

美国被拖入二战正是为了保卫中国。美国曾反对日本 1931 年入侵中国东北三省；1937 年，在日本侵华战争中，大多数美国人站在中国一边[②]，许多人志愿加入了飞虎队（“美国第一志愿航空队”，简称 AVG），用印有中国国旗的美国飞机攻击日本飞机。今天在中国的湖南、四川、云南和广西都有飞虎纪念馆或博物馆。

1941 年，美国试图切断主要石油供应以阻止日本对中国的袭击，导致日本偷袭珍珠港。从那时起，美国公开与中国并肩作战。

1943 年，美国通过了《中美关于取消美国在华治外法权及处理有关问题条约》，结束了美英对华的不平等条约权利，使美英在华期间受中国法律管辖。

战后，在 1948 年，美国国务卿马歇尔（Marshall）在国会秘密会议上声称，国民党永远不能在战斗中打败共产党，他敦促美国调停中国内战。但他在中国“败走麦城”，而后美中关系一直中断到 1979 年，那时我已在驻台湾的空军服役两年。

尽管强大的特殊利益集团和媒体的煽动引起恐慌和不信任，中美关系自 1979 年以来一直在改善。消除这种恐慌的唯一办法是摒弃这种无知，消除无知的最好办法是增加交流，特别是像中美两国在过去 170 年的大部分时间里进行的教育交流。

② 昆西・赖特，卡尔・ J. 内尔逊 . 1937—1938 年美对中日态度【J】. 舆论季刊，1939，3（1）：46-62.

容闳（1828–1912），1854年毕业于耶鲁大学，是第一个从一所北美大学毕业的中国人。1876年，耶鲁大学授予他荣誉法学博士学位，1878年他捐给耶鲁1200册藏书，这些书后来成为耶鲁著名的东亚图书馆的最重要部分。容闳在1854年写道：

“中国的年轻一代应当享受与我同样的教育利益；这样通过西方教育，中国将得以复兴。”

自1868年中美签订《蒲安臣条约》，许多中国人开始追随容闳的脚步。这是中国与西方国家签订的第一个平等条约，它规定：“嗣后中国人欲入美国大小官学学习各等文艺，须照相待最优之人民一体优待。”1872年，清政府派出30名中国青少年赴美留学，启动了它的第一个留学项目。

美国传教士、外交官和其他官员在中国各地创办或共同创办一些素质教育机构，其中最著名的是清华大学，它培养了像钱学森这样的杰出人才。上世纪40年代，钱学森成为加州理工学院著名的火箭科学家；在50年代的“赤色恐慌”中受到无端指责后，他回到中国成为“中国火箭之父”，大大推动了中国第一颗原子弹的发射进程。

我的家乡厦门就是美国对中国教育影响的缩影。从1900年到1920年，据说鼓浪屿有着地球上最富有的一平方英里，但它可能也是地球上最有才华的一平方英里。这个小岛上有20所教育机构，包括美国驻厦门领事巴詹声（A. Burlingame Johnson）创办的同文学院。小小的鼓浪屿出现了中国现代体育之父马约翰、现代中国医学圣母林巧稚博士、拼音与标点之父卢戆章、著名天文学家余青松、著名指挥家陈作煌、两次获得诺贝尔文学奖提名的林语堂和中国最伟大的钢琴家殷承宗等一大批杰出人才。

新中国成立后，中美学术交流合作停止，但在1978年，邓小平要求派遣300名中国学生赴美留学时，卡特（Carter）总统回答说，中国派遣10万名学生来美国都不是问题。到1981年，在美国的中国学生超过8000名，在中国也有数百名美国学生，两国间有八十几所姐妹学校。③

2019年，在美留学的369548名中国学生（主要是商科，其次是工程、数学和计算机科学）占美国109万留学生的1/3。中国现在是美国学生的十大留学目的国——不过，如果美国人对中国的了解能赶上中国人对美国的一半，那么至少在一个间隔年里，中国将是美国学生的第一留学目的地。

20世纪60年代以来，世界成千上万的青年人在大学毕业前通过去国外旅游、做志愿者或参加体育活动、文化交流等形式度过“间隔年”。这种方式让他们停下来，重新思考自己的身份、愿景和目标。也许是因为美国教育成本高昂，就业压力大，很少有美国人选择间隔年，但我鼓励自己尽可能在高中毕业后到中国待一年。中国很有趣，让人大开眼界，且花销相对便宜。在当今，在中国学习一年普通话的经历放在任何简历上看起来都不错，不管你是什么职业。从以往经验看来，一旦中国融入学生的血液，他们的职业规划很可能会改变。

③ https://www.chinadaily.com.cn/a/201911/22/WS5dd6c738a310cf3e355791e1.html.

1999 年，我帮助厦门大学主办了一学期面向美国学生的中国研究项目，多年来，25% 的参与者在大学毕业后返回中国深造或工作。我一点也不奇怪这些美国年轻人和我一样喜欢中国。我相信大多到过中国的美国人或者到过美国的中国人都会被当地的民众打动——就像习近平主席本人 1985 年和 2012 年在爱荷华州马斯卡廷（人口为 2.2 万）那样，被当地的农民打动。

2012 年习近平主席重访爱荷华州时，马斯卡廷市长说："我们不仅向这位世界领导人展示了我们的职业道德，还展示了我们对友谊的重视。"

习近平主席谈到马斯卡廷人时说："对我来说，你们就是美国！"④

我同意习主席的看法。

美国人每周投入工作的时间比任何其他发达国家的都多，和中国人一样，美国人也为实现梦想努力工作。他们友好、包容、热情，也有恐惧或无知——但所有国家的人都有这样的一面，包括中国人。恐惧和无知是和平与繁荣最大的威胁，唯一的办法是加深彼此的了解。

小时候，我怀揣着美国梦。长大后，我见证了中国梦的实现。我现在的梦想是，中美两国为实现世界梦共同努力——但除非我们更好地向世界讲述中国故事，否则这种梦想不会实现。所以，学好英语，讲好中国的故事——并访问美国。

潘维廉

2020 年 5 月 14 日

④ http://www.xinhuanet.com/world/2015-09/19/c_128246345.htm.

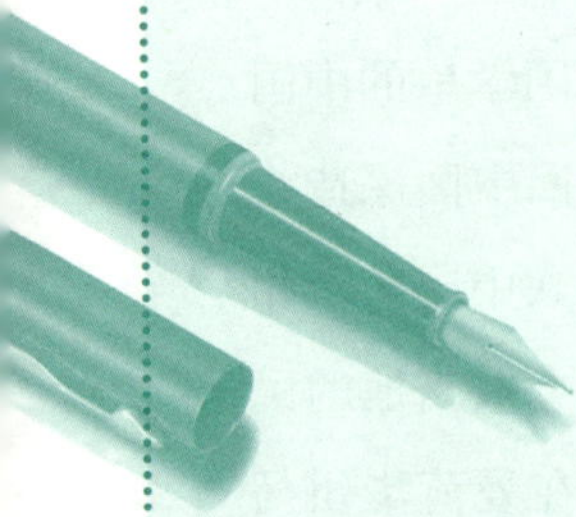

扫一扫

看老潘读信视频

Health, Then Wealth!

May 20, 2020

Dear Chinese friends,

"Our nation is wanting in strength" was the 20-year-old Mao Zedong's first sentence in his first published article. His concern was not military or economic weakness but the Chinese themselves.

"The physical condition of the population deteriorates daily," Mao wrote in "A Study of Physical Education" (April, 1917). "Physical education complements education in virtue and knowledge... Without the body there would be neither virtue nor knowledge. Those who understand this are rare... Nowadays students generally dislike exercise."

Mao gave several reasons that people neglected health, the first being that they did not truly see the need. I understood the problem. I too had taken health for granted until I ended up in a Hong Kong hospital for two months in 1999 struggling with cancer.

From my hospital bed I gazed out the 14th floor window at people in the park far below. I longed to just walk in the sunshine – or even just eat a morsel of food, as I had no food or drink by mouth for two months. How true, I realized, that only sick people appreciate health.

American visitors asked me, "If you are able to leave, will you return home?"

By "home," they meant the U.S., but I'd hoped to return to China, though it seemed unlikely, given my condition. And then our Fujian governor, Xi Jinping, and Xiamen mayor Hong Yongshi, sent people with flowers and wishes that I'd recover quickly and return home – and by home they meant Fujian. I started improving from that day, determined to return home to my Xiamen home and family. But the doctor gave me a stern warning before I left.

"You had a 50/50 chance this time," he said, "but you won't survive a second time. Colon cancer is partly hereditary but the biggest cause is lifestyle: poor diet, lack of exercise, lack of rest and sleep, and stress. You aren't superman. If you take care of your body, it has a chance of overcoming even hereditary problems, but if you don't change your lifestyle, you won't have a very long life."

That was the first time a Western doctor had spoken to me about healthy lifestyle. Chinese medical philosophy has of course emphasized prevention over cure for thousands of years but it is not as common in the West. Most Westerners sabotage our body's miraculous natural defenses with the unhealthy lifestyle that, sadly, is also becoming prevalent in China.

When I came to China in 1988, people walked or took a bus – or rode a bicycle if they were rich enough to own one. Most Chinese don't cycle today. Many barely even walk except to hop in a taxi or bus. They spend their days at a desk and spend their evenings with eyes glued to a TV, computer or mobile phone, and fuel their sedentary lifestyle with fast food often delivered right to their door. Not surprisingly, obesity in China has risen from 3.3% in 2004 to 14% in 2014 (with abdominal obesity over 31%). Rural boys' obesity shot up from 0.03% in 1985 to 17.2% in 2014.①

Ji Chengye wrote, "China has entered the era of obesity. The speed of growth is shocking."②

To see where Chinese will be a few years down the road, just look at U.S. statistics. In 2020, 3/4 of Americans are overweight and 42.4% are obese – up from 30.5% only 8 years earlier. Obesity is almost 50% in some age groups. And the problem with obesity is not people's appearance. For most of history we've viewed heavier people as better looking than the stick figures foisted on us today by the fashion industry. The problem with obesity is simply that it is deadly. With over 300,000 deaths per year, obesity is the 2nd leading cause of preventable death in the U.S., surpassed only by tobacco.

Obesity not only leads to heart disease, stroke, cancer, type 2 diabetes and other chronic illnesses but also increases the risk of mental disorders such as mood swings, anxiety and depression. A 2015 study revealed that 62% of American adults suffer from stress-induced chronic health problems.

In Britain, now known as "Europe's fattest nation," the percentage

---

① "Explosion in Childhood Obesity in China 'Worst Ever,' Expert Says of New Study Findings," *South China Morning Post,* 27 April 2016.

② MacLeod, Calum, "Obesity of China's kids Stuns officials," *USA Today,* 1 August 2007.

of adults overweight or obese grew from 53% to 63% between 1993 and 2018, but children are suffering as well. A February 2019 headline read, "British young 'more likely to be fat and sick' than other Europeans."③ Between 2008 and 2016, the percentage of British youth aged 16 to 24 with chronic health problems grew from 13.5% to 18.5%.

This obesity epidemic has spawned an $82 billion industry of weight-loss regimens and products but dieting usually fails because perpetual hunger is not a sustainable choice – at least for sane people. Besides, food is only one of many factors behind obesity. The only cure for the unhealthy lifestyle behind obesity is to change the unhealthy mindset – which my wife and I did in Napa Valley, California.

10-Day Miracle Cure

How much would you pay for a miracle medicine that, within weeks, cured my wife of borderline type 2 diabetes and decades of debilitating pain from fibromyalgia, migraines, and irritable bowel syndrome? For almost 3 decades, Sue had tried both Chinese and Western medicine but doctors could only give her painkillers as there was no cure. As her condition deteriorated, she ate more, walked less, and her weight increased. In 2017, in sheer desperation, we spent 10 days at the St. Helena Lifestyle Medicine Institute – and it changed our lives.

The program not only cured Sue's illnesses but also my high blood

③ https://metro.co.uk/2019/02/20/british-young-more-likely-to-be-fat-and-sick-than-other-europeans-8683758.

pressure. It also gave us more energy, better moods, more enthusiasm for life, family and work – and helped Sue lose 35 pounds over the subsequent two years without dieting.

For 10 days, we listened to fascinating health lectures and ate nothing but the healthy, tasty meals that their chefs taught us to prepare. They even took us to a grocery store to show us how to decipher the deceptive labels and avoid the highly processed foods that have been proven to cause health issues ranging from high-blood pressure and cholesterol to cancer, obesity and depression.

The Lifestyle Medicine Center shared extensive peer-reviewed research that reaffirmed my Hong Kong doctor's claim in 1999 – that most "chronic" illnesses like type 2 diabetes are caused not by disease or DNA but lifestyle. But, frankly, I was still skeptical that a change in lifestyle could actually reverse such conditions. It sounded too good and too simple to be true. Yet within weeks, Sue quit taking medicines she'd used for decades, and 3 years later and 35 pounds lighter, she feels so good that she has no temptation at all to sabotage her newfound health with a return to the old ways.

The 10-day St. Helena Lifestyle Medicine program was life-changing, but even as I took notes I marveled that I had already read about much of the basic philosophy in ancient writings of both East and West.

Hippocrates (460-370 BC), the Father of Western medicine, said, "Let food be your medicine," and he often prescribed foods as medicine, but his ancient wisdom has long been disregarded.

In China, however, the medicinal value of foods and herbs has been touted for over 4,000 years, with practitioners stressing that nutritional needs vary with age, gender, and even climates or seasons. After 3 decades in China, we're no longer surprised when our Chinese neighbors drop by on the first day of Spring or Winter with a fortifying soup to keep us hale and hearty.

Ancient Chinese also emphasized stress relief through herbs, meditation, acupuncture, massage and exercise. FIFA recognizes *cuju* (蹴鞠), described in the over 2000-year-old *Annals of the Warring States* (《战国策》) as the world's first version of football. But the most common exercise today is seen in parks each night when Chinese of all ages practice tai chi or dance gracefully to rhythmic music, their willowy movements forceful yet graceful, energizing yet calming.

Some people, of course, do have physical limitations, but that hasn't stopped people like my quadriplegic friend Dr. Zhang. Paralyzed from the neck down as a young medical doctor in Africa, he can email me only by blowing through a tube clamped between his teeth, but he is positive and persistent, and passionate about the organization he founded to encourage other physically challenged people. Dr. Zhang is also extremely health conscious because life is very fragile for a quadriplegic – but whose life is not fragile?

Xi Jinping visited Fujian's Pingtan Island in November 2014 and said, "An excellent eco-environment is Pingtan's precious asset. 'A true treasure' should never be exchanged for any other 'fake treasures' that may harm the environment."

Xi Jinping would agree, I'm sure, that your true treasure is health, and should never be exchanged for a fake treasure.

Stay healthy, stay the course, and dream!

Bill Brown

Quotes from Lao Pan:

老潘金句：

Stories are not just entertainment but also powerful tools for teaching all ages, from kindergartners to graduate students.

故事不仅可用于娱乐，还是有效的教育方式，从幼儿园到大学都是如此。

From my hospital bed I gazed out the 14th floor window at people in the park far below. I longed to just walk in the sunshine – or even just eat a morsel of food, as I had no food or drink by mouth for two months. How true, I realized, that only sick people appreciate health.

躺在病床上的我，透过14楼的窗户眺望着楼下公园里的人们。那时，我渴望到阳光下走一走，甚至一丁点食物都让我心心念，要知道我已经两个月没法正常吃喝了。于是，我真切地体会到，只有病了才懂得珍惜健康。

健康、致富！

亲爱的中国朋友们：

20 岁的毛泽东在他发表的第一篇文章的第一句话写道“国力茶弱”，他担心的不是军事或经济上的弱点，而是中国人自己。

“民族之体质，日趋轻细。”他在《体育之研究》（1917 年 4 月）中写道，“体育一道，配德育与智育……无体是无德智也。顾知之者或寡矣……今之学者多不好运动。”

毛泽东提出人们忽视健康的几个原因，第一是他们没有看到健康的必要性。对此，我深有体会。我也曾把健康当作理所当然，直到 1999 年底我在香港的一家医院挣扎两个月后才“醒悟”。

躺在病床上的我，透过 14 楼的窗户眺望着楼下公园里的人们。那时，我渴望到阳光下走一走，甚至一丁点食物都让我心心念，要知道我已经两个月没法正常吃喝了。于是，我真切地体会到，只有病了才懂得珍惜健康。

美国游客问我：“如果可以，你会回家吗？”

他们说的“家”是指美国。我本来希望回到中国大陆，然而我的情况似乎不太允许。后来，时任福建省省长的习近平和厦门市长洪永世托人送来了鲜花，希望我能尽快康复。回家，他们说的是福建。于是从那天起我就开始有了转变，决心回到厦门的家和家人身边。但医生在我离开前给了我一个严厉的警告。

“这次你有50%的存活率，”他说，“但下次就不一定了。结肠癌部分是遗传的，但最大的原因是生活方式，如饮食不良、不做锻炼、缺乏休息睡眠以及压力过大等。你不是超人。如果你照顾好自己的身体，甚至有机会克服遗传疾病，但如果你不改变生活方式，你就活不长。”

那是西医第一次跟我谈健康生活方式。几千年来，中国的医学一直强调预防胜于治疗，但在西方却并不常见。大多数西方人用不健康的生活方式破坏自己身体神奇的自然防御功能，遗憾的是，这种不健康的生活方式也逐渐横行中国。

当我1988年来中国时，中国人常步行或坐公共汽车出行，有点余钱的会买辆自行车代步。但今天大多数中国人不骑自行车。许多人除了步行去坐出租车或公共汽车，几乎都不走路。他们白天坐在桌前，晚上盯着电视、电脑或手机，久坐不动，饿了点份外卖。因此，中国的肥胖率从2004年的3.3%上升到2014年的14%（腹部肥胖率超过31%）就毫不奇怪了。在2014年，农村男孩肥胖率已从1985年的0.03%飙升至17.2%。[①]

健康专家季承业写道：“中国已经进入肥胖时代。增长速度令人震惊。”[②]

要想知道中国未来几年的发展方向，只需看看美国的数据。

① 新研究发现，中国儿童正遭遇“最严重”的肥胖激增现象【N】. 南华早报，2016-4-27.

② 卡勒姆·麦克劳德. 中国儿童肥胖现状引发政府震惊【N】. 今日美国，2007-8-1.

到 2020 年，3/4 的美国人超重，42.4% 的人肥胖，而肥胖人口 8 年前只有 30.5%。在某些年龄段肥胖人口几乎占 50%。肥胖的问题不在于外形。历史上，很多时候我们以微胖为美，认为这种体型比时尚界今天强加给我们的杆状身材好看。肥胖的问题仅在于它的致命性。在每年三十几万死亡人口中，肥胖是美国可预防死亡的第二大死因，仅次于烟草。

肥胖不仅会导致心脏病、中风、癌症、二型糖尿病和其他慢性疾病，还会增加情绪波动、焦虑和抑郁等精神障碍的风险。2015 年的一项研究显示，62% 的美国成年人患有因压力导致的慢性健康疾病。

在如今被称为“欧洲最胖国家”的英国，1993 年至 2018 年间，成年人超重或肥胖的比例从 53% 上升到 63%，与此同时儿童也未能“幸免”。2019 年 2 月有一个头版头条这样写道，《英国年轻人比其他欧洲人“更容易肥胖和生病”》③。在 2008 年至 2016 年间，16 至 24 岁患有慢性健康疾病的英国青年从 13.5% 增长到 18.5%。

肥胖症的流行催生了价值 820 亿美元的销售减肥方案和产品的产业。节食通常不管用，至少对正常人来说，长期不吃东西不是一个可持续选择。此外，食物只是众多因素中的一个。肥胖背后有不健康生活方式在作祟，要改变不健康生活方式唯一的方法就是改变不健康心态，就像我和妻子在加州纳帕谷时做的那样。

③ https://metro.co.uk/2019/02/20/british-young-more-likely-to-be-fat-and-sick-than-other-europeans-8683758.

10天奇迹疗法

你愿意花多少钱买一种在几周内可治愈我妻子苏的二型糖尿病和根除她数十年来因纤维肌痛、偏头痛和肠易激综合征导致的虚弱疼痛的神奇药物呢？近30年，苏看过中医和西医，但都只是治标不治本。病情恶化后，她食量增加运动量减少，体重大增。2017年，情急之下我们去了圣赫勒拿生活方式医疗研究所呆了10天，我们的生活由此得到了改变。

这个项目不仅治好了苏的病，还治好了我的高血压；带给我们更多的能量、更好的情绪，以及对生活、家庭和工作的热情；还帮苏在随后的两年里在不节食的情况下减掉35磅。

在那里的10天，我们听精彩的养生讲座，吃的是厨师教我们做的健康可口的食物。他们甚至带我们去杂货店，展示如何识别欺骗性标签，避免食用那些已被证明会导致高血压、高胆固醇、癌症、肥胖和抑郁等健康问题的精加工食品。

医疗中心分享了它们大量已由同行评议的研究，证实了我1999年时在香港的医院听到的说法，即大多数“慢性”疾病，如二型糖尿病不是由疾病或DNA造成的，而是生活方式。坦白地说，至此我仍怀疑生活方式的改变是否真的能扭转局面。因为听起来太好，太简单了，做起来可能就不是那么回事。然而几周内，苏不再依赖几十年来一直服用的药物；3年后，她的体重减轻了35磅，她感觉也非常好，没有任何东西可诱惑她破坏新找到的健康，重回过去的恶性循环。

为期10天的圣赫勒拿生活方式医疗项目改变了我们的生活方式。做笔记时，我惊奇地发现，这些内容有许多是我读过的东西方古代著作的基本理念。

西医之父希波克拉底（Hippocrates）（公元前460—公元前370年）曾说“让食物成为你的药”，并且他经常为病人采用食物疗法，但他古老的智慧长期被人们忽视。

在中国，食品和草药的药用价值已被推广4000多年，从业者强调营养的输入需随年龄、性别甚至气候、季节的变化而变化。因此，在中国生活30年后，当中国邻居在春季或冬季的第一天带着滋补汤来拜访我们时，我们已不再感到惊讶。

中国古人强调通过草药、冥想、针灸、按摩和锻炼来缓解压力。2000多年前《战国策》里提到的蹴鞠，就是国际足联认定的足球雏形。今天在中国最常见的运动见于每晚的公园，不同年龄段的人们在公园随着音乐节奏，优雅地打着太极拳或跳着舞步，他们动作柔软，富有力道，却十分优雅，充满活力却又心平气和。

当然，有些人确实有身体缺陷，但也不能阻止像我的四肢瘫痪的朋友张医生这样的人。作为一名年轻的驻非内科医生，他颈部以下全部瘫痪，只能通过夹在牙齿间的管子给我发电子邮件，但他积极向上、坚持不懈，热情投身于自己建立的助残组织，开展爱心工作。作为一名四肢瘫痪的患者，他知道生命的脆弱，非常注重健康——但谁的生命不脆弱？

2014年11月，习近平主席视察福建平潭岛时说：“优良的生态环境是平潭的‘真宝贝’，不能毁了‘真宝贝’，引来一些损害环境的‘假宝贝’。”

我相信，习主席会认同，你真正的宝贝是健康，健康永远不该用假宝贝给换走。

保持健康，坚持到底，梦想成真！

潘维廉

2020年5月20日

Quotes from Lao Pan:

老潘金句：

The most common exercise today is seen in parks each night when Chinese of all ages practice tai chi or dance gracefully to rhythmic music, their willowy movements forceful yet graceful, energizing yet calming.

今天在中国最常见的运动见于每晚的公园，不同年龄段的人们在公园随着音乐节奏，优雅地打着太极拳或跳着舞步，他们动作柔软，富有力道，却十分优雅，充满活力却又心平气和。

During my decades in China, Chinese have come to know the world but the world still does not know China. But as my grandfather used to say, "We can either get bitter or better."

在中国生活的几十年里，我发现中国对世界的了解日益加深，但世界对中国仍是知之甚少。但正如我祖父过去常说的，我们要么变得痛苦，要么变得更好。

扫一扫

看老潘读信视频

Bravery of Storytellers

August 6, 2020

Dear Chinese friends,

When CETV held a launch ceremony on January 15, 2020 for "Stories of China Retold in English," no one imagined that a pandemic would turn the world upside down, but nothing could dampen the spirit of the over 100,000 entrants, from preschool to college, or the small army of people that pulled the amazing event together.

The future of the event was in doubt, but on January 31, the organizing committee held its first online meeting and Prof. Hu Min, founder and CEO of New Channel International Education Group, and one of the competition's initiators, said, "We will proceed as planned, but move it online!"

Contestants began signing up the very next day through New Channel branch schools in over 40 cities, UBest English, and through co-organizers 21st Century English Newspaper, iQiyi, Bank of China and Mastercard.

As Prof. Hu Min predicted, the event was a great success, with the epidemic forcing organizers and contestants alike to embrace new methods and technology. In fact, the epidemic itself was a great story to share with the world as China defeated the disease with precision even as it has tackled poverty and other problems with precision to realize the China Dream.

By the end of the preliminary registration on March 31, the event had over 100,000 entrants not just from China but also from the U.S., Australia, the UK, Singapore and other areas. Each of them was eager to share their own China Story with passion, boldness – and courage!

I was honored to be a judge for the 44 finalists, but in my eyes each of the 100,000+ entrants were winners because each one overcame what to this day is Americans' greatest fear.

What Most Americans Most Fear?

For decades, many surveys of Americans' Top 10 Fears have shown that numbers two to ten may vary but number one is always the same – and I shared that same fear myself.

The National Social Anxiety Center revealed in February 2017 that fear of public speaking is Americans' most common fear and affects 73% of Americans. They fear it even more than spiders, heights – or even death![①]

In "The Thing We Fear More Than Death," in *Psychology Today* (November 29, 2012), Dr. Glenn Croston noted that the fear of public speaking is rooted in a fear of rejection and ostracism – a fear common

① https://nationalsocialanxietycenter.com/2017/02/20/public-speaking-and-fear-of-brain-freezes.

not just to people but to all social animals (even though I've yet to hear animals speak in public).

Croston wrote that Signe Dayoff, a social psychologist and teacher, feared speaking so much that he froze every time he had to give a class! "My tongue stuck to the roof of my dry mouth and I couldn't swallow, I blushed, sweated and trembled," he said. He finally got professional help.

I can relate to him. I was so shy as a child that I rarely spoke even to my own family. They nicknamed me hermit because I spent almost all of my time alone with my animals, or in the library. I could mimic the animals well – cows, chickens, horses, pigs, turkeys, monkeys. (I was born in the Year of the Monkey, and had a squirrel monkey.) But I didn't talk to people. And to this day, after teaching in China for 32 years, I still feel nervous before each class – but I love teaching so I do it anyway, and once I'm in front of my students, fear is forgotten.

Do You Fear Public Speaking?

A few years ago, the UK's Prince William was asked what he feared most, and he said, "Speaking in public." The British Council noted that 75% of people fear public speaking and 10% are "genuinely terrified."[②] The Council noted that those who feared public speaking included Winston Churchill, Abraham Lincoln, Thomas Jefferson and Gandhi – but they did not let their fear stop them! The billionaire Sir Richard Branson is afraid of speaking in public, and so are golfer

---

② https://www.britishcouncil.org/voices-magazine/how-overcome-fear-public-speaking.

Tiger Woods and actor and former California governor Arnold Schwarzenegger. And over 2,000 years ago, Cicero, the Roman statesman, lawyer and philosopher admitted,

> "Personally, I am very nervous when I begin to speak. Every time I make a speech I feel I am submitting to judgment, not only about my ability but my character and honour."

Warren Buffett was also "terrified" of public speaking, but he finally overcame it at age 21 when he took a Dale Carnegie course on public speaking. Buffett wrote,

> "You have to do it. And the sooner you do it, the better. It's so much easier to learn the right habits when you're young. If you have a fear of associating with people, you have to go out there and do it, and it's painful..."

I can relate to Buffett. Until I was 14, I was also "terrified" of public speaking, but by the time I'd moved to China in 1988, I had given talks about leadership to groups as large as 15,000. So as I tell my MBA students, if I can do it, anyone can – and should.

I was often bullied in school because I was not only very quiet but also small for my age, so when I turned 14 I decided I'd had enough of being everyone's punching bag. But when I entered a public speaking contest, my sister laughed. She was an outgoing, popular cheerleader, and she said, "Who will you give your speech to? The animals?"

I practiced alone before a mirror for hours and shocked students and teachers alike by winning the school contest, the district contest, and coming in 4th in the state contest. By then, many people were saying, "You are a natural speaker!" That was nonsense, of course. I was a natural hermit, not a speaker – but I did well because I practiced until I'd mastered the speech, going beyond mere memorization and mimicry and actually embodying the speech until I gave it naturally and fluidly.

As people discovered that I communicated well in writing and orally, I was asked to help many groups, and by grade 12, I was president of 2 clubs, a junior member of the city government, publicity chairman for the Florida MidState Lung Association, and I had attended an awards dinner with our governor.

In high school, and later in the military and business, many told me, "You are a natural leader!" That was nonsense, of course. I was a hermit, not a natural leader – but one of the leader's most important skills is communication. After all, a leader is only someone with followers, and people follow you because you can communicate to them how you can help them if you work together. So because I was a good communicator, I did become a leader in many areas – not because I was a natural leader but because I worked hard. And those communication skills have helped me in China as well – teaching, representing Chinese cities in overseas competitions, and telling China's Story to as many people as I can.

No one was born a good communicator, or a leader. Read the history books. You'll find they started out just like you, and me – young, inexperienced, afraid. But those you read about never quit. They pressed forward, and improved. As for those who did quit... that's exactly why you've never read about them!

You need to improve your speaking abilities for your own career, of course. But as 100,000 entrants in the recent "Stories of China Retold in English" event know, you also need to improve your public speaking skills, especially in English, so you can share China's story with the world.

I hope New Channel and CETV will hold this competition again – and I hope to hear your personal China Story as together we work to help the China Dream also become the World's Dream.

Persistence Brings Success! Àipīn cáihuì yíng!

Bill Brown

Quote from Lao Pan:

老潘金句：

I've known from childhood that stories can be powerful and life-changing, but only after moving to China did I learn that stories are also a powerful language learning tool, as well as a means for overcoming cultural misunderstandings and prejudices.

从小我就领略到故事有着强大力量，能够影响人生，但只有搬到中国后，我才知道故事也是一种强大的语言学习工具，也是消除文化误解和偏见的重要手段。

Bill serving as a judge at the first “Stories of China Retold in English” event, 2020
老潘担任首届“用英语讲中国故事”活动评委（2020 年）

Bill greeting players, 2020
老潘向活动选手打招呼（2020 年）

Bill communicating with a reader, 2020
老潘与读者交流（2020 年）

勇敢的故事讲述者

亲爱的中国朋友们：

2020年1月15日“用英语讲中国故事”活动在中国教育电视台发布时，没有人料想到世界会被小小的新冠病毒搅得天翻地覆。但即使如此，也没有什么能浇灭10万余名从学前到大学的各年龄段参与者的热情，或者说阻止这场令人叹为观止的活动的进行。

尽管活动前途未卜，但在1月31日活动组委会举行的第一次网络会议上，新航道国际教育集团创始人兼首席执行官，即活动发起人之一，胡敏教授说道：“活动按原计划进行，初选全部挪至网上！”

仅在第二天，参赛者就通过新航道在40多个城市的分校网点、优加青少英语以及活动的合办方《21世纪英文报》、爱奇艺网站、中国银行以及万事达信用卡中心等渠道报名。

尽管受疫情影响，组织者、报名者不得不采纳新方法和新技术，但正如胡敏教授所料，活动举办得非常成功。事实上，中国的新冠疫情本身就是一个可向世界分享的宏伟故事——中国有效控制了疫情，恰逢它在采取精准扶贫等措施实现中国梦的进程中。

截至 3 月 31 日报名截止日期，该活动吸引了 10 万余人报名参与，其中不仅有来自中国本土，还有来自美国、澳大利亚、英国、新加坡等地区的国际选手。他们每个人都渴望向世界分享自己饱含激情、无畏勇气的中国故事！

最后 44 名选手入围全国总决选，我很荣幸担任总决选评委一职，但在我看来，这 10 万多名报名者都是获奖者，因为每一位选手都克服了迄今为止最令美国人恐惧的事情。

大多数美国人最害怕什么？

尽管在过去几十年大量的调查中，第二大至第十大最令美国人恐惧的事情在排名上不尽相同，但第一大总是“毫无争议”——这也是我最恐惧的。

美国国家社交焦虑中心（National Social Anxiety Center）在 2017 年 2 月透露，害怕公开演讲是美国社会最常见的恐惧，73% 的美国人受此影响，其程度超过对蜘蛛、高度，甚至死亡的恐惧！①

2012 年 11 月 29 日《今日心理学》发表了一篇名叫《比死亡更令我们害怕的事情》的文章，格伦·克罗斯顿（Glenn Croston）博士在此指出，对公众演讲的恐惧源于对拒绝和排斥的恐惧，这种恐惧普遍存在于人类当中，甚至对所有群居动物都是如此（尽管我还没听到过动物发表公共演说）。

克罗斯顿写道，社会心理学家兼教师西格尼·戴霍夫（Signe

① https://nationalsocialanxietycenter.com/2017/02/20/public-speaking-and-fear-of-brain-freezes.

Dayhoff）极其害怕说话，每次给学生上课时他都会紧张得说不出话来！他这样描述当时的情形："舌头粘在干涸的上颚下，让我无法吞咽，我的脸涨得通红，与此同时，汗流浃背，浑身发抖。"最终，他得到了专业的帮助。

我对此深有体会。小时候我很害羞，甚至不敢和家人说话。在近乎所有的时间里，我不是和我的小动物们待着，就是独自在图书馆看书，于是家人给我安了个"隐士"的绰号。我很擅长模仿动物，像牛呀，鸡呀，马呀，猪呀，火鸡呀，猴子呀（我属猴，养过一只松鼠猴）。但我鲜和人说话。在中国我已执教了 32 年，每次上课前我仍会感到紧张，不过对教学的热爱让我克服了这些，一旦和学生面对面，恐惧就被我抛诸脑后了。

你害怕公众演讲吗?

几年前，英国威廉王子被问到最害怕什么时，他回答公共演讲。英国文化协会（British Council）指出，75% 的人害怕公众演讲，10% 的是"打心底里恐惧"。[②] 英国文化协会指出，这个名单上包括温斯顿·丘吉尔（Winston Churchill）、亚伯拉罕·林肯（Abraham Lincoln）、托马斯·杰斐逊（Thomas Jefferson）和甘地（Gandhi），但他们却没有让人生止步于这种恐惧！不仅如此，亿万富翁理查德·布兰森爵士（Sir Richard Branson）、著名的高尔夫球手泰格·伍兹（Tiger Woods）、演员兼前加州州长阿诺德·施瓦辛格（Arnold Schwarzenegger）也面临同样的恐惧。2000 多年前，罗马政治家、律师和哲学家西塞罗（Cicero）就承认过：

② https://www.britishcouncil.org/voices-magazine/how-overcome-fear-public-speaking.

> “在私下里讲话时，我都感到非常紧张。每次发表公众演讲时，我甚至觉得是将自己的能力、品格、声誉公之于众，任人评判。”

沃伦·巴菲特（Warren Buffett）也曾对公众演讲感到“恐惧”，但他在21岁参加戴尔·卡内基（Dale Carnegie）的公开演讲课程后，终于克服了这一点。巴菲特写道：

> “你必须采取行动，且行动越早，效果越好。年轻时培养出好的习惯要容易得多。如果你害怕与人交往，你就得走出去，这很痛苦……”

我很能理解他的说法。14岁前我对公众演讲心生“恐惧”，但到我1988年搬到中国前，我就已经给涉及1.5万名人员的不同团体做过关于领导力的演讲。所以，正如我对自己MBA的学生说的那样，如果我能做到，任何人都可以，并且也应该做到。

我在学校时经常被人欺负，这不仅因为我性格安静，也跟我当时个儿小有关。但14岁时，我决心不再任人欺负，真是受够了做出气筒的日子。当时我参加一个公开演讲比赛，却招致我姐姐笑话。她性格外向，是位颇受欢迎的啦啦队队长，她说：“你要给谁演讲？动物们吗？”

赛前，我独自在镜子前练习了很长时间，结果在学校、地区的比赛中都获得了优胜，并最终名列所在州的第四名，这让老师和学生大感震惊。于是，很多人开始说我天生是演说家的料，但这毫无根据。我是一个天生的隐士，而不是一个演说家，但我之所以在演讲方面表现出色是因为通过大量的练习掌握了演讲的能力，这不是单纯依靠机械记忆和模仿，而是真正做到将演讲内容内化，再自然流畅地表达出来。

当我的书面和口头表达能力得到人们的认可时，我也应邀加入了不少团体。12 年级时，我已担任过两个俱乐部的主席、市政府的青少年成员、佛罗里达中州肺脏协会（Florida MidState Lung Association）的宣传主席，还和州长共进过颁奖晚宴。

在高中以及后来在部队和商业领域的工作中，很多人告诉我："你是天生的领导者！"那当然是毫无根据的。我是个隐士，不是天生的领导者，但领导者最重要的技能之一就是沟通。毕竟，有追随者的人才叫领导者，人们跟随你，就是因为你们共事时你能通过沟通给他们带去帮助。所以，凭借良好的沟通能力，我成了许多领域的领导者，但这种能力并非天生，而是源自我为此付出了许多后天的努力。这些沟通技巧也帮助了我在中国的生活，如教学，代表中国城市申请国际宜居城市，向世界讲述中国故事等。

没有人生来就善于沟通，或生来就是领导者。不信？读读历史。你会发现那些历史人物起初也与你我一样，年轻、缺乏经验、心有恐惧，但他们从不言放弃，奋力向前，于是扭转人生局面。至于那些放弃的人……这就是你在历史书中见不到他们身影的原因！

当然，你需要为自己的事业提高口语能力。此外，正如刚参加完"用英语讲中国故事"活动的 10 万余名参赛者体会到的那样，你还需要提高公共演讲技巧，尤其是用英语演讲的技巧，这样你才能向世界讲述中国故事。

我希望能再次举办这个活动，也希望听到你们个人的中国故事。我们一起努力，帮助中国梦成为世界梦！

我坚持，我成功！爱拼才会赢！

潘维廉

2020 年 8 月 6 日

Quote from Lao Pan:

老潘金句：

In retrospect, much of my life seems to have come together with sheer luck – or Yuánfèn. But in reality, I was able to build upon seemingly unrelated experiences because, in everything I've done, I've learned all I could and done my best to weave a "thread of success" through everything, even when doing things I did not really enjoy. As the saying goes, "The harder you work, the luckier you are" – and I am certainly very lucky!

回头看，我人生的许多际遇似乎纯运气使然，或者说全凭缘分。但事实上，我能够在看似不相关的经历上获得发展，是因为我尽可能从中进行学习，并在复盘的过程中尽最大可能找到"成功的线索"，哪怕是做那些我并不喜欢的事情时也是如此。俗话说："越努力，越幸运"——我当然很幸运！

扫一扫

看老潘读信视频

Two Keys to Successful Public Speaking

August 7, 2020

Dear Chinese friends,

I am confident that the "Stories of China Retold in English" event will be held again, and when it is, you can improve your chances of success with a strategic focus on two keys: content and delivery. And a mastery of strategic communication will not only improve your storytelling but also help you win at virtually everything else you put your head and heart to – whether it be marketing a product, leading a sports or business team, or asking for your sweetheart's hand in marriage (which, by the way, I did very badly. She laughed at me!).

Strategic Content: Audience/market-oriented!

In business, the customer is king, so we must know their demands and expectations and design products to meet them.

In public speaking, the audience (or judge) is king, and we must know their expectations as well – and meet them – and every word and action counts. Everything we say and do either reinforces our message or distracts from it. Consider the recent "Stories of China Retold in English" contest.

Many contestants began by introducing themselves in Chinese but not in English, even though the point of the contest was to tell China's story to foreigners. Even a brief self-introduction in English would have helped build a relationship and rapport between the storytellers and their foreign judges or audience. It helps for the audience to know a little about you because all storytelling is autobiographical. It says something about you.

The first element of the China Story contest was recitation of a story from New Channel's delightful bilingual series, *Stories of China Retold in English*, which is a rich collection of stories from both ancient and modern China. Although students did not write these stories, they were still somewhat autobiographical because their choice of story revealed what was important to them.

The second element, sharing their own China Story, was clearly autobiographical, but the best contestants integrated the first and second sections. For the recitation, they shared a story that set a foundation for their own China Story. This helped the audience better understand and identify with them and their story, and was far more effective than simply delivering two entirely unconnected and disjointed stories.

The third element, the talent show, was yet another opportunity to reinforce the message, in English (remember – foreign audience) of the first two elements, and some did just that. But some students shared a talent that was entirely unrelated to their stories, or had no English explanation. A piano recital, for example, may be beautifully performed, but without an explanation of the choice of song, how does it help tell China's story in English? This is entertainment, and well done, but this is not storytelling.

One student performed martial arts – which at least was Chinese – but without any English explanation of the performance, or of why the student loves martial arts, and its importance to China, it was nonverbal entertainment but not storytelling. I loved it because I've practiced martial arts, but it did little to help the world better understand China.

The talent shows would have better told China's story had the students focused on "edutainment," in which audiences are both entertained and educated. In my home of Xiamen, for example, Xiamen orchestra conductor Madame Zheng Xiaoying explains to audiences the story behind the songs they perform – and the audience loves it! I've even heard Chinese opera performed in English. Granted, it does sound funny, but foreign audiences appreciate understanding the story, just as Chinese audiences like seeing Chinese subtitles for Italian opera. So at the least, the talent videos should have had English subtitles explaining what the foreigners were seeing, and why it was important to China.

In summary, given the contest was about telling China's story in English, the storytellers should have ensured that each of the 3 stages focused clearly on 1) telling China's story, 2) in English, and 3) making their story more compelling by integrating all three elements to reinforce a common, unforgettable theme.

Strategic Delivery!

Once we decide what to say (content), we must decide how we

will say it (delivery).

"How is your Chinese?" I ask Chinese students, and they often laugh and reply, "My Chinese is great, of course! I'm Chinese!"

But just because they can "speak" Chinese does not mean they can effectively communicate in Chinese.

Albert Mehrabian, a professor of Psychology at the University of California, has shown that when communicating feelings and attitudes (which are important when sharing China's Story to foreigners who have strong preconceived ideas about China), only 7% is communicated with words, while 55% is facial expressions and 38% is tone.

In the same way, foreigners have preconceived ideas about China, so in Telling China's Story in English, you need to be very strategic in not just what you share but how you share it! This is why judges focused not just on English fluency but also on the storytellers' body language and expressiveness.

The best storytellers stood erect but not stiff, like a robot, and some walked about the stage, relaxed, making eye contact with different members of the audience.

Hand gestures also reinforce or detract from the message. Some finalists stood with their arms stiffly at their sides, as if at attention in the army. A couple contestants clasped their hands together in front of them for the entire time, as if they were Xiamen Airlines stewardesses. But some, aware of the importance of hand gestures, waived their hands all over the place as if they were Harry Potter casting a spell. The best storytellers' hand gestures were natural and relaxed – neither rigid and mechanical nor so wild that they distracted from the message.

Eye contact is also very important in building rapport with the audience. The best speakers look at different members of the audience throughout the talk. When they look at the audience, the audience looks at them. This creates a personal, even emotional, connection – and helps break barriers to communication.

As Prof. Mehrabian discovered, facial expressions are extremely powerful in conveying emotions. Some storytellers never smiled, even when they were talking about happy subjects, but a couple contestants smiled the entire time, regardless of the content of their talk. Such over-rehearsed body language can convey insincerity, as if they were acting out a story they did not quite believe. And if they don't believe it, neither will their audience – or the judges.

English fluency is of course also important, but by the finals, most contestants had little problem with English fluency. Their primary problems were one, choice and organization of content, and two, poor delivery, which is why some students with poorer English performed better than others whose pronunciation was flawless but appeared robotic or insincere in their posture, gestures and expressions.

Strategic content, strategic delivery – these are the two keys to not only performing better in the next "Stories of China Retold in English" event but in every other form of communication. Whether you're helping the world to better understand China, or marketing a product, or helping a Chinese city win a global competition for livable communities – or asking the boy or girl of your dreams for a date or to marry you, success depends not just on English fluency but on how strategically you choose what to say (and what not to say!), and how you say it!

But above all, be passionate. History has many stories of people who were poor communicators but they were passionate – people like Gandhi and Lincoln – and over time they improved, and they changed the world. And of course there are people like me. When I asked Susan Marie to marry me, I did it so badly that she laughed! A rejection is bad enough, but to have the girl of your dreams laugh in your face?

"I ask you to marry me and you laugh at me?" I replied.

"You're joking, right?" she said.

"I would never joke about marriage!" I said. Wow – I'll never forget that kiss!

That was the worst marriage proposal in history but it was passionate and she said yes and she's still my best friend 40 years later. But even after 40 years, we still have misunderstandings and miscommunications. Communication is something you must work on for the rest of your life.

Keep learning – and I hope to see you at the next New Channel's "Stories of China Retold in English" event!

Bill Brown

成功进行公共演说的两大法宝

亲爱的中国朋友们：

我相信，“用英语讲中国故事”活动还会再次举办。届时你们将战略重点放在展示内容和展示方式这两个关键点上，会提高你们在这个活动中胜出的可能性。拥有战略性沟通能力不仅能提高你们讲故事的能力，还能有助于你们在所有自己全身投入的事情上取得胜利，无论是营销产品、领导体育或商业团队，还是向你的爱人求婚。（顺便说一句，我在这件事上做得很糟糕，竟然遭到我爱人的嘲笑！）

以观众、市场为导向选择展示内容

在商业经营中，顾客至上，我们必须了解他们的需求和期望，从而设计出满足他们的产品。

在公共演讲中，听众（或评委）至上，我们也必须了解他们的期望并加以满足，因此我们的一言一行都需要加以考虑。我们所说所做要么强化我们的信息，要么弱化它们的输出。想想最近的“用英语讲中国故事”活动，就可见一斑了。

活动的目的是向外国人讲述中国故事，但许多选手一开始进行自我介绍时采用的都是汉语。其实，哪怕是一段简短的英语自我介绍，也有助于选手和外国评委或观众产生联结，拉近彼此距离。

该活动的第一环节为朗诵《用英语讲中国故事》丛书的章节片段。这是一套古今中国故事集，采用双语编写故事，引人入胜，虽然这些故事并非选手亲自编写，但他们的选择展示了个人偏好，某种程度上可视为他们的自传。

第二环节是分享个人的中国故事。尽管这个环节明确要求选手讲述自己的故事，但表现最佳的选手会将前两个环节有机结合起来，在挑选朗诵章节时，有意识地为之后的个人故事作铺垫，加深观众对他们本人和他们故事的理解与认同，这比简单陈述两个完全不相干的故事要有效得多。

第三环节是才艺展示（切记面对外国观众，一定要用上英语）。这是加深观众对前两个环节印象的又一机会，有些选手就妥妥地抓住了。但有些学生的展示和先前分享的故事完全脱节，或者对自己的表演不作任何英语解释。一段钢琴独奏也许能让观众感受到精湛技艺，但如果对曲目不加英语解释，这段演奏怎能帮助选手“用英语讲中国故事”呢？这是娱乐，是有着出色表演的娱乐，但这样跟讲故事离得就远了。

一位学生选择进行武术表演，但如果对它不作一点英语解释，不介绍个人喜欢武术的原因，或武术对中国的重要性等，同样地这只能属于非语言的娱乐，而不是讲故事。这样的表演能打动我是因为我练过武术，但在让世界更好地了解中国层面却只会收效甚微。

如果选手们能注重“寓教于乐”，让观众有所乐有所学，他们的表演会更好地展现中国故事。例如，在我的家乡厦门，著名的管弦乐团指挥家郑小瑛女士会现场讲解演奏曲目背后的故事，大受观众欢迎！我还听过英语版的中国戏剧。诚然，这听上去有些好笑，但外国观众的确喜爱以这种方式欣赏京剧，就像中国观众喜欢边听意大利歌剧边看中文字幕一样。所以这些展示才艺的视频至少该配上英文字幕，用以向外国观众讲解选手所展示的内容以及这些内容对于中国的重要性。

综上，鉴于本次活动的主题是用英语讲中国故事，讲述者应该确保在这三个环节做到以下几点：1）讲述中国的故事；2）使用英语讲述；3）整合三大环节使其形成主线，加强故事的吸引力。

战略性选材和展示中国故事

一旦想到要说什么（内容），我们就必须确定说话的方式（展示）。

“你的中文怎么样？”我经常这样问中国学生。他们通常会笑着回答：“我的中文当然很棒！我是中国人耶！”

但会说中文并不意味着他们可以用它进行有效的沟通。

加州大学心理学教授阿尔伯特·梅拉宾（Albert Mehrabian）指出，感情和态度的交流（向先入为主对中国抱有过激观念的外国人分享中国故事时，它们有着十分重要的作用）只有 7% 是通过文字，55% 依靠面部表情，剩下的 38% 依靠语气。

同样，外国人因交流不畅对中国也抱有先入为主的想法，所以用英语讲中国故事你需要具备战略眼光，选取恰当的内容和方式！这就是评委不仅会关注选手英语流利程度，还关注他们的肢体语言、表达能力的原因。

最佳的故事讲述者身姿笔挺却不显僵硬，绝非呆板得像个机器人；他们在舞台上自如走动，与不同的观众进行眼神交流。

手势既能强化信息，也能弱化它。一些决赛选手将手臂僵硬地垂在身体两侧，就像正在立正的军人。还有几个选手将双手紧紧攥在身前，站立得如同厦门航空的空姐。过犹不及的是，一些选手意识到手势重要性，则不停地挥动手臂，就像哈利波特在施法一样。那些最佳的讲述者，手势自然且自如，既不僵硬、机械，也不盲目挥动，让人不知所踪。

与观众建立融洽关系的另一重要方式是眼神交流。最佳演讲者全程下来会与不同的观众有着眼神交流。受演讲者的感染，观众也会给予眼神反馈，这样就创造出一种亲密的甚至情感上的联系，继而打破沟通障碍。

正如梅拉比安教授发现的那样，面部表情在传达情感方面十分有效。但有些讲述者全程无笑，哪怕是讲到快乐的事情时；也有几个参赛者全程带笑，全然不顾此举是否与谈话内容相适宜。这种过度预演的肢体语言传达不出真诚，他们就像在表演一个连自己都不太相信的故事。而如果他们自己都不相信，观众或评委又怎么会被打动呢?

当然，英语的流利度也是无法忽视的因素，但到了总决选，大多数选手在这方面表现良好。他们的问题主要在选材和内容的组织展示上，这就解释了那些发音完美但姿势、手势、表情呆板得如同机器人或因此显得不甚真诚的学生，表现反倒不及那些英语较差的选手的原因。

用战略性眼光选材和讲述中国故事，不仅对提升选手在下届“用英语讲中国故事”活动中的表现，对其他任何形式的交流也都起着关键作用。无论是你帮助世界更好地了解中国，还是推销一款产品，又或者是帮助中国城市赢得国际宜居城市的竞赛，甚至是邀约你的意中人或求婚时，是否获得成功不仅取决于语言的流利度，还取决于你说什么（不说什么）以及你怎么说！

但最重要的是，持有激情。历史上不少名人，如甘地和林肯，虽然沟通能力欠佳，但充满激情。随着时间的推移，他们弥补了自身的不足，最终改变世界。当然也有像我这样的求婚者。我向苏珊·玛丽（Susan Maria）求婚时表现得过于糟糕，令她忍俊不禁！被拒已经够糟糕的了，被梦中女孩当面嘲笑简直难以想象！

“我向你求婚，你却嘲笑我？”我答道。

“你是在开玩笑，对吗？”她说。

“我绝不会拿结婚开玩笑！”我说。但，我永远都忘不了那一吻！

尽管我是历史上最糟糕的求婚者，却充满激情，最终赢得美人归，在40年后她仍然是我最好的搭档。但即使一起走过了40年，我们仍会有误解和沟通不畅的时候。沟通，是需要你用余生努力经营的事情。

坚持学习！期待在下届新航道“用英语讲中国故事”活动上看到你们精彩的表现！

潘维廉

2020年8月7日

扫一扫

看老潘读信视频

Have Our Eating Habits Changed in China?

August 14, 2020

Dear Chinese friends,

I am often asked if my eating habits have changed over my 3 decades in China. The answer is no, I still eat every day! Haha!

Actually, I'm happy to answer that question because I love Chinese food. In fact, when a Beijing reporter asked me why I moved to China, I said it was because Chinese food is too expensive in America! Haha. Actually, Chinese food is cheap in America, but as I'll explain later, it's not real, authentic Chinese food.

Almost 400 years ago, the French playwright, actor and poet, Moliere, warned, "Man should eat to live, not live to eat." Hm, I doubt that Moliere ever ate Chinese food. If he had, he too would have lived to eat!

But authentic Chinese food, in China, is nothing like Chinese food in the West, much of which is deep fried and coated in sweet 'n sour or lemon sauces. Chinese have tried, of course, to serve genuine Chinese food in the West, and failed. A friend from Xiamen emigrated to Canada decades ago and proudly opened a restaurant serving real Chinese food!

Sadly, although the local Chinese loved it, there weren't enough of them to keep it in business. So after a few weeks he started serving Canadian Chinese food, with Chinese fortune cookies (which I've never seen in China) – and then he prospered.

But we have the same problem here in China. For one thing, there is no one kind of Chinese food. It varies from province to province, region to region, even county to county. Even in Fujian, oysters and fish balls are prepared differently in North Quanzhou and South Quanzhou. And we have Shaxian snacks in Xiamen but they are nothing like the real ones in Sanming, where they originated. And Changting's Hetian chicken is completely different when served in Sanming 60 kilometers away.

When we first came to Xiamen, one reason we loved Chinese food was that it was so healthy. Fast-paced Westerners are often so busy that they just shop for food once a week – so they buy frozen, canned and dried foods, eat lots of junk snacks (chips, cookies, soft drinks) and eat out a lot. Chinese however, at least when we first came, shopped daily for fresh veggies, eggs and meats. They had to because we didn't have refrigerators, and those who did buy refrigerators could not use them because the power went out all the time.

It was time-consuming – we spent hours each day just on food – but it was tasty and healthy, and no one minded because eating fine Chinese food together is such a part of Chinese family and culture.

And I admire how Chinese can quickly cook a feast with simple ingredients and simple kitchen tools – a wok, a cleaver, and a pot or two. Americans, by contrast, often have an entire kitchen full of gadgets and hi-tech appliances – and still don't cook, but eat fast food.

Sadly, today's Chinese are busier than ever so, like Westerners, many buy groceries only once or twice a week and cook with more frozen, canned and dried foods. Many in fact, don't cook at all, but eat out at junk food places – or use their phone to have it delivered to their doorstep.

This poorer diet, combined with less exercise (less walking and biking, more cars and buses) means that Chinese are starting to develop the same chronic diseases that Westerners suffer from – heart problems, type 2 diabetes, cancer, which with obesity are all rooted in an unhealthy life style.

This is sad, and ironic, because Chinese have for over 2,000 years emphasized healthy lifestyle and prevention of disease instead of cure. In the West, only in the last couple of decades have doctors come to admit that healthy lifestyle is important. Maybe this is because doctors make a lot more money curing someone than keeping them healthy (in ancient China, by the way, many people did pay their doctor to keep them healthy).

My wife, Susan Marie, certainly understands the importance of healthy life style. For almost 30 years, neither Chinese nor Western doctors could cure her migraines, IBS (Irritable bowel syndrome), and fibromyalgia. She was in great pain almost 24/7 – but since she spent 10 days at St. Helena Hospital's Lifestyle Medicine program, in Napa Valley where we ate healthy, delicious vegetarian food and learned about the latest advances in healthy lifestyle, she no longer needs the medicines, and she feels better than she has in 30 years! And, amazingly, much of what we learned in Napa Valley was said centuries ago by Chinese, and even by the Romans. It seems that the ancients had a lot more common sense than us so-called modern folks.

It's a shame it took Sue and me 3 decades to awaken to the fact that we really are what we eat. Everything we eat, drink or breathe either strengthens or weakens us. It's logical, of course, but in today's busy life, we often overlook this, or we make excuses.

So our eating has indeed changed during our time in China. We of course eat more Chinese food than we did in the U.S., but we also emphasize eating healthily. So for breakfast we usually eat oatmeal (extremely healthy, and cheap) with soymilk, blueberries, bananas and apples – and a couple spoons of chia and hemp seeds. For lunch – healthy Chinese food cooked by Lixi, an Anxi lady who has been with us since 1988! And for supper, Sue's amazing salad – tasty and healthy, and very filling because she adds so many ingredients.

But, in closing, I'd like to reply to those Chinese who too often naively say, "You [Americans] eat bread and beef and potatoes." While our favorite food is Chinese, Western cuisine is in fact very diverse. Just like in China, it can vary from state to state, or even city to city. And as a nation of immigrants, the U.S. has every kind of cuisine imaginable. And there are literally hundreds of ways to fix beef and potatoes, and countless varieties of breads. So to simply say, "You people eat potatoes, bread and beef" is like saying "Chinese eat rice." In fact, many Chinese in the Northeast or the West don't eat rice – they eat flour-based noodles, *jiaozis*, flatbreads, etc.

I've traveled abroad with a dozen Chinese delegations and their entire itinerary centered on going from one Chinese restaurant to the next. They had no desire to even taste the local foods. Now, I must admit that I too would not want to eat those foreign foods daily. I never tire of Chinese food, whereas I can't imagine eating other foods every day. But I like at least to explore what's out there.

So I encourage you to try other countries' foods – and not just fast food! So many Chinese judge American food by McDonalds or KFC. How would you feel if I said I disliked Chinese food because I'd gone to a cheap Chinese noodle shop? But even fast food can be good. If you want a real hamburger, go to places like Cassells, opened in Los Angeles in 1948. They've been rated 5-stars for decades because they choose choice beef, grind it themselves, bake their own bread, make their own sauces. It is worlds apart from McDonalds. (Though being vegetarian, I make veggie hamburgers that I think are even better than Cassells.)

So I do love American food too, which is infinite in variety if you take the time to explore it. But our family favorite is Chinese. Our oldest son, Shannon, is married to Miki from Xiamen and they eat Chinese food daily. And our youngest son, Matthew, does volunteer medical work with his wife in Africa, and his big concern was that he would not find the things he needed to cook Chinese food in Africa. But he wrote, excitedly, "Dad, even this tiny remote African village has a family selling Chinese spices from their house because Chinese are here helping to raise Africa from poverty through China's 'Belt and Road Initiative.' " Those Chinese were shocked to meet a blonde American who cooked Chinese food – and our 2-year-old granddaughter who spoke Chinese to them!

So, yes, Chinese is our favorite, as I'm sure it is yours. But do explore what else is out there in this little world of ours.

Thanks for listening!

Bill Brown

Quotes from Lao Pan:

老潘金句:

As a child, I cherished the American Dream. As an adult, I've witnessed fulfillment of the China Dream. My dream now is that China and the U.S. can work together for a World Dream – but that won't happen unless we do a better job of telling China's Story to the world.

小时候，我怀揣着美国梦。长大后，我见证了中国梦的实现。我现在的梦想是，中美两国为实现世界梦想共同努力——但除非我们更好地向世界讲述中国的故事，否则这种梦想不会实现。

Even today, trade is not borderless, and probably never will be – but the coronavirus truly knows no borders. Rich and poor alike fall before it – though the elderly, the weak and the poor fall hardest.

即使到今天，贸易也不是没有国界，也许还将永远存在——但新冠病毒确实没有国界意识。无论贫富都会受到它的侵袭——但年老、体弱、贫穷之人是它主要的攻击对象。

在中国，我们的饮食习惯发生改变了吗？

年轻的中国朋友们：

经常有人问我：“在中国生活 30 年，你的饮食习惯发生改变了吗？”并没有，我还是每天会吃东西！哈哈！

我很乐意回答这个问题，因为我喜欢中国食物！一位北京的记者曾问我搬到中国的原因，我说因为中国食物在美国卖得太贵，买不起！哈哈。其实中国食物在美国卖得很便宜，但正如我稍后解释的那样，它们不正宗。

大约 400 年前，法国剧作家、演员和诗人莫里哀提醒世人：“人应当是吃而为生，而不是生而为吃。”嗯，我怀疑莫里哀没吃过中国菜！如果尝过，他会改变想法，为了吃而生的！

西方的中餐馆卖的根本就不是正宗的中国食物，做法通常是先油炸，再将食材抹一层糖醋或沾点柠檬汁。当然，有中国人曾尝试开设正宗的中餐馆，但没有成功。几十年前，我的一位厦门朋友在移民加拿大后，颇为自豪地开了一家正宗的中餐馆，但令人遗憾的是，尽管正宗的中国菜深受当地华人喜欢，但这还不足以让这家店维持生计。几周后，他转而供应加拿大风味的中餐，并配上中国幸运饼（这种饼干我在中国从未见过）——他成功了。

在中国，我们也遇到了同样的问题！首先，中国不止一种食物，不同省份，不同地区，就连不同县区之间，人们吃的食物也不尽相同。例如，在福建省泉州市的南北部，人们就采用不同的方式制作牡蛎和鱼丸；我们在厦门吃的沙县小吃，就和发源地三明市沙县的正宗沙县小吃一点都不像；而长汀的和田鸡到了60公里外的三明，口味也大不相同。

初到厦门我们就爱上了中国菜，原因是它非常健康。快节奏的西方人通常因为工作忙碌，一周只买一次食物，所以冷冻、罐装、脱水食品就成了常规储备，垃圾零食（薯条、饼干、软饮料）常不离口，外出就餐也是常有的事。然而，至少在我们刚到中国时，中国人还会天天上街买新鲜蔬菜、鸡蛋、肉类。这也是因为那时没有冰箱，即使买了冰箱的，也因为一直停电无法使用。

做饭很费时间——我们每天仅在做饭上就得花上几个小时——但自己做的东西确实美味又健康。中国人并不介意花这些时间做饭，因为和家人一起吃饭是他们家庭文化的一部分。

我很佩服中国人仅用简单的食材、一个炒锅、一把切菜刀和一两个汤锅就能快速做出一顿大餐。相比之下，美国人的厨房里经常是摆满了小器具和高科技玩意，但他们仍然不做饭，喜欢吃快餐。

令人遗憾的是，今天的中国人比以往任何时候都要忙，许多中国人像西方人那样，一周只买一两次食物，越来越喜欢冷冻、罐装和脱水食材。事实上，有很多人根本就不做饭，要么去垃圾食品店应付一顿，要么就是图方便点个外卖到家。

饮食不健康、运动量减少（走路、骑自行车的时间锐减，更多是坐汽车和公共汽车）意味着中国人开始像西方人一样遭受心脏病、二型糖尿病、癌症等慢性病的困扰，这些疾病和肥胖都源于人们不健康的生活方式。

这令人遗憾，也颇具讽刺意味，因为2000多年来，中国人一直强调健康的生活方式，认为预防重于治疗。而在西方，直到几十年前医生才开始承认健康生活方式的重要性。这也许是因为治病比养生让医生更有利可图吧（顺便说一句，在古代中国，确实有不少人会花钱请医生传授养生之道）。

对于健康生活方式的重要性，我的妻子苏珊·玛丽自然是深有体会。过去30年，她饱受偏头痛、肠易激综合征和纤维肌痛的折磨，中医和西医带来的疗效都不佳，每天她几乎都处在巨大的疼痛中。但自从在纳帕谷的圣赫勒拿医院接受了10天的生活方式医疗项目后——哇！在那里，我们吃健康美味的素食，了解最新的健康生活方式——她不再依赖药物，获得了30年来前所未有的舒适感！令人惊讶的是，我们在纳帕谷学到的很多东西，在很多个世纪前，中国人甚至罗马人就提倡过。这样看来，古人似乎比我们所谓的“现代人”更具常识。

遗憾的是我和苏花了30年才意识到人如其食。我们吃的喝的呼吸的既能使我们强壮，也能使我们虚弱。当然，尽管道理易懂，在今天忙碌的生活中，我们却常忽视这一点，或者以此为借口。

这样说来，我们的饮食习惯确实发生了变化。当然，我们比在美国时吃了更多的中国食物，但我们也更强调健康饮食。早餐我们通常吃燕麦片（非常健康，价格也便宜！），再加上豆奶、蓝莓、香蕉和苹果，以及几勺奇亚籽和大麻籽。中午吃的是李西做的健康中餐（她来自安溪，自 1988 年就开始和我们在一起生活！）。晚餐吃的是苏做的美味又健康的沙拉，在里面她还加了许多食料，所以吃起来很饱。

最后，我想回答那些天真地以为“你们（美国人）就吃面包、牛肉和土豆”的中国人。虽然中餐是我们的最爱，但西餐实际上也是种类繁多。就像中国一样，在美国的州与州之间，甚至城市与城市之间，人们吃的食物也会有所不同。作为一个移民国家，美国汇聚了各式你能想到的美食。 实际上烹饪牛肉和土豆的方法有上百种，面包的种类也是巨多无比。简而言之，说“你们就吃土豆、面包和牛肉”就像说“中国人就吃大米”一样。在中国东北或西部，就有许多中国人并不以大米为主食，他们吃的是面条、饺子、饼子等。

我曾和十几个中国代表团结伴出行，他们以中餐馆为中心，整个行程是从一家中餐馆赶往另一家中餐馆。他们对于品尝当地食物并无兴趣。现在，我必须承认，我也不愿每天吃那些外国食物。我每天吃中国食物都不会感到厌倦，而如果换成别的，简直令我无法想象。但即使如此，我至少还希望去看看外头还有什么好吃的。

所以我鼓励你们多尝试其他国家的食物，而不仅仅是快餐！很多中国人对美国食物的评价局限于在麦当劳或肯德基的消费经历。如果我说我不喜欢中国菜，只是因为去了一家便宜的中国面条馆，你会做何感想？但快餐里也有值得推荐的。如果你想吃到正宗的汉堡，就该去洛杉矶卡塞尔汉堡餐厅。这家店开于 1948 年，几十年来口碑炸裂，一直是五星，他们用的是精选牛肉、自制牛肉馅，汉堡的面包是自家烘烤，酱汁也是自家调制。这和麦当劳有着天壤之别（我是素食主义者，我认为自己做的蔬菜汉堡甚至比卡塞尔的汉堡更好吃）！

所以我也很喜欢美国食物，如果你花时间去探索的话，你会发现它也是种类繁多。但我们家还是最爱中国食物。大儿子山农取了厦门姑娘米琪做媳妇，他们每天都吃中国菜。小儿子马修和他的妻子在非洲做志愿医生，他曾十分担心在非洲找不到做中餐的炊具！但有一天他兴奋地写道："爸爸，在这个偏远的非洲小村庄，竟然有商家在卖中国香料，因为中国人正在通过'一带一路'倡议帮助非洲脱离贫困。"那些中国人看到一个金发美国人做着中国菜，听到我们两岁的孙女跟他们说中文时，一定很震惊。

是的，中国食物是我们的最爱了，我确信如此。但是，一定别忘了去探索我们这个小小世界里还有什么别的好吃的。

谢谢你们的聆听！

潘维廉

2020 年 8 月 14 日

Quote from Lao Pan:

老潘金句：

One of the biggest reasons I love China is that I have a very big family here!

我爱中国最大的原因是我在这里有很多家人！

扫一扫

看老潘读信视频

Bill or William: Trouble in Hong Kong

August 20, 2020

Dear Chinese friends,

This morning I saw that our OneMBA students were surprised to learn that Bill Gates is also William Gates, and Bill Clinton is also William Clinton, and Bill Brown is also William Brown. In English speaking countries, we take it for granted that people know this, but in December, 1981, when Sue and I flew to Taiwan to get married, this issue caused us a lot of grief!

Our flight from Los Angeles to Taipei took us through Seattle, Anchorage and Hong Kong, and months before our wedding a friend from Taiwan warned us to book two rooms in the Hong Kong YMCA because flights to Hong Kong were often late, and if we missed the connecting flight to Taipei, it would be very expensive to get a room at the last minute. As a penny-pinching student, I wasn't keen on paying in advance for rooms we'd probably not use, but I took his advice.

Sure enough, we missed our Taipei plane, but when we got to the YMCA, they said they had no reservations for us.

"Of course you do!" I said. "I paid in advance, months ago!" Unfortunately, I'd forgotten to bring the receipt, and after fruitless arguing, Sue and I went in search of another hotel but could not find any we could afford. We finally returned to the YMCA and sat on the lobby floor, exhausted. After a few minutes, a man at the desk came over and said, "Excuse me, but is 'Bill' the same as 'William'?"

I'd reserved the room as William Brown but when I checked in told them I was Bill Brown – clueless that Chinese did not know Bill is simply the informal version of William.

Chinese say these nicknames are strange, but no stranger, I think, than the Chinese custom of using a childhood name such as Dingding or Dongdong or Poopoo – and then switching to an adult name. Different places, different customs. But for the record, I'll try to explain why we say Bill instead of William – even for the president of the U.S.

Will is short for William, but in the middle ages people began saying Bill because one, it rhymed with Will, and two, phonetics makes Bill slightly easier to say than Will.

Bob is short for Robert because it began as Rob but "B" is easier on the tongue than "R."

Sally is short for Sarah; the "r" was changed to an easier to say "l," though today most girls prefer Sarah, which was the original Hebrew name.

And Molly is a common nickname for Mary – again, because an "l" rolls off the tongue more easily than an "r."

Peggy is short for Margaret; it evolved from Meg, Mog and Maggie.

Dick is short for Richard because it rhymes with Rick (also short for Richard) and a "d" is easier to say than an "r."

Hank and Harry are short for Henry, though Harry is more popular now because of the English Prince – or former prince? Now I think he's retired from royalty and is simply henpecked.

Jack is short for John, so U.S. President John Kennedy was often called Jack. But his wife's nickname was Jackie, short for Jacqueline, so they were Jack and Jackie.

Chuck is short for Charles because Charles was pronounced Chukken in Middle English, which was spoken from 1066 AD until the late 15th century. And this brings up an interesting point. Books in Middle English, such as *Canterbury Tales*, are hard to read today even thought they were written just over 600 years ago. For example, Chaucer wrote in *Canterbury Tales*, "I knowe ynogh, on even and a-morwe," which today is written, "I know enough, in the evening and in the morning."

If you think Middle English is hard, try Old English – and that's not English used by old people like me, it was English used from the mid-5th century until 1066, when it was replaced by Anglo-Norman, a relative of French that evolved into Middle English. In *Beowulf*, "I wish to declare to the son of Healfdene..." was written as, "Wille ic asecgan sunu Healfdenes..." Sounds like something from the *Lord of the Rings* – Elvish.

But although English has changed greatly, most Chinese characters have remained relatively unchanged for almost two thousand years, and even Korea, Japan and Vietnam at one point used Chinese as their official written language. A few years ago, the Seoul Government showed me a museum of Korean history and I read an ancient script. "You can read ancient Korean!" they said.

"It's Chinese," I said!

"Oh. Right," they said.

But did you know that people in South America also used ancient Chinese writing – over 2,000 years ago?

Bill Brown

Quote from Lao Pan:

老潘金句:

None of us chose where to be born, or when, and I could not imagine being alive in a more exciting period. What a privilege to witness China lift more people from poverty than any other nation in history – and through the Belt and Road Initiative, to help dozens of other nations.

我们无法选择出生的时间、地点，但我认为我正生活在一个最好的时代。在这里，我见证了历史上最大规模的扶贫计划得以实现，也见证了"一带一路"倡议让沿线数十个国家获得建设发展方面的帮助。能够亲历这些历史时刻，是多么荣耀的事情呀！

在香港遇上麻烦的是比尔还是威廉①

亲爱的中国朋友们：

今天早上，我们OneMBA的学生“惊奇”地发现比尔·盖茨（Bill Gates）也叫威廉·盖茨（William Gates），比尔·克林顿（Bill Clinton）也叫威廉·克林顿（William Clinton），比尔·布朗（Bill Brown）也叫威廉·布朗（William Brown）。在英语国家，我们一直认为这是地球人都知道的事，正因为如此，我和苏在1981年12月飞往台湾结婚时，就给自己惹了大麻烦！

当时从洛杉矶飞抵台北需途经西雅图、安克雷奇和香港，在结婚前几个月，一位台湾朋友就叮嘱我们在香港基督教青年会预订两个房间，因为飞香港的航班经常晚点，一旦错过从香港转飞台北的航班，临时预订房间很不划算。作为一名“抠门”的学生，我不想为这种可能性预付费用，但我还是接受了他的建议。

果然，我们完美地错过了飞台北的飞机，但辗转至香港基督教青年会后，却被告知没有接到我们的预订。

“我确定我们预定了！”我说，“我提前付了款，还是提前了好几个月呢！”不幸的是，我忘了带收据。双方各执一词，争

① 这里采用的是常规译法威廉，但潘教授给自己起的中文名是维廉。

吵无果，于是我和苏重新去找住处，但没有找到一间我们住得起的。我们折回基督教青年会，筋疲力尽地坐在大堂的地板上。不一会儿，前台有人向我们走了过来，然后他问道：“请问比尔和威廉指的是同一个人吗？”

预定时，我用的名字是威廉·布朗，但登记入住时，用的却是比尔·布朗，我竟然“蠢到”忘了中国人并不一定清楚比尔就是威廉的非正式叫法。

中国人认为这些叫法很不可思议，但我认为这还比不上中国人先叫个丁丁、东东、便便等风格的乳名再换成学名的取名风俗怪异。地域不同，风俗习惯也不尽相同。请听好了，我将要解释一下英语国家的人们为什么使用比尔而不是威廉，即使称呼美国总统也是如此。

威廉简称威尔，但中世纪以来，人们开始把威尔叫作比尔，因为比尔与威尔押韵，又比威尔更容易发音。

相似的例子还有不少。

罗伯特（Robert）简称鲍勃（Bob），因为鲍勃的首字母 B 不用发卷舌音。

萨拉（Sarah）简称萨莉（Sally）。萨拉的字母 r 被换成更容易发音的 l，尽管如此，现在大多数女孩更喜欢最初希伯来语的叫法——萨拉。

玛丽（Mary）通常又叫莫莉（Molly），原因与上面相似，字母 l 比 r 更容易发音。

玛格丽塔（Margaret）简称佩吉（Peggy），后者是由梅格（Meg）、莫格（Mog）和玛吉（Maggie）演变而来。

理查（Richard）又叫迪克（Dick），原因是迪克与瑞克（Rick，理查德的另一简称）押韵，并且字母 d 比 r 更容易发音。

亨利（Henry）简称汉克（Hank）或哈里（Harry），但因为英国王子或者曾经的英国王子（我认为这位英国王子退出皇室只是因为怕老婆）也叫哈里，哈里这个叫法更受欢迎。

约翰（John）简称杰克（Jack），所以美国总统肯尼迪（Kennedy）又常被叫作杰克。他妻子杰奎琳（Jacqueline）的简称是杰姬（Jackie），所以人们又称呼他们为杰克和杰姬。

查尔斯（Charles）简称查克（Chuck），因为查尔斯在中古英语中读作 Chukken，这个叫法从公元 1066 年一直沿用到 15 世纪末。这就引出了一个有趣的现象：像《坎特伯雷故事集》这样的中古英语书籍，距今只有 600 多年，现今读来却晦涩难懂。例如，乔叟写道“I knowe ynogh, on even and a-morwe”，换成今天的说法就是“我知识广博，无论是在晚上还是早上”。

如果中古英语就叫难了，试试古英语就知道什么真的叫难懂了——即使像我这样的老人也看不懂古英语。古英语活跃于 5 世纪中叶到 1066 年，后来被法语语支盎格鲁—诺曼语取代，并最终演变成中古英语！在《贝奥武夫》中，“我想向哈夫丹（Healfdene）之子宣布……”就被写作“Wille ic asecgan sunu Healfdenes...”，听上去就像《指环王》中的小精灵在念咒语。

尽管英语发生了翻天覆地的变化，但近 2000 年的时间，大部分汉字却几乎没有变化，在韩国、日本、越南它也一度用于官方书写。几年前，首尔市政府官员带我参观了韩国的历史博物馆，听到我当场念了一篇古文后，他们惊叹道：“你竟然认识古韩语！”

“这是汉语！”我说。

“哦，没错，”他们说。

但你知道吗，2000多年前南美洲的人们也使用中国古代文字？

潘维廉

2020年8月20日

Quotes from Lao Pan:

老潘金句：

Except for writing stories, few of my childhood goals worked out as I had hoped, but if I had scripted my life from cradle to grave, I could not have penned a more exciting or rewarding life.

除了写故事，我童年的目标很少能像我所期待的那样实现，但如果我一早就被剧透我人生的剧本，怎能书写出更加令人兴奋或富有意义的生活呢？

Dream big, and set goals, but be flexible and open to new opportunities that may far surpass what you could have planned yourself.

拥有远大梦想，并设定目标，但灵活应对、乐于接受新的机会——这些机会带来的可能性有时远超你的预期。

Chapter 3
Family Education

第三章
家庭教育

扫一扫
看老潘读信视频

Better to Teach Children a Skill than Give Money

May 4, 2020

Dear Chinese friends,

Hello parents – and grandparents, too, because now I have two grandchildren!

Our sons were only 2 years old and six months old when we came to China in 1988, so it was quite an experience watching them grow up in two cultures. But it was also a great opportunity to help them learn the best of both East and West – though sometimes it was also confusing.

When Matthew was 3, he asked while we were eating, "Dad, how do you say 'cài' (菜， vegetables) in Chinese?"

" 'Cài' is Chinese, Matt," I replied.

He looked surprised, then asked, "So how do you say it in English?"

We had initially planned for our sons to attend Chinese schools but though they liked kindergarten, first grade did not work out. They were the only foreign children so not just the adults but even other children would pinch their rosy cheeks and tug on their blonde hair and say, "So cute!" Shannon was under so much stress we had to take him to a doctor in Hong Kong, so we reluctantly decided to homeschool – and that turned out to give a perfect balance of East and West.

Over 100 years ago, an American family in Fujian for 51 years used a correspondence program called Calvert Schools, which was started in 1899 to help families who lived outside of the U.S. Calvert had rich experience and a great reputation so we used that curriculum to homeschool our sons for 8 years. Calvert provided books and materials and Sue and I proctored exams and mailed their homework assignments back and forth.

Many people warned that homeschooling was ineffective and our sons would not be socialized, but public schools with large classes are fairly new in the West. One or two centuries ago, some of the brightest minds were tutored at home – and it worked well for Shannon and Matt as well (and as I'll show you at the end, public education in the U.S. is not that effective). Our sons finished their daily Calvert materials in about 4 hours, and then they spent time with Chinese tutors for higher math, piano and martial arts.

The only electives that I absolutely insisted they take were music and sports. Shannon, the oldest, has a personality like mine. He's not good at sports with balls but loves music, so I'd tell him to practice piano for 20 minutes and he'd practice for an hour, but I had to force him, at first, to play sports. Matthew's personality is like his mom's. He did not like music but loved sports. If I said to practice piano for 20 minutes, he'd practice for 5 and then cry, "I'm tired!"

"Fifteen more minutes," I'd insist.

"I'm tired!" he'd cry, and I'd glare, and he'd pound the keys unhappily.

I battled Matt for three years but I knew music and math were both important for intellectual development and they were too young to make that kind of decision, so I did not give in.

Matt slowly improved, and by high school had taught himself guitar and drums, played in groups, written songs, and he won his university's award as their best pianist.

Today, both boys are excellent at both music and sports – and both boys have thanked me, many times, for forcing them to do both when they were too young and undisciplined to appreciate it.

Except for music and sports, I never tried to influence their interests, but I did try to give them as much exposure as I could to many things in life so they could determine for themselves what they were passionate about. After all, what a pity that so many people spend their one life pursuing a career they don't even like! And sometimes it takes awhile to discover your interests. After all, I'm 64 and I still don't know what I want to do when I grow up.

I also taught them to use computers when they were only 3 or 4 (I had to make my own computers in those days with parts I brought in from Hong Kong), and I bought them a telescope, microscope, and of course musical instruments – guitars, piano, drums. We also took them camping, roller skating, skateboarding, swimming and body surfing. I constantly exposed them to new things but was careful never to press anything. If they liked it, I'd help them pursue it; if they had no interest,

I did not press it again – except for music and sports.

In 1997, I helped Xiamen's Mayor Hong and Madame Yangying start Xiamen International School, which has a high quality IB program, but the boys' home studies with Chinese tutors for language, math and sports were so effective that we turned down free tuition to continue with Calvert.

For grades 9 to 12, they used a high school correspondence program that the University of Nebraska had developed for children who lived in remote rural areas. In 12th grade, they took the SAT tests for college – and both boys scored so high that they were given full university scholarships, and in college they did well because they had 12 years of self-discipline in studying largely on their own.

In looking back, I can't imagine a better environment for learning. Had they pursued the education in the Chinese schools, they'd have studied morning to night 6 or 7 days a week for 12 years to pass the Gaokao (College Entrance Examination) – and very few electives. My sons' piano teacher, a music professor at XMU, wanted her own son to learn piano but did not dare teach him because it would distract the 8-year-old from preparing for the Gaokao!

My MBA classes have had both Chinese and foreign students, and though many of the foreign students had hobbies like guitar or juggling, very few Chinese students had such hobbies. I learned why when I built a treehouse.

When I built a treehouse for the boys, Chinese asked, "What are you doing in that tree?"

"I'm building a tree house so when my wife gets angry I can sleep here," I said. Within 24 hours everyone on campus knew my wife was so strict that I had to sleep in a tree when she was angry. When she heard the news, she really was angry.

When I added slides and swings to the treehouse, neighbors realized it was not a hideout for me from my wife but a place for kids to play, and they were very upset. "If you do this, our children will also play on it and won't do their school work. Besides, it's a waste of money because in another 8 or 10 years they'll go to college and no one will use it."

A couple years later, a neighbor destroyed the tree house.

After this incident, I wrote an article comparing the pros and cons of Eastern and Western education and urging a balance between the two. But years later, I found that I was mistaken in assuming my Chinese students had no creativity!

Confucius said that if he showed a student one corner and they could not deduce the other three corners, he would not repeat the lesson, but with my MBA students, I felt that even if I showed them 3 corners they could not deduce the 4th! But years later, I found that these "uncreative" students were in fact very innovative, and I learned that both East and West face the same problem with creativity.

A lengthy study of 16,000 American children found that between ages 3 to 5, 98% were "creative geniuses," which essentially means we are all born very creative. But by age 25 it was only 2% – and this was in a society where education supposedly fosters creativity!

The whole world faces this problem because, by age 7, children begin to "fear failure." I remember reading aloud in first grade, almost

60 years ago, and how embarrassed I felt when other students laughed at me mispronouncing the word "enough." In school and society, we learn to give the right answer and fear making the wrong answer – even as Chinese students of oral English fear to open their mouths lest they make a mistake. But I've also learned that even if it appears this creativity has been quashed, it is still deep inside of us awaiting an opportunity or a challenge.

Some of my most "uncreative" Chinese students were later in life very creative and innovative when they faced problems or opportunities. In this, they were like ancient Chinese. The West says rigid education kills Chinese creativity but why didn't it kill the creativity of ancient Confucian scholars who were the most creative people in history?

Even so, I still think a balance of East and West is best, but if I was forced to choose only one – I'd choose East for the simple reason that suppressed creativity can be rekindled but if we don't build a solid foundation for critical thinking when we're young, it will be too late when we're older.

Henry David Thoreau wrote, "If you have built castles in the air, your work need not be lost; that is where they should be. Now put the foundations under them."

But according to some astonishing statistics that I shared in an article 25 years ago, Western children have no foundation. Research showed that 61% of American 17-year-olds could not read high school texts[①] and 80% of 21-year-olds could not understand a college

① Zinn, Howard, *A People's History of the United States*, Longman, NY, 1980, p.109.

textbook.[2] *Newsweek* revealed that 1/2 of American 8th graders could barely pass a 5th-grade math test and warned:

> "There is even compelling evidence that the longer kids stay in school, the farther they fall behind... Only 46% of 12th graders can do 7th-grade work and only 5% can do precalculus work."[3]

By 1988, the U.S. school dropout rate had soared to 28.5 %, compared with Japan's 5% and the Soviet Union's 2%.[4] Fully 44% of U.S. adults did not read even one book per year.[5]

The 1980 census revealed that in Detroit, the heart of America's automotive industry, 200,000 out of 1 million adults were illiterate.[6]

U.S. News and World Report found, "One of every 5 employees on the job now cannot even read at an eighth-grade level."[7]

Lastly, lest my Asian readers feel smug, a final quote from my article,

> "Not surprisingly, first generation Asians in America, hailing from nations that still stress academic fundamentals,

---

② "Literacy: Profiles of America's Young Adults," Princeton, NJ: National Assessment of Educational Progress, 1987.

③ "A Dismal Report Card," *Newsweek*, June 17, 1991,

④ "The Annual School Scoreboard," *USA Today*, February 26, 1988, p.5D.

⑤ *USA Today*, May 13, 1986, p.1 (Based on the D'Arcy Masius Benton & Bowles survey).

⑥ "We Daydream About One Life, Live Another," *International Business Weekly*, July 16, 1990.

⑦ *U.S. News and World Report*, June 3, 1991.

score the highest on American educational tests. It's no less surprising that second and third-generation Asian Americans, products of progressive education, inexorably settle to the level of their creative but illiterate peers."[8]

In summary, it seems that Americans fantasize about sand castles in the air but can't build foundations under them, and Chinese can build foundations but aren't dreaming about what to build upon them. But if I must choose, I choose foundations. As Ralph Waldo Emerson wrote, "The base determines the height of the pinnacle."

Almost all of us, fully 98% of us, are born creative geniuses, and as China's ancients and my modern Chinese students have all proven, that spark of creativity is only dampened, not extinguished, and an opportunity or challenge can rekindle it. But if we fail to build a foundation in our youth, it is not likely we'll ever build one later.

But having said that, I do encourage parents to follow my own example and give your children exposure to as much in life as possible so that they can discover for themselves what they are passionate about. I think I've learned much more from teaching my sons than they ever learned from me. My sons have finally chosen their careers – even though I still haven't figured out what I want to do when I grow up.

Bill Brown

---

⑧ "A Dismal Report Card," *Newsweek*, June 17, 1991.

Shannon loves reading, 1989
爱读书的山农（1989 年）

Shannon and
Mathew studying by
correspondence at
home, 1991
山农和马修在家接受早期
远程教育（1991 年）

Mathew at school, 1992
马修在学校（1992 年）

Shannon (front, left) winning a Beijing Opera award, 1999
山农（前，左）获得京剧表演奖项 (1999 年）

赐子千金不如教子一艺

亲爱的家长朋友们（和爷爷奶奶们）：

我现在也是两个孩子的爷爷了呢！1988年我们来中国时，我们的大儿子还只有两岁，小儿子才半岁，看着他们在两种不同文化中长大是一段非比寻常的经历。这也是帮助他们了解东西方文化精髓的绝佳机会——当然有时这也会让人困惑不已。

马修3岁时，在一次吃饭时问道：“爸爸，用中文怎么说‘菜’（蔬菜）？”

“‘菜’就是中文，马修，”我回答道。

他看上去有些惊讶，然后问道：“那用英语要怎么说呢？”

我们原本是计划让两个孩子上中国学校的，但无奈他们刚度过快乐的幼儿园时光，就在小学1年级时遇到了问题。当时，学校里外国孩子很少，因此不只是大人，孩子也喜欢捏捏他们俩红润的脸颊、扯扯他们金色的头发，然后赞叹道：“好可爱呀！”这给我的大儿子山农带来了很大压力，我们不得不带他到香港就医咨询，最后无奈决定让两个孩子在家接受教育——结果却证明这是东西方的完美平衡。

100多年前，一个在福建生活过51年的美国家庭就使用了卡尔弗特学校的函授课程。学校建于 1899 年，旨在帮助旅居国外的美国家庭解决教育问题。卡尔弗特经验丰富，声誉良好，所以在长达 8 年的时间里，我们一直为孩子选用它的课程。函授给孩子们提供书籍和教辅用品，我和苏则负责为孩子监考，用邮件向学校传递孩子的家庭作业。

许多人告诫我们，这种方式不会奏效，还会让孩子们变得孤僻。但其实在西方，公立学校大班教学模式才是新近的做法。一两个世纪前，一些最聪明的人物就是在家接受教育的——这对山农和马修也特别管用（其实美国的公共教育并没有那么奏效，这个我会在文末讲到）。我们家的孩子大约每天花 4 小时在卡尔弗特学校的课程上，然后再跟着中国家庭老师学习高等数学、练习钢琴和武术。

我坚持让他们选修的课程只有音乐和体育。山农是老大，个性和我相似，不擅长球类运动，但是很喜欢音乐。每当让他练 20 分钟钢琴时，他会练习一个小时，但说到体育运动，刚开始我要使用强制手段才行。马修的性格和他妈妈相似，不喜欢音乐，喜欢运动。让他练 20 分钟钢琴，才练 5 分钟就哇哇大哭，直喊：“太累了！”

“再练 15 分钟，”我坚持不让步。

“太累了！”他继续哭喊。我便瞪着他，见此，他重重地敲着琴键以示不情愿。

我和马修斗智斗勇 3 年，我深知音乐、数学对智力的发展至关重要，但年幼的他们还无法体会，所以我“坚持己见”，绝不退让。

马修慢慢有了进步，到了高中，不仅自学了吉他、架子鼓，还参加了乐队，自己写歌；在大学期间，他甚至拿到了“校园最佳钢琴家奖”。

现在这两个男孩在音乐和体育方面都表现出色——还多次向我表达谢意，感谢我“强迫”他们在年幼缺乏自律不懂事时不放弃他们。

除了音乐和体育，我从未试图干预他们的兴趣，但我确实尽力让他们接触到更多事物，这样他们就可以找到自己所热衷的。毕竟，那么多人花一辈子时间去追求一个连自己都不喜欢的事业，实在令人遗憾。但有时找到兴趣也不是一两天的事，就像我尽管今年 64 了，但还是不知道以后想做什么。

我也教过他们使用电脑，那时他们才三四岁（当时组装电脑要从香港买零部件），还给他们买了望远镜、显微镜；当然，少不了吉他、钢琴、架子鼓等乐器。我们还带他们去露营、滑冰、玩滑板、游泳和冲浪。我不断让他们接触新事物，但我非常注意方式，以免他们产生被强迫感。他们喜欢，我会帮他们追求；他们没有兴趣，我也不会施加压力——除了音乐和体育。

1997 年，我协助厦门洪市长和杨英女士创办了厦门国际学校。这所学校的国际文凭课程质量出众，而且愿意为我家两个孩子免除学费。但孩子们在家庭中文、数学和体育老师的指导下学习已颇有成效，我们便婉拒了学校的好意，让他们继续在家学习。

高中阶段，他们使用的是内布拉斯加大学为偏远地区的孩子开发的函授课程。12 年级时，他们参加了美国高考，分数都很高，还获得了全额奖学金；大学期间，凭借过去 12 年里依靠自学养成的自律习惯，他们表现得也很优异。

回顾过去，我想象不出更好的学习环境了。如果在中国学校里接受教育，为了高考，他们就得在那 12 年里每周花六到七天从早学到晚——并且几乎没有选修课。他们的钢琴老师是厦门大学的音乐教授，尽管这位老师想让自己的小孩学习弹钢琴，但却不敢教，担心这会妨碍一个 8 岁的孩子准备高考！

我的 MBA 学生中既有中国人也有外国人，很多外国学生喜欢弹吉他或玩杂耍，但近乎没有中国学生会如此。而了解到个中缘由，是我在修建树屋时。

当时有人看到我在建树屋，就问："你在树上干什么？"

"我正在建造一座树屋，以后我妻子跟我生气了，我就可以睡这儿了，"我回答道。于是，一天之内"我的妻子很凶悍，她一生气我就得睡树上"的说法就传遍校园，当传到她耳朵里时，她可真生气了。

见我给树屋加滑梯、上秋千，邻居们才恍然大悟，原来这不是我的"避难所"，而是给孩子们的"乐园"。为此他们十分不安。"如果你加上滑梯秋千，我们的孩子就会来玩，一玩就没心思做功课。并且这样很浪费钱呢，过个十年八年，他们就上大学去了，这些滑梯秋千到时谁来用呀？"

几年后，一位邻居把这座树屋给拆掉了。

为此，我专门写了篇文章，比较东西方教育的利弊，呼吁大家寻找两者的平衡点。但几年后，我发现自己对班上的中国学生持错误的看法——他们不是没有创造力！

孔子曾说，他教授学生一个知识点后，如果他们不能举一反三以此类推，他就不会再教；而我曾觉得，即使教给我的工商管理硕士 3 个知识点，他们还是不能推导出新的！但几年后，我发现这些"没有创造力"的学生其实很有创新精神，东西方在创造力方面也都面临着同样的问题。

根据一项对1.6万名美国儿童进行的长期研究发现，在3到5岁期间，98%的研究对象是“富有创造力的天才”，实质上这意味着我们生来就富有创造力。但到了25岁，这一比例就只有2%——这还是在一个据称教育能培养创造力的社会！

全世界都面临这个问题，因为到了7岁，孩子们就开始“害怕失败”。距今虽然已近60年，但我仍记得小学1年级大声朗读念错“足够”引得同学哄堂大笑时内心的尴尬。无论是在学校还是社会，我们学着给出正确答案，害怕做出错误回答——正像是学习英语口语的中国学生担心犯错而害怕张嘴那样。但我也了解到，即使这种创造力似乎已经被碾压，但它仍潜藏在我们内心深处，等待机遇或挑战把它唤醒。

我的一些最“缺乏创造力”的中国学生，在后来的生活中面对问题或机遇时，展现了出色的创造力和创新力。在这点上，他们就像古代中国人。西方社会认为僵化的教育扼杀了中国人的创造力，但为什么历史上最具创造力的古代儒家学者却表现得截然相反呢？

即便如此，我仍然认为平衡东西方教育是最好的选择，但如果只能二选一——我会选择东方的教育，原因很简单，压抑的创造力可以重新被点燃，但年轻时没能为批判性思维打下坚实的基础，以后就为时已晚。

亨利·大卫·梭罗（Henry David Thoreau）写道：“如果你的梦想只是空中楼阁，不必摧毁它；那本就是它的位置。现在你要做的只是在它下面垫上基石。”

25年前，我在一篇文章中分享了一些数据，表明西方儿童基础知识薄弱，这些数据令人十分惊讶。有研究发现，在美国有61%的17岁孩子看不懂高中课本[①]，80%的21岁青少年看不懂大学课本。[②]《新闻周刊》曾披露，美国8年级学生竟然有一半只能勉强通过5年级数学考试，于是该周刊警告道：

> "甚至有令人信服的证据表明，孩子在学校待的时间越长，他们落后的程度就越大……只有46%的12年级学生能做7年级的作业，只有5%的学生能解答初级微积分的题目。"[③]

到1988年，美国辍学率飙升至28.5%，而日本、苏联仅分别为5%、2%。[④]美国成年人年读书量不到一本的足足占比44%。[⑤]

据1980年人口普查显示，在美国汽车产业中心底特律，每100万成年人中有20万是文盲。[⑥]

《美国新闻与世界报道》发现："现在每5名职员就有1人甚至未能掌握8年级水平的阅读能力。"[⑦]

最后，为了防止我的亚洲读者自鸣得意，我再从那篇文章中引用如下一段：

① 霍华德·津恩. 美国人民的历史【M】. 纽约：朗文出版社，1980: 109.
② 读写能力：美国年轻人的侧画像【R】. 新泽西州普林斯顿市：美国国家教育进展评估，1987.
③ 惨不忍睹的成绩单【J】. 新闻周刊，1991-6-17.
④ 学校年度计分板【N】. 今日美国，1988-2-26（5D）.
⑤ 根据达西·马修斯·本顿和波尔斯的调查【N】. 今日美国，1986-5-13 (1).
⑥ 我们梦想着一种生活，却过着另一种生活【J】. 国际商业周刊，1990-7-16.
⑦ 美国新闻与世界报道，1991-6-3.

“第一代美国亚裔来自那些仍然强调学术基础的国家，他们能在美国教育体系的考试中拿下最高分不足为奇。但令人错愕的是，作为先进教育的产物，第二、三代美国亚裔却不可避免地甘于和他们的同龄人一样——富有创造力但满纸别字、病句连篇。”⑧

总而言之，美国人似乎幻想在空中建立沙堡，却无法在其下面筑起地基，而中国人能够筑起地基，但似乎并不梦想在上面建些什么。但如果必须做出选择，我会选择地基。正如拉尔夫·沃尔多·爱默生（Ralph Waldo Emerson）所写：“顶峰的高度是由基石决定的。”

几乎所有人，高达98%，天生富有创意；中国古人和我的中国学生都证明了，创意的火花只会受到抑制，而不是熄灭，一个机会或挑战就可以重新点燃它。但如果我们不能在青年时代打下根基，日后将难以建立根基。

话虽如此，我却非常鼓励家长朋友们参考我的亲身经历，尽可能多地让孩子接触生活，让他们发现自己的激情所在。在我看来，从孩子那学到的远比我教给他们的要多得多。他们最终都按自己意愿选择了职业——然而我还没有弄清楚以后想做什么。

潘维廉

2020年5月4日

⑧ 惨不忍睹的成绩单【J】. 新闻周刊，1991-6-17.

扫一扫

看老潘读信视频

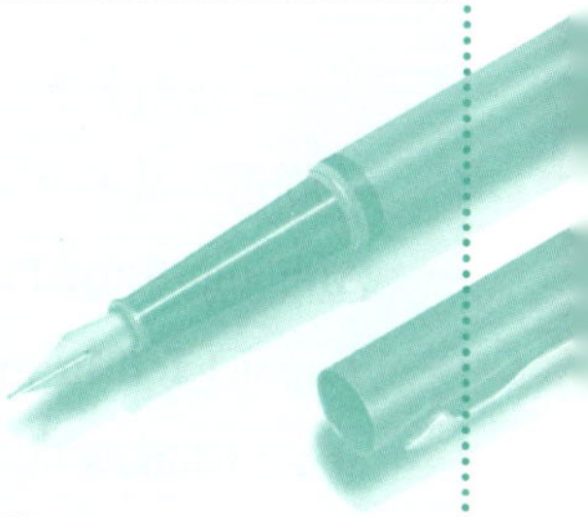

How to Choose Your Ideal Life

May 13, 2020

Dear Chinese friends,

My childhood goal was to visit Australia and Africa, not China, quite simply because I knew nothing about China. Today, I've still not been to either Australia or Africa, but life in China has been far more fulfilling than I could have ever imagined. This has taught me an invaluable lesson: dream big, and set goals, but be flexible and open to new opportunities that may far surpass what you could have planned yourself.

After high school, I joined the Air Force simply because they'd pay for my college expenses and I'd get to travel – but my first assignment was only 50 miles from home! I was so upset that I volunteered for Greenland because no one else wanted to live on a sheet of ice for two years. My friends, however, all volunteered for the "dream assignment" of Taiwan. I had no interest in Taiwan or Asia, so of course the Air Force sent me to Taiwan and sent my friends to Greenland. I was as furious as they were – but it was Yuánfèn (fate).

In 2019, Xi Jinping said during the national congress that he had Yuánfèn with Fujian. In the same way, I had Yuánfèn with Taiwan. Although I tried to cancel the assignment, within days of my arrival in Taipei I fell in love with the place and the people. As I learned more about China's history, I set a goal of leaving the Air Force after Taiwan and studying Chinese – but then I spent three years as an OSI special agent in the U.S. and Turkey.

As a youth, I'd not had any interest in the military but that experience taught me discipline and persistence and also led me to Taiwan. My experience as a special agent, including time spent with the Shah of Iran, opened my eyes to what was happening to people in developing countries and led me to study cross-cultural studies in Los Angeles. And while studying in Los Angeles, I met a blonde-haired, blue-eyed American girl who had been born and raised in Taiwan and lived in Taizhong, where I'd lived. But though we had the same friends, Sue had returned to the U.S. the year I moved to Taiwan so we didn't meet until 3 years later in Los Angeles. Yuánfèn! We both dreamed of going to Mainland China, and at Christmas we were married in Taipei, but it took 7 years to get to Xiamen.

While we waited to move to China, I started a business to pay off school loans, then got a PhD in business – never imagining that the experience and degree would enable me to help XMU start one of China's first MBA programs. Yuánfèn again.

When I came to Xiamen 32 years ago, my sole goal was to study Chinese. I had no idea I'd also teach MBA, write over a dozen books, write and film hundreds of TV episodes, be an international spokesman for many Chinese cities, and serve as New Channel's Retelling Chinese Stories in English Ambassador – a position I especially enjoy because I've been writing and telling stories since I was 7. Yuánfèn!

Except for writing stories, few of my childhood goals worked out as I had hoped, but if I had scripted my life from cradle to grave, I could not have penned a more exciting or rewarding life. But in retrospect, I can see how each stage of my life built upon the previous stage because, consistently, whether I liked what I was doing or not, I did my best and learned all I could from it. And as the ancients in both East and West have long said, "You reap what you sow" – though in China, I've reaped far more than I've sown.

Over my decades in Xiamen I've had over 10,000 graduate students, and a handful of those have gone on to be very successful. In interviewing them, and successful people in other countries, I've found that our "success secrets" are all fairly similar!

1. Read widely and gain broad experience. When Xi Jinping was sent to the countryside, other youth took warm clothes and extra food but he took books. Long after the food was gone and the clothes were threadbare, Xi still had his books, and they gave him the intellectual foundation to excel at anything he faced later. As a youth (and today as well), I especially enjoyed biographies, which gave me confidence as I read how ordinary people like myself overcame adversity. I also learned some foundational subjects that I knew would help in any pursuit – such as music (for intellectual development) and

a second language. By college I had no idea what I wanted to do so I studied law, criminal justice, psychology, philosophy, oceanography, astronomy – and of course languages, which I've come to love. I never used most of what I learned but it broadened my perspective and made it easier for me to adapt rapidly to challenges.

2. Set goals, with action steps – but remember that goals evolve over time. My childhood dream was Australia, not China, because I knew nothing at all about China, but my goals evolved as I gained knowledge and experience. Even my China goal, initially, was simply to study Chinese; it wasn't until I arrived in Xiamen that I was asked to help start an MBA program, which led to so many other things. Yuánfèn.

3. Weave a "thread of success" in your life by doing your best at everything, even if forced to do something you don't care for. In 1990, I asked a girl student how she scored 100 on all 8 of my exams in 4 courses, and also excelled in sports, student leadership and everything else. She said, "My parents are poor teachers but they taught me when I was young that if I did small things badly, I'd never have a chance to do bigger things, so do my best at everything." A simple philosophy, but she went on to become a bank executive overseas and very successful. Another XMU student came from a very poor family but learned a similar lesson from her grandfather. After XMU, she graduated from Harvard, worked for McKinsey, and became an executive at Google Headquarters. When I was in business, the one thing I looked for in hiring was that "thread

of success," even if it was in an entirely different field. I learned that if a person can excel in one thing, they may possibly excel in another.

4. Never quit (永不放弃). Prof. Hu Min, CEO of New Channel, has a personal motto "Strive until succeed," and I've seen the same persistence in every successful person I've known, including my former business associate who was a high school teacher and went on to become a billionaire. As Edison said, "Genius is 1% inspiration and 99% perspiration." Like my two most successful students, I learned early on to do my best and never quit – but also to be open and flexible because there's a fine line between persistence and sheer obstinacy.

5. Be open and flexible. As the ancients said, the mountain won't turn but the road might. We should not lightly give up on anything we've started but as we gain more experience or the situation changes, our goals or methods may evolve. But we must be cautious that the change is planned and purposeful, and not simply a retreat from difficulty – and this is where it helps to have a team of people you trust.

6. Master team. As Confucius said, "Where 3 walk together, 1 may be my teacher." Always learn from others. Like many successful people that I've known or read about, I always sought advice on difficult decisions from a small core of mature, experienced people that I trusted. Their diverse experience and perspectives often helped keep me from making disastrous mistakes. And a few times when I felt like quitting, they gently but firmly reminded me of why I started in the first

place. As Xi Jinping has often said, "Don't forget your original intent (不忘初心)."

In retrospect, much of my life seems to have come together with sheer luck – or Yuánfèn. But in reality, I was able to build upon seemingly unrelated experiences because, in everything I've done, I've learned all I could and done my best to weave a "thread of success" through everything, even when doing things I did not really enjoy. As the saying goes, "The harder you work, the luckier you are" – and I am certainly very lucky!

So in summary, broaden your knowledge and experience so you have more choices before you, then set goals and create action steps to judge your progress. But also be open to redefining those goals as your own experience and abilities evolve or the situation changes. And don't rush it and make irreversible decisions before you know what you are really passionate about. My youngest son took six years to finish a 4-year degree because he studied three majors before settling upon medicine. Matt was worried about spending too long in college and my wife was worried about spending too much money, but I warned them both, "Better to spend the time and money now than to waste a life on something you are not passionate about."

Lastly, in your drive to make it big in life, don't try to go it alone. The Hollywood movie *Into the Wild* was about a young man, Alex McCandless, who in 1992 gave away his money and left his family to travel alone. He eventually ended up stuck, alone, in an abandoned bus in remote Alaska and starved to death. The movie makes him out to be some kind of hero, quoting his dying words, "I have had a happy life..."

But he also wrote in his journal just before his death, "...an unshared happiness is not happiness... Happiness is only real when shared. I was wrong. I think it is time for me to return home, to right the wrongs."

It was too late for McCandless, but hopefully not for you and I. All across the world, people on their deathbeds have been asked what they most regret and none have ever regretted not making more money or spending more time in the office, but many did regret, with tears, that they did not spend more time with family.

One of the biggest reasons I love China is that I have a very big family here! Chinese throughout the ages have treasured healthy social relationships and are always there for friends and family. As a Fujian man told me, "If I ignored someone in my village who needed help, I could not live with myself." Set goals that enrich not just yourself but those around you, and after you too have gone, you will live on in the lives of those you've touched.

Dream with no regrets!

Bill Brown

Bill's family photo, 1989
老潘一家人（1989 年）

Bill's family singing together, 1994
老潘一家人大合唱（1994 年）

Happy family, 2012
幸福的一家人（2012 年）

如何选择理想生活

亲爱的中国朋友们：

小时候，我想去澳大利亚和非洲，而不是中国，因为当时我对中国全无概念。至今我还没去过澳大利亚和非洲，但在中国的生活比我想象的要充实得多。这给了我一个宝贵的教训：拥有远大梦想，并设定目标，但灵活应对、乐于接受新的机会——这些机会带来的可能性有时远超你的预期。

高中毕业后我加入了空军，原因很简单，可以免交大学费用，还可以到处旅行。令我失望的是，我的第一个任务离家只有 50 英里，于是我主动申请去格陵兰岛，当时鲜有人愿意在这冰天雪地的岛屿上生活两年。我的朋友都主动申请参加台湾的“梦想任务”。而我对台湾，甚至亚洲都没有兴趣，所以空军当然会把我送到台湾，把我的那些朋友送到格陵兰岛。我很愤怒，他们也一样，但那是缘分。

2019 年，习近平主席在中国的全国人民代表大会上说，他与福建有缘分。我与台湾也是如此。虽然我曾试图阻止被分到驻台湾的空军部队，但到达台北几天后，我就爱上了那里，爱上了那里的人们。随着对中国历史了解的加深，我决定在台湾服完兵役后就退伍去学中文，但随后我被派遣到美国、土耳其，做了3年空军特别调查办公室（OSI）特别探员。

年轻时我对军事并不感冒，但从军的经历教给了我纪律和毅力，也让我有机会去台湾。如包括与伊朗国王共事在内的特别探员生涯，让我有机会了解发展中国家的生活，并让我下定决心在洛杉矶学习跨文化研究。又因为在洛杉矶读书，我遇到了一位金发碧眼的美国女孩苏。她在台湾出生长大，我们还有共同的朋友，但不巧她在我去台湾的那一年回了美国。3年后我们在洛杉矶相见，缘分呀！我们还都梦想着来中国大陆。同年圣诞，我们在台北结婚，但7年后才到厦门。

等待去厦门的那几年，我经营了一家公司偿还上学贷款，然后拿到商科博士学位，但从没想过我的这段经历和商科博士学位会在日后厦门大学开办中国第一批MBA课程时派上用场。缘分呀！

32年前我到厦门时，一心只想学好汉语，没想过还会成为MBA老师、十几本书的作者，参与编写、拍摄几百集电视剧，成为许多中国城市的国际代言人，甚至成为新航道“用英语讲中国故事”活动的形象大使——我特别乐于担任这个形象大使，因为我从7岁起就在撰写和讲故事。挡不住的缘分呀！

除了写故事，我童年的目标很少能像我所期待的那样实现，但如果我一早就被剧透我人生的剧本，怎能书写出更加令人兴奋或富有意义的生活呢？回头看走过的路，我能看到自己生命中的每一阶段是如何建立在前一阶段之上，无论喜欢与否，对于正在做的事情我一直在尽最大努力，并从中尽可能多地汲取养分。东西方古人早就说过，“种瓜得瓜，种豆得豆”——但我在中国的收获远远超过种下的。

在厦门的几十年里，我带过1万多名研究生，其中少数学生已经非常成功。结合对他们和其他国家成功人士的采访，我发现“成功秘诀”都十分相似：

1. 学无止境。习近平主席下乡时，一般年轻人带得最多的是衣服和食物，他带的是书，这为他日后出类拔萃夯实了知识基础。年轻时（今天也是如此），我尤其喜爱阅读传记，每读到像我这样的普通人如何克服差异时，常常信心大增。我还学了一些在我看来对任何追求都有帮助的基础学科，比如音乐（促进智力发展）和第二语言。上大学时，我不知道自己想做什么，所以我学了法律、刑事司法、心理学、哲学、海洋学、天文学——当然还有后来爱上的语言学。我仅用到了学的一小部分知识，但广泛涉猎拓宽了我的视野，提升了我快速适应挑战的能力。

2. 设定目标，制定行动步骤——记住目标会随时间而变化。我儿时梦想去澳大利亚，而不是来当时一无所知的中国，但随着知识和经验的增长，我的目标发生了变化。甚至到中国，最初也只是为了学习汉语，直到来了厦门，受邀参加开办MBA课程后才有了一连串的故事。缘分呀。

3. 找到自己“成功的线索”——尽最大可能做好一

切，即使是那些你不愿意做的事情。1990年，我问班上的一名女学生是如何在我教的4门课的8门考试中都拿100分，同时还能在体育、学生领导力和其他方面都表现出色。她说："我的父母都是收入不高的老师，但他们从小就教导我，如果小事做不好，就永远没有机会做更大的事，所以无论做什么都尽力而为。"尽管理念很简单，但却引领她成为一名外资银行的高管，且做得十分出色。还有一名厦大的学生，家庭非常贫穷，但她从祖父那里学到了类似的经验。她后来去了哈佛，从哈佛毕业后去了麦肯锡，之后在谷歌的总部担任高管。我经营公司招人时只看对方身上是否有"成功的线索"，哪怕线索分布在完全不同的领域。因为我知道一个人如果能在一件事上表现卓越，在另一件事上也可能如此。

4. 永不放弃，大器晚成。新航道首席执行官胡敏教授有一句个人座右铭："我坚持，我成功"，我在所有认识的成功人士身上都看到了同样的坚持，包括我以前的商业伙伴——他曾是一名高中老师，后来成了亿万富翁。爱迪生说："天才是1%的灵感和99%的汗水。"和我那两个十分成功的学生一样，我很早就学会了尽力而为，永不放弃，但我也学会了开放和灵活，因为坚持和固执之间的界限并非清晰。

5. 开放灵活。古人常说，"山不转那路在转"。因此，尽管不能轻言放弃，但随着自身经验的增长或外部情况的变化，我们的目标或方法可能需要做相应调整。但是，我们必须谨慎，改变是有计划和目的的，不是简单地逃避困难——这也是一支靠谱的团队发挥作用的地方。

6. 与优秀的人为伍。孔子说："三人行，必有我师焉。"不要停止向他人学习。像我认识的或从书中了解到的许多成功人士一样，面临艰难抉择时，我总是会向自己信任的成熟且富有经验的人士寻求建议。他们不同的经验、观点常能帮助我有效避免犯下灾难性错误。有几次想放弃时，他们都会温柔但坚定地提醒我当初"出发"的原因。这就像习近平主席常说的，"不忘初心"。

回头看，我人生的许多际遇似乎纯运气使然，或者说全凭缘分。但事实上，我能够在看似不相关的经历上获得发展，是因为我尽可能从中进行学习，并在复盘的过程中尽最大可能找到"成功的线索"，哪怕是做那些我并不喜欢的事情时也是如此。俗话说："越努力，越幸运"——我当然很幸运！

总而言之，拓宽知识和经验，让自己有更多选择，然后再设定目标，制定行动步骤，并据此判断是否进步。但也要随着自身经验、能力的增长或外部情况的变化，接受目标的更新。在你知道自己真正热衷什么前，不要急于做出不可逆转的决定。我小儿子马修 6 年才读完 4 年的学位，因为他在攻读了 3 个专业后才转向医学。当时，他担心再学医会花太长时间，我妻子则担心会花太多钱，但我告诫他们两个"与其把生命浪费在自己不热衷的事情上，不如现在就花上时间和金钱"。

最后，在你努力实现梦想时，不要单打独斗。在好莱坞电影

《荒野生存》中，一位名叫亚历克斯·麦克坎德莱斯（Alex McCandless）的年轻人在1992年捐出了自己的钱财后，离开家人独自去旅行。最后，他在遥远的阿拉斯加独自一人被困在一辆废弃的公共汽车里，不幸饿死。这部电影让他成为某种英雄，他在临终时曾说道：“我度过了幸福的一生……”

但他临死前在日记中这样写道：“……无法分享的幸福不是幸福……只有能分享的才是真正的。我错了。我想是时候让我回家，弥补曾经犯下的错了。”

对麦克坎德莱斯来说为时已晚，但希望这对你我来说不是如此。世人在临终前被问到最大的遗憾是什么时，往往没人会说没赚到更多钱或花更多时间工作，但确实有许多人流下悔恨的泪水，后悔曾经没有花更多时间陪伴家人。

我爱中国最大的原因是我在这里有很多家人！古往今来，中国人都很珍惜健康的社会关系，总是为朋友和家人考虑。一位福建人告诉我：“如果我忽视了村里需要帮助的人，我就会心生愧疚。”你设定的目标如果不仅丰富了你自己，也能使你周围人的生活变得丰富充实，那么即使在你离开后，那些你曾触动过的人将一直记得你。

无怨无悔追梦！

潘维廉

2020年5月13日

扫一扫

看老潘读信视频

Big Rocks First – Key to Your Success!

May 26, 2020

Dear Chinese friends,

I love juggling because it's a relaxing exercise, and an added benefit is that science has proven that juggling increases the brain's white and gray matter[1] – which is great news for me because I need all the help I can get.

I've seen some people juggle 6 or 7 balls at a time, and Alex Barron of the UK won the Guinness World Record by juggling 11! For me, juggling 3 balls is hard enough – so imagine juggling 583 balls – or tasks – each day? Yet that's exactly what the average American manager did in the 1970s. And nowadays, thanks to the internet, mobile phones and social networking, we're probably juggling ten times that.

Whether you're a manager trying to keep a company together or a student seeking time to practice oral English, you need to stop juggling and put your Big Rocks first. This won't guarantee success, but failure

① Scholz, J., Klein, M., Behrens, T. et al. "Training Induces Changes in White-Matter Architecture," *Nat Neurosci*, 2009 (12): 1370-1371.

to discover your Big Rocks and put them first will probably guarantee your failure.

583 Balls

In the 1970s, Canadian Professor Henry Mintzberg found that executives and managers typically believed that they spent their day planning, organizing, leading and controlling, but in reality they averaged 583 activities a day – one task every 48 seconds![②] A study of 160 British managers found that only once in every two days were they able to spend over half an hour on one task.[③]

With such a schedule, managers not only have no time to plan, they don't even think. They simply react to problems, trying to keep everything going like a juggler with 583 balls in the air. With no time to think, reactions are based not on what is really happening but on the manager's expectations, based on their experience – but in our rapidly changing world, yesterday's experience may be outdated today.

If managers juggled 583 tasks a day in the slower 1970s, just imagine life today with email, mobile phones and social media. And it's not just managers who are juggling impossibly complex schedules and competing demands. Everyone, including teachers and students, face the same issues, and you'll never be fully effective unless you learn to identify the "big rocks" and put them first.

② Henry Mintzberg, *The Nature of Managerial Work,* New York: Harper & Row, 1973.
③ Rosemary Stewart, *Managers and Their Jobs*, London: Macmillan, 1967.

The Rock Jar Story

Years ago, an American professor filled an empty glass jar to the brim with rocks and asked, "Is it full?"

"Yes," the students answered. The professor smiled, and then added tiny rocks as he shook the jar gently, letting the pebbles sift to the bottom.

"It is full now?"

"No!" said the twice-burned students. Twice-burned means you learn from mistakes. If you burn yourself on a hot stove, you don't touch it twice unless you're one of those few people who actually enjoy pain.

The professor slowly added fine sand until it was full. "Is it full now?"

"No!" shouted the students.

He added water to the very brim and asked, "Is it full now?"

"Yes!" said most students, though a chemistry major said "No!" because he knew that adding salt could actually decrease water's volume.

"So what is the lesson of this demonstration?" asked the professor.

We knew it was about time management, so I said, "There is always more time!"

"Nonsense," he said. "There are only 24 hours in a day, and once it is gone, it is gone forever. If you lose money, you can earn it back, but if you lose time, it is gone forever."

"The lesson," he said, "is that you must put the big rocks in first, because if you first add water, sand and little rocks, you'll never get the big rocks in later."

That was one of the most important lessons I learned in 20 years of school. Big Rocks, of course, are your greatest priorities. Small rocks must also get done but later – or delegate them if you can. Sand is the daily chores, which should always be delegated. Water is the time wasters that you should ignore.

Find Your Big Rocks with an Activity Survey

To put your big rocks first, you must first discover what they are. You can do this by making two columns on a sheet of paper, the left one labeled Theory and the right one Reality. Under Theory, list all tasks that you believe you must do, and rate their importance on a 1 to 5 scale. Under Reality, use the same 1 to 5 scale (so you can compare the two sides) to rate how much time you really spend on those tasks. For example, under Theory, you may rate "practice oral English 20 minutes a day" as 5, but under Reality give it a 1. Or you might rate "WeChat" as a 2 under Theory but a 5 under Reality.

After your survey, ask yourself 3 questions (what, why and how):

1. What are the biggest imbalances?
2. Why do I have them?
3. How can I fix them, or at least compensate for them?

It Takes Time to Save Time

"It takes money to make money" is common knowledge but few understand that it also "takes time to save time." I was running a business while doing a PhD full time, and struggling with 20 hour days. So as soon as I heard the Rock Jar Story, I began each day locked in my office while my secretary told everyone I was in my morning meeting – which was just me and a cup of coffee.

I reviewed each day's activities and scheduled my big rocks early in the day, and I either delegated the rest or scheduled them in the afternoon. When I proactively put my big rocks first, I almost always finished that day's key tasks. People still dropped in with unexpected demands but I would sigh and say, "I'm so sorry (though I wasn't sorry at all) but I have this at 10 AM, and this at 1 PM – no time! Sorry! Please see Mr. Edwards..."

But if I did not put the big rocks first, my day would fill up with little rocks, sand and water and by 4 or 5 PM I'd find I had not even thought about the big rocks, much less attempted to finish them, and I'd either work late or take my work home – or have even more to do the next day.

Big Rocks First is a powerful but simple concept, but it only works when done consistently over time, which is why most people fail – but as the saying goes, "You either fail to plan or you plan to fail."

Today is far more hectic than the simpler 1970s when managers juggled 583 tasks per day, but the most effective people I know, including a few billionaires, do not come close to 583 tasks a day. They know that success is not doing more things; success is doing fewer things, but doing them better. That's why I remind my students that business is spelled with an "i," not a "y" (busyness).

In the late 1990s, in spite of my best intentions, I too got caught up in what Mintzberg calls the "activity trap." When my health broke down I began to say no to many of the demands made upon me, focusing on my three priorities: family, students, telling China's story. The only time I agreed to other activities was when they were either uniquely suited to my experience and interests, or they were something I wanted to learn more about. Since I began saying no, I've done much less yet accomplished far more than I did during the days when I said "yes" to everyone.

Lastly – many of my students say they want to become leaders in their fields, but you cannot be a leader if you cannot even lead yourself. If you don't manage your time, others will happily manage it for you, so whatever your goal in life, take back control of time, your most precious and irreplaceable resource. And if you have a goal – improve oral English, write a book, learn martial arts – stop making excuses and make it one of your Big Rocks, and then put that Big Rock First.

It's that simple – but simple isn't always easy because you need persistence in putting the Big Rocks First today, tomorrow and every day until you accomplish your dream. And even then it does not end because, in my experience, once I've achieved one dream, there's always another dream building upon what I've just learned. To stop learning and dreaming is to abandon one's whole reason for living.

Dream – and then make sure that dream is a Big Rock so it is not just a day dream!

Bill Brown

Bill with Chinese kids, 2006
老潘和中国孩子们（2006 年）

Bill with Chinese kids, 2009
老潘和中国孩子们（2009 年）

Bill with Chinese kids, 2020
老潘和中国孩子们（2020 年）

先放好大石头——你成功的关键！

亲爱的中国朋友们：

我喜欢玩杂耍，它让人身心放松，另一个好处是，有科学依据证明玩杂耍能增加大脑的白质和灰质[①]——对我来说是个好消息，这正是我需要的。

我见过一些人一次可抛玩6到7个球，英国的亚历克斯·巴伦（Alex Barron）凭借同时抛玩11个球，登上了吉尼斯世界纪录！对我来说，3个球已经够难的了——玩583个球或每天处理583项任务简直难以想象！然而，这就是上世纪70年代美国经理人的日常。现在多亏互联网、手机和社交网络的便捷，我们每天处理的事务数量翻了10倍。

无论你是一个运营公司的经理人，还是一个寻找时间练习英语口语的学生，你都需要停止杂耍，得把你的大石头放在第一位。尽管这并不能保证成功，但如果你不能发现自己的大石头，并将它们放在第一位，就很有可能注定失败。

① 简·肖尔茨，米里亚姆·克莱因，蒂莫西·贝伦斯等．训练可引起脑白质结构变化【J】．自然神经科学，2009（12）：1370-1371.

583个“球”

上世纪70年代，加拿大教授亨利·明茨伯格（Henry Mintzberg）发现，高管和经理们通常认为自己一天的时间花在了计划、组织、领导和控制上，但事实上，他们平均每天有583项活动，每48秒一项任务！[②]一项针对160名英国经理人的调查发现，他们能够花半个多小时完成一项任务的机会每两天才一次。[③]

这样安排日程，经理们不仅没有时间做计划，甚至连思考的时间都没有。他们只是对问题做出反应，试图运转这一切，就像个玩杂耍的人在空中同时抛着583个球。没有时间思考，做出的反应不是基于实际发生的，而是基于经理人自身的期望和经验——但在瞬息万变的世界里，昨天的经验今天可能就已过时。

在节奏相对缓慢的20世纪70年代，管理者如果每天要处理583项任务，那么想象一下如今被电子邮件、手机和社交媒体充斥的生活，又会是一番怎样的场景。不仅仅是经理人每天要面对十分繁忙的日程安排和十分复杂的紧急性需求，包括老师和学生在内的所有人都有着同样的问题——除非你学会识别那些“大石头”并把它们放在第一位，否则你永远不会达到高效。

石头罐的故事

几年前，一位美国教授把一个空玻璃罐装满石头，然后问道：“现在满了吗？”

“满了，”学生们回答道。教授笑了笑，然后添加一些小石块，

② 亨利·明茨伯格．管理工作的本质【M】．纽约：哈珀与罗出版公司，1973.
③ 罗斯玛丽·斯图尔特．管理者和他们的工作【M】．伦敦：麦克米伦，1967.

再轻轻摇晃一下，这些鹅卵石就被筛到了底部。

“现在满了？”

“没有！”有了前车之鉴，学生们否定回答道。前车之鉴意味着你从错误中吸取教训。如果被热炉子烫着了，除了为数不多的享受疼痛的人，否则人们都不会再次碰那个灼热的炉子。

教授慢慢地加入细沙，直到玻璃罐满了。“现在满了吗？”

“没有！”学生们喊道。

教授沿着罐沿往里再加水，然后问道：“现在满了吗？”

大多数学生都给出了肯定答案，除了一个化学专业的学生说“没有！”，因为他知道加一些盐就可以减少水的体积。

“那你们从这次示范中学到了什么？”教授问道。

因为这是节关于时间管理的课，所以我说：“时间挤一挤总是有的！”

“胡说！”他说，“一天只有24小时，消逝了就永远回不来。丢了钱，你可以赚回来，但丢了时间，就永远丢了。”

他说：“它告诉我们你必须先放大石头，因为先加水、沙子和小石子，以后就永远无法装大石头了。”

这是我20年的学生生涯里最重要的一课。当然，大石头是那些值得你最优先考虑的事情。小石头也必须放进去，但晚些时候，或者有可能的话就委托他人来放。沙子是日常琐事，应该总是交给别人来做。水代表浪费时间的小事，应当忽略。

展开活动调查，找到你的大石头

把大石头放在第一位，首先你必须了解它们是什么。要解决这个问题，你可以将一张纸分成两栏，左边一栏标上理论，右边一栏标上现实。在理论这一栏，列出所有你认为必须完成的任务，用 1 到 5 的数值来评定它们的重要性。在现实这一栏，用相同的等级（以便对两边进行比较）评估你在这些任务上实际花费的时间。例如，在理论那一栏，你可把“每天练习 20 分钟英语口语”评为 5，但在现实那一栏，可把它评为 1；或者你可以在理论那一栏，把“微信”评为 2，而在现实那一栏评为 5。

调查结束后，问自己三个问题（什么，为什么和怎么做）：

1. 最失衡的是什么？
2. 为什么会这样？
3. 怎样解决，或者至少怎样才能亡羊补牢？

节省时间需要花时间

“赚钱需要钱”是常识，但很少有人知道“节省时间也需要时间”。攻读全日制博士学位时，我还经营着一家公司，一天下来我得努力 20 个小时。所以听到那个摇晃玻璃罐的故事后，我就每天早上将自己锁在办公室，让我的秘书告诉别人我在开早会——那时办公室里其实只有我和一杯咖啡。

每天一早我便评估当天的任务，并安排好我的“大石头”，余下的事情，我要么委托他人，要么安排到下午做。主动把大石头放在第一位，我几乎总能完成当天的主要任务。遇到不速之客，我会惋惜地说道：“很抱歉（然而我完全不这么认为），我早上 10 点安排了事情，下午 1 点也安排了——真没时间了！抱歉！去找找爱德华兹先生吧……”

不先放置好大石头，我的一天就会被一些小石头、沙子和水给塞满，到下午四五点，才发现竟然把大石头给忘了，更不用说试图完成它们了。这样一来，我要么工作到很晚，要么得把工作带回家——或者推到第二天。

大石头第一的理念非常有用，实践起来一点都不复杂，但它的作用只有在人们坚持不懈的情况下才会凸显出来，这解释了大多数人失败的原因——俗话说，“凡事预则立，不预则废。”

今天人们远比上世纪 70 年代忙碌，当时经理人每天要处理 583 项任务，但据我所知，最有效率的人，包括一些亿万富翁，每天所处理的事情远没有 583 项。他们知道成功不是做更多的事情；成功是做更少的事情，并将它们做得更好。这就是为什么我会提醒学生，生意（business）这个英文单词上写的是“i”，而不是“y”（busyness 忙碌）。

上世纪 90 年代末，尽管我有着美好初衷，但还是陷入了明茨伯格说的“活动陷阱”。当健康出现问题时，我开始拒绝他人的许多要求，把重心放在三个优先事项上：家庭、学生、讲述中国故事。只有在遇到那些和我的经验兴趣特别匹配，或是我希望进一步了解的活动时，我才会同意。学会拒绝后，我参与的事情比“来者不拒”时要少很多，但我能完成的事情却要多得多。

我的许多学生告诉我，他们想成为所在领域的领导者，但如果你连自己都领导不了，又怎能成为某个领域的领导者呢！如果你管理不了自己的时间，别人会乐意为你“代劳”，所以无论人生目标是什么，收回对时间的控制权，因为这是你最宝贵和无法替代的资源。如果你有目标——提高英语口语、写一本书、学武术——就不要找借口，而是把它当成你的大石头，然后把它放在第一位。

道理很简单——但实践起来不总是这么回事，因为你不仅需要在今天将大石头放在第一位，明天以及以后的每一天都是如此，直到你实现梦想。并且，即使一个梦想实现了，你仍旧需要将大石头放在第一位——根据我以往经验，一旦实现一个梦想，总有另一个梦想随之而来。停止学习，停止梦想，就是否定生活的全部意义。

坚持梦想——确保它是一块大石头，而不只是一个白日梦！

潘维廉

2020 年 5 月 26 日

Quote from Lao Pan:

老潘金句：

The world has never had two great nations as powerful and unique as 5,000-year-old China and the 250-year-old U.S., and though they are vastly different on the surface, they are both inhabited by people who share the same values and dreams; we differ mainly in how we seek to accomplish those dreams.

世界上从未有两个国家像有着 5000 年历史的中国和 250 年历史的美国这样强大和独特，这两个国家表面看去有着天壤之别，但这两片土地上的人们却分享着共同的价值观和梦想；我们的主要分歧是在于如何实现这些梦想。

Chapter 4
Lessons from Prevention and Control of COVID-19

第四章
抗疫经验

扫一扫

看老潘读信视频

I Wish I Were in China Now

January 31, 2020

Dear Chinese friends,

I just returned to the U.S. to help my 90-year-old mother-in-law only a couple of days before the world realized the coronavirus was so serious. On the one hand, I should feel lucky, as many foreigners are scrambling frantically to leave. Yet on the other hand, I regret that I am not there in China to help. Had I realized the situation was so dire, I would have preferred to stay.

But I see two reasons that the world is lucky this happened in China and not elsewhere: 1) the Chinese government, and 2), the Chinese people. No other government would have had the ability, resolve or courage to act so decisively or quickly. Within two weeks of seeing an unknown virus, Chinese scientists had isolated and published the virus' genetic sequence needed to make a vaccine! While China's reaction to SARS in 2003 was slower, the nation has certainly learned a lot since then – which is not surprising. Never before in history has there been such a large nation with so many people, and so many lives have improved so quickly. With no historical precedent, China must of course learn as it goes. But this present challenge underscores that China is using what it learns to help not only China but the rest of the world as well.

But what really moves me is the Chinese people's response to the virus. While the rest of the world is panicking (and I don't blame them), Chinese are stoically dealing with the situation. People the world over are amazed at media reports of how, even in the virus' epicenter of Wuhan, people shout from windows to people on the streets, "Jiāyóu! (加油！)" "Press forward!" My WeChat messages from Chinese friends are not fearful but positive. "Our government and our people will overcome this!" one said, and another wrote, "We are careful but not afraid!"

They remind me of the Chinese that an English author, Ann MacKenzie Grieves, encountered when she lived in Amoy in the 1920s. She felt Chinese, "immense vitality the moment I first set foot in Amoy... It was a life, at times, frightening in its force. It needed to be strong to survive such human miseries as it daily faced."

This frighteningly powerful Chinese spirit is why China has survived not just centuries but millennia, and today it will carry not just

China but the rest of the world through this present crisis.

Our hearts are with all of you, and we hope to see you all again soon! Jiāyóu !

Bill Brown

Quotes from Lao Pan:

老潘金句:

On the one hand, I should feel lucky, as many foreigners are scrambling frantically to leave. Yet on the other hand, I regret that I am not there in China to help. Had I realized the situation was so dire, I would have preferred to stay.

对比许多争相离开这片土地的在华外籍人士，我应该感到幸运，但我也后悔此时未能在中国同大家并肩作战。如果我能更早意识到事态的严重性，我更希望此时是身在中国。

This frighteningly powerful Chinese spirit is why China has survived not just centuries but millennia, and today it will carry not just China but the rest of the world through this present crisis.

这种强大的中国精神也正是中华文明得以流传几千年而不是短短几个世纪，昙花一现的原因，到了今天，它将引领中国及全世界穿越当下这场危机……

我更希望此时身在中国……

亲爱的中国朋友们：

就在新型冠状病毒的危急性为世界所知晓的前几天，我回到了美国去探望我90岁高龄的岳母。对比许多争相离开这片土地的在华外籍人士，我应该感到幸运，但我也后悔此时未能在中国同大家并肩作战。如果我能更早意识到事态的严重性，我更希望此时是身在中国。

对于此次疫情发生在中国而非别的地方，我相信世界应该感到幸运。对此理由如下：1. 中国政府；2. 中国人民。因为没有其他任何一个政府有这样的能力、决心和勇气，能如此果断迅速地采取行动。在发现新型冠状病毒的两周内，中国的科学家就已成功地将病毒进行分离，并公布了它的基因序列用以疫苗的研制。尽管2003年时，中国政府对非典的反应相对滞后，但这个国家也获得了许多应对公共卫生事件的经验。这并不令人惊讶。回望历史，从未出现过一个拥有如此众多人口的大国，且该国民众的生活水平能如此迅速地得以提升。既然史无前例，中国当然是在自身的发展中不断学习。而当下的挑战也正强调了这一事实——中国以往的经验不仅帮助了本国此次疫情的抗击，也给其他国家提供了借鉴。

但真正打动我的是中国人民对疫情的响应。此时，尽管外界心存恐慌（我并无指责之意），但中国人民却展现了极具坚忍的一面。当世界通过媒体听到身处疫情中心的武汉人民透过窗户对街上的同胞大喊“加油”时，深为震惊！而从中国朋友发来的微信中，我感受到的也非恐惧，而是满满的正能量。其中一位用微信说道：“我们的政府和人民定会赢取这场战役！”另一位则写道：“我们并非害怕只是谨慎待之！”

他们让我想起了英国作家安·麦肯齐·格里夫斯（Ann Mackenzie Grieves）笔下的中国人。那时是 19 世纪 20 年代，她正居住在厦门。一到厦门，她就感受到中国人“充满着巨大的生命力……那种生命力有时所折射的力量甚至令人震撼。要在日复一日的苦难中生存下来，除了坚强别无选择”。

这种强大的中国精神也正是中华文明得以流传几千年，而不是短短几个世纪昙花一现的原因，到了今天，它将引领中国及全世界穿越当下这场危机……

我们的心与你们同在，希望能尽快再次见到大家！加油！

潘维廉

2020 年 1 月 31 日

扫一扫

看老潘读信视频

Flying Home to the Safest Country on the Planet!

March 1, 2020

Dear Chinese friends,

I hope that your online studies are going well, so that together you and I can do an even better job of telling China's Story to the world – and this year we certainly have two great stories to tell the world.

First, of course, is how China so efficiently handled this virus. But to me, of more importance long term is that this year, 2020, is the year that China ends absolute poverty – something that no nation has ever even attempted, much less succeeded at. Amazing!

I feel so fortunate to live in this day and age, in China, and to witness such achievements. But today, I'd like to share the good news that Sue and I are flying home to Xiamen!

A hearty thanks to Xiamen Airlines for our new tickets from Los Angeles to Xiamen. Given how well China has managed the virus, and the rest of the world is mismanaging it, Sue and I are confident that China is indeed the safest place on the planet.

But I'm also thankful that this trip from Los Angeles to Xiamen will be about 60 hours faster than our first one in 1988, when we spent over 50 hours on 3 planes from Los Angeles to Hong Kong, and then we rode a boat for 18 hours up the coast to Xiamen.

Today, it's only 12 or 13 hours from Los Angeles to Xiamen. I'm not sure why one direction is faster than the other; maybe coming home is downhill?

It is amazing that Xiamen Airlines is continuing weekly flights between Los Angeles and Xiamen because the U.S. isn't even letting Chinese into the country, so it loses money on every flight.

But Xiamen Airlines, like all of China, is making sacrifices because Xiamen Airlines puts passengers first – which is probably why it has also been one of the most profitable airlines in history.

China's first privately-owned airlines, Xiamen Air has not only set records in China for the most consecutive quarters and years to make profits, it has also been honored as China's Best Airlines for 19 consecutive years.

But most importantly to me, Xiamen Air is like family because 1) it is based in my home of Xiamen, and 2) many of the staff and pilots have been my MBA students. Not many airlines send pilots to MBA programs, but this is probably why Xiamen Air has excelled in both passenger satisfaction and profits.

So thank you Xiamen Airlines for flying us home – but is it safe to return to China?

A Xiamen University official just suggested we stay in the U.S. until we're sure it is safe to return. We do appreciate his concern, but

Sue and I both think it is far safer in China than in any other country!

It is a miracle to me that the most populous nation on the planet has been able to contain such a contagious virus so thoroughly. As I've said, the world is lucky this happened in China and nowhere else because only the Chinese government and people have the resolve and courage to tackle this so resolutely – and the international news over the past few days' proves me right.

Western media has complained that China delayed a few days before taking action, but China waited only long enough to be sure it was a real threat. As I've told friends, you don't shout fire in a crowded room, and you don't panic 1.4 billion people unless you're certain there is a threat. But how is the rest of the world handling the virus?

While the Western media complains about China's delay of a few days, the rest of the world has had two entire months to prepare, yet they are still arguing over whether there is really a threat, and if so, how to respond. Just this morning, the U.S. attorney general told Americans that they do not need masks – that these are only needed by health professionals.

Stock markets kept rising until a week ago because no one believed it was really serious. Now the market has crashed because they could no longer pretend there was no problem, and many health officials are even saying there is no hope of containing the virus. But of course they still criticize how China has handled it, even though China is the only nation that has actually tackled the problem in a scientific and professional manner.

Years ago, Akio Morita, co-founder of Sony, said that Americans look ahead 10 minutes but Japanese 10 years. I like to add to that, saying Chinese look ahead for centuries! But with this virus, world leaders are not looking ahead at all but acting like children who think they can hide by covering their own eyes.

That the most populous nation on earth has done so well in containing this virus is little short of a miracle – but after 3 decades in China, it does not surprise me at all. I am surprised, though, by the utterly confused response from the rest of the world. I hope they will take some lessons from China.

Some have asked me: "What if you get the virus in China?" Well, if I do end up getting it, I'd rather get it in China than anywhere else because Chinese have shown they can handle it.

Thank you China! See you soon!

Bill Brown

Quote from Lao Pan:

老潘金句：

That spark of creativity is only dampened, not extinguished, and an opportunity or challenge can rekindle it. But if we fail to build a foundation in our youth, it is not likely we'll ever build one later.

创意的火花只会受到抑制，而不是熄灭，一个机会或挑战就可以重新点燃它。但如果我们不能在青年时代打下根基，日后将难以建立根基。

A cartoon drawn by Bill, 1988
老潘手绘漫画（1988 年）

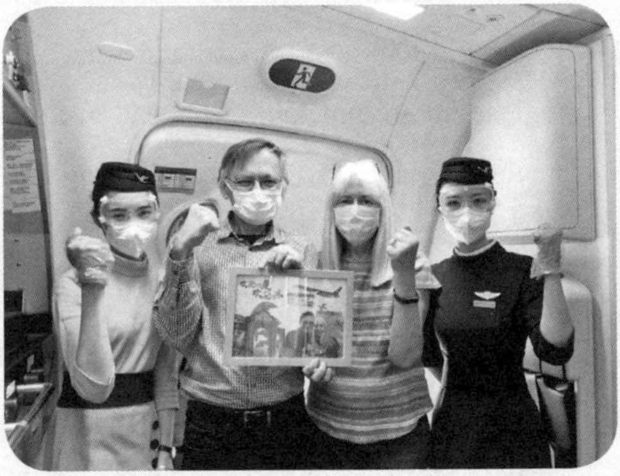

Bill with Susan flying back to China, 2020
老潘和苏在飞回中国的飞机上（2020 年）

Bill under quarantine, 2020
老潘下飞机后接受“隔离”（2020 年）

从美国飞行回家，回到地球上那个最安全的国家！

亲爱的中国朋友们：

希望线上教育进展顺利，这样的话，我们就可以更好地向世界讲述中国故事——今年我们有两个伟大的故事要向世界讲述。

当然，首先要讲述的是中国为何能如此有效应对新型冠状病毒的故事。而另一个故事，在我看来更具重要的长期意义，它就是中国在今年（即2020年）将彻底脱贫——这种尝试在世界尚属首次，更别提要获得成功有多难。这太令人震撼了！

能在这个时代的中国生活，见证如此伟大的成就，我感到非常幸运。而现在，我迫不及待想告诉大家的是，我要回家，回到厦门来了！

衷心感谢厦门航空（简称“厦航”）为我们改签成从洛杉矶直飞厦门！纵观世界，中国“战疫”表现突出，我和苏珊充分相信中国是目前世界上最安全的地方。

比起1988年我们第一次到厦门用的时间，这趟洛杉矶到厦门的旅程缩短了大约60个小时，对此我心存感激。要知道，1988年时我们可是花了五十几个小时，转机两次，才从洛杉矶抵达香港，然后再沿着海岸线花18个小时乘渡轮北上辗转到厦门。

而今天，只需要十二三个小时。我为何会感到飞回厦门的航班更快一些？这可能是我归心似箭吧！

虽然美国方面目前禁止中国公民入境，而厦航每周仍有洛杉矶—厦门的直飞服务，这令我感到十分惊讶，因为每次飞行都意味着厦航在赔钱。

正如它的国家那样，厦航也在牺牲自己的利益，将乘客的利益放于第一位——这可能解释了厦航为什么也是历史上最赚钱的航空公司之一。

作为中国首家获得民航局批准成立的民营航空运输企业，它不仅在中国创下了最长连续季度和年度的盈利记录，还连续多年被评为中国“最佳航空公司”。

对我而言，最重要的是，它就像家。这不仅因为它总部设在我的家乡厦门，还因为那里有不少管理人员和飞行人员是我MBA项目的学生。将飞行员送去学习MBA项目可不常见，但这也许是厦航能在客户满意度和盈利能力上实现双优的原因。

因此，谢谢厦航将我们接回家——但是，回中国安全吗？

厦门大学的一位领导建议等我们确定中国无事了才回来。我们非常感谢他的关心，但我和苏珊一致认为中国比其他国家都安全得多！

中国人口如此众多，它却能够如此彻底地控制传染性这样强的病毒，在我看来就是奇迹。正像我之前所说，世界应该庆幸疫情最初暴发在中国而不是别的地方，因为只有中国政府和人民才有这样的决心和勇气能如此坚决地应对——我的这个看法在近几日也得到了国际舆论的佐证。

西方媒体抱怨中国没有更早采取行动，但中国所“耽误”的时间仅是确定疫情性质必需的时间。我和朋友说，不要在拥挤的房间大喊“着火”，即在问题完全确认前，不要以此给这 14 亿人民制造恐慌。而世界其他国家是如何应对病毒的呢？

西方媒体抱怨中国拖延了几天才采取行动，但其他国家有整整两个月的时间准备，至今却仍在争论病毒是否具备威胁力，如果真有威胁，又该怎样应对的阶段上。就在今天早上，美国司法部长宣称普通民众不需要佩戴口罩——只有医务人员才需要。

没人相信疫情会如此严重，直到一周前美国股市才开始下跌。而现在，人们不得不面对疫情，甚至有医务官员声称控制病毒无望，导致美国股市全线受挫。当然，他们仍旧指责中国的应对方式，然而中国是唯一一个真正利用科学、专业的方式应对这个问题的国家。

许多年前，索尼的联合创始人盛田昭夫（Akio Morita）说，美国人会提前考虑 10 分钟后的事情，日本人是 10 年后的事情。我想加上一句，中国人会提前考虑几百年后的事情。在这次疫情肆虐的情况下，世界许多领导人不再朝前看，而是像个孩童，认为捂上自己的眼睛别人就看不到了。

世界上人口最多的国家，在控制病毒传播方面表现如此之好，无异于奇迹——但在中国生活了 30 年后，我认为这是情理之中的事。我惊讶的是世界其他一些国家目前对于病毒的反应，希望他们能从中国借鉴一些经验。

有些人问我："如果你在中国感染上了病毒该怎么办？"嗯，如果真是命该如此，我宁愿那时身在中国，因为中国人民已显示出完全可以应对病毒的能力。

谢谢中国！希望很快能再见！

潘维廉

2020年3月1日

Quotes from Lao Pan:

老潘金句：

Years ago, Akio Morita, co-founder of Sony, said that Americans look ahead 10 minutes but Japanese 10 years. I like to add to that, saying Chinese look ahead for centuries!

许多年前，索尼的联合创始人盛田昭夫说，美国人会提前考虑10分钟后的事情，日本是10年后的事情。我想加上一句，中国人会提前考虑几百年后的事情。

It is a miracle to me that the most populous nation on the planet has been able to contain such a contagious virus so thoroughly.

中国人口如此众多，它却能够如此彻底地控制传染性这样强的病毒，在我看来就是奇迹。

扫一扫

看老潘读信视频

Virus Lesson from China

March 17, 2020

Dear Chinese friends,

Today I'd like to share with you some ideas about important life lessons we can learn from China's response to the coronavirus. And at the end, I'd like to share some encouraging insights from foreigners who lived in China over a century ago.

If you understand the spirit of ancient China, and why foreigners had such great respect for both China's government and people, you'll also understand why Chinese today are able to tackle such formidable foes as poverty, hunger, and the borderless battle with the coronavirus.

An American asked his friend, "Did you quit shaking hands because of the virus?"

"No," he said, "I quit because everyone is out of toilet paper."

I'm glad people still have a sense of humor! But what is not at all funny is that some of the wealthiest nations not only lack toilet paper but also still don't have virus test kits even 10 weeks after China shared the virus' genome with the world. Why on earth are these nations so unprepared?

Even a little logic should have suggested the virus was coming, but they not only did not prepare but also went to great lengths to explain why their "democracies" could not take China's lead.

Even a week ago, Western media was writing of how China's draconian measures such as quarantines and restrictions on travel deprived people of their basic rights of freedom of movement. But fast forward to today and the news is trumpeting that the epidemic is now a pandemic and governments are falling over themselves to take many of China's measures.

Of course, places like San Francisco are careful to avoid the word "quarantine," which violates people's inalienable right of movement, but they did order people to "shelter in place," which may sound kinder and more "democratic" but violations are a "misdemeanor punishable by fine, imprisonment, or both."

Sounds to me like, however you word it, it is still restricting people's movement – and these restrictions are needed, so why pretend they are not?

The only logical reason that nations could spend months criticizing China while doing nothing themselves is that they naively felt they were in no danger. But this is understandable, given our immersion today in an artificial world of social media. We are bombarded daily with so much bad news that tragedies afar off are no more real than a reality TV show or a movie.

It also seems that people living in comfort in the wealthier nations have a sense of entitlement, and believe that their wealth will continue to shield them from some far-off virus even as for decades their wealth and militaries have insulated them from the wars, crimes and political unrest that kill tens of millions every year in poor nations.

As the younger President Bush once declared, "Nothing will change our American way of life!" But it appears the coronavirus never got Mr. Bush's message.

In 1990, I thought it ironic that a Japanese strategist, Kenichi Ohmae, would write a book entitled, *The Borderless World*. He claimed that trade was open and free for all nations, even though his own home of Japan has some of the most rigid cultural, political and economic barriers in the world.

Even today, trade is not borderless, and probably never will be – but the coronavirus truly knows no borders. Rich and poor alike fall before it – though the elderly, the weak and the poor fall hardest.

Fortunately for the world, China acted immediately, without excuse or apology or mincing words, to protect peoples' most fundamental right – the right to life.

And only yesterday, China began testing a vaccine and has already promised that, if successful, they will share it freely with the world.

And even as the Chinese government resolutely sacrificed its economy to tackle the problem head-on, the Chinese people also rose to the occasion and cooperated because, quite frankly, they well know they are mortal.

Chinese value comfort and convenience as much as any other

people, but they remember all too vividly the poverty and sickness that haunted their nation only decades earlier. Chinese agree with their government that if they lose that most fundamental right of life, all other rights are useless.

And to preserve that most precious gift of life, Chinese have always been able to tighten their belt and endure hardships like no other people in history.

In closing, I will share foreigners' comments about China and Chinese from some of my hundreds of 19th and 20th century books. You will be as astonished as I was at how much the Westerners admired the Chinese nation and people over the centuries.

And if you understand the spirit of China through the ages, then you'll also understand how and why the world's most populous nation today dared to tackle and defeat this epidemic head-on.

So now some quotes from foreigners who lived in 19th and 20th century China.

Mackenzie Grieves, an English lady who lived in Xiamen in 1920s, wrote,

> "In this, our first year in China, an astonished excitement possessed us... I had felt the impact of this immense vitality the moment I first set foot in Amoy (Xiamen). I came upon it by no rational process, no social studies. I met the tide of lusty and abundant life full in the face, with all its primitive urges undiluted. It was a life, at times, frightening in its force. It needed to be strong to survive such human miseries as it

daily faced."

Talman, an Amoy missionary from 1916 to 1930, she wrote in her unpublished memoirs,

> "To their conditions the Chinese have developed responses – frugality (nothing is wasted in China), patience, industriousness, sense of humour – a philosophical approach to the realities of life. These are the qualities that make the Chinese tough and persevering and give them the will to love and fight against poverty. The Chinese enjoy few luxuries in material things. They are not an acquisitive society. The people yearn more for peace and stability – a climate for work rather than affluence or wealth for the sake of pleasure. There is a great difference in the psychology of Eastern and Western society."

And now a Chinese at Fukien Christian University in 1926 wrote about the right attitude to life. He said,

> "Fukien (Fujian) has taught me how to live. Material things can be acquired anywhere in this material world, but an attitude to life can only be mastered in the right environment. Fujian provided such an environment for me."

I too am proud of the way Fujian reared me.

John Macgowan, a Scottish missionary in Xiamen, wrote in 1907 in one of his main books about China that Chinese were like "Oriental Spartans." He said,

"Take the matter of pain. The Chinese bears it with the composure of a saint. The heroic never seems to come out so grandly in him, as when he is bearing some awful suffering that only a martyr could endure.

"...It is this same absence of nerves that enables the Chinese to bear suffering of any kind with a patience and fortitude that is perfectly Spartan. He will live from one year's end to another on food that seems utterly inadequate for human use; he will slave at the severest toil, with no Sunday to break its wearisome monotony, and no change to give the mind rest; ...with a sturdy tread and with a meditative mystic look on his face, that reminds one of those images of Buddha that one sees so frequently in the Chinese monasteries or temples... The staying power of the Chinese seems unlimited. The strong, square frames with which nature has endowed them are models of strength."

He also wrote in 1907 about the adaptable Chinese:

"The strength of the Chinaman lies in his power to adapt himself to the circumstances in which he may be situated. Place him in a northern climate where the sun's rays have lost their fire, and where the snow falls thickly and the ice lays its wintry hand upon the forces of nature, and he will thrive as though he had descended from an ancestry that had always lived in a frozen region. Transport him to the torrid zone, where the sun is a great ball of molten flame, where the air is as hot as though it had crossed a volcano, and where the one thought is how to get cool in this intolerable maddening heat, and he will move about with an ease and a comfort just as if a sultry climate was the very thing that his system demanded.

"He is so cosmopolitan in his nature that it seems to be a matter of indifference where he may be or what his environment. He will travel along lofty peaks, where the snows of successive winters lie unmelted, or he will sleep in a grass hut where the fever-bearing mosquitoes will feast upon him the livelong night to the sound of their own music, and he will emerge from it next morning with a face that shows that the clouds of Anopheles have left him a victor on the field. He will descend into the sultry tin mines of Siam, and at night he will stretch himself on the hard, uneven ground, with a clod for his pillow, and he will rise as refreshed as though he had slept on a bed of down."

He also wrote of China's timeless people:

"One advantage the Celestial [or the Chinese] has over the Occidental, the westerner, is what may be called his absence of nerves. The rush and race and competition of the West have never yet touched the East. The Orient is sober and measured, and never in a hurry. An Englishman, were all other signs wanting, could easily be distinguished, as he walks along the road, by his rapid stride, the jerky movements of his arms, and the nervous poise of his head, and all so different from the unemotional crowd around him, who seem to think that they have an eternity before them in which to finish their walk, and so they need not hurry."

Mary Gamewell in 1919 wrote about the ancient people of the future. She said,

"China is not like ancient Egypt, whose greatness has departed though she still lives on. China is a vital force whose largest possibilities of development lie before her and not behind her. A new fresh life is beginning to course through the nation's veins..."

In Fuzhou in 1861, 160 years ago, the scottish missionary Maclay wrote about "eternal China":

"It is a noteworthy fact that of all those ancient empires founded immediately subsequent to the deluge China alone remains. The Assyrians, Egyptians, and, in later times, the Grecians, have severally attained to a comparatively high degree of intelligence and refinement; but their star soon culminated and sank into utter darkness. China, however, has never been wrecked, her civilization has never retrograded; paradoxical though it seems, her star has remained in its zenith for at least three thousand years. Through all this long lapse of centuries the Chinese have kept up, fairly and steadily, to their original civilization; and today they present all the essential elements of those social, literary, and political traits which characterized them in those early epochs when the Assyrians built their magnificent cities, the Egyptians developed their subtle theory of the metempsychosis, or the Greeks were thundering at the gates of Troy.

"The permanence of Chinese institutions is worthy of notice in this connection. It is a significant and singular fact that, from the earliest period of their authentic history to the present time, the Chinese have preserved intact and inviolate every important feature and principle of their government and civilization. The successive irruptions of northern barbarians have neither abrogated nor essentially modified Chinese institutions. The conquering races who have overrun those fertile plains have stood abashed in the presence of a superior civilization; and after subduing the empire, they have invariably adopted its government, laws, civilization, and language."

If the above insights on China don't make you proud and confident, nothing will!

Àipīn cáihuì yíng!

Jiāyóu, China!

Bill Brown

Bill with Sue celebrating the Chinese New Year, 2020
老潘和苏在美国唐人街过新年（2020 年）

Bill “snapping up” toilet paper，2020
老潘“抢购”厕纸（2020 年）

Bill with statues wearing masks, 2020
戴口罩的“雕像”（2020 年）

中国给世界的抗疫经验

亲爱的中国朋友们：

今天想和大家分享的是，中国抗击新冠病毒带给世界的经验。文末我将附上百年前侨居中国的外国人士对中国的一些鼓舞人心的看法。

如果你能了解古代中国的精神，明白外国人曾对中国政府及其人民如此尊重的原因，你就能找到今天中国能够应对贫穷、饥饿，与新冠病毒进行无国界斗争的原因。

一位美国人问他的朋友："你是不是因为害怕病毒而不与人握手？"

他回答道："不，我不和别人握手是因为大家都没有卫生纸了。"

很高兴人们的幽默感不减当初！但一些最富裕的国家不仅缺少卫生纸，而且在中国公开病毒基因组序列10周后，仍然缺少病毒检测试剂盒，这就一点也不好笑了。

怎么会这样措手不及呢？

但凡有点逻辑就知道病毒马上要来了。但他们不仅毫无准备，反倒不遗余力地解释"民主国家"不能"跟风"中国的原因。

就在一周前，西方媒体还在报道，中国政府采取隔离、限制旅行等严厉措施剥夺人们基本行动自由权。但仅仅几天后，在各大媒体上见到的却是这一传染病已成为全球性流行病，各国政府正忙不迭地大量借鉴“中国措施”救治病人的消息。

当然，像旧金山这样的地方会谨慎使用“隔离”这个词，因为该词侵犯了人们不可剥夺的行动权，但是他们命令人们“就地避难”。这个词听上去可能更亲切、“民主”，而“侵犯”意味着行为不当，是种轻罪，可处以“罚款或监禁，或者罚款加监禁”的惩罚。

不过，在我看来，无论怎样称呼，人们的行动都受到了限制——既然限制是必要的，为何要不承认呢？

这些国家花两个月的时间批评中国，自己却无所作为，对此唯一行得通的解释是，他们天真地认为自己会免于危险。这是可以理解的，因为我们正沉浸在一个人造的社交媒体世界里，每天处在坏消息的狂轰滥炸下，远方上演的悲剧不过是电视真人秀或电影罢了。

此外，那些富裕国家过着舒适日子的人们似乎有一种权利意识，认为自身的财富将一如既往地使他们免受远方某种病毒的侵害。尽管几十年来，这些让他们免于卷入战争、遭遇犯罪以及经历政治动荡的财富和军队，每年在一些贫穷落后的国家造成了数千万人的死亡。

小布什总统曾宣称：“没有什么能够改变美国人民的生活方式！”但新冠病毒似乎从未领会其心意。

1990年，日本战略家大前研一（Kenichi Ohmae）出版了《无国界的世界》，颇为讽刺的是，在书里他声称贸易对所有国家都是开放自由的，但他的家乡日本有着世界上最僵化的文化、政治和经济壁垒。

即使到今天，贸易也不是没有国界，也许还将永远存在——但新冠病毒确实没有国界意识。无论贫富都会受到它的侵袭——年老、体弱、贫穷之人是它主要的攻击对象。

值得庆幸的是，中国政府不找借口、不作道歉，也不含糊其辞，迅速反应保障民众最基本的权利——生命权。

就在昨天（3 月 16 日），中国开始进行新冠疫苗临床试验，并承诺疫苗如证实有效，将与世界免费分享。

当中国政府毅然牺牲本国经济直面疫情时，它的全体人民也携手合作，成功应付这一困难局面。坦率地说，他们深知自己不是永生之躯。

和他国人民一样，中国人民也重视生活的舒适和便利，但对于几十年前让国家陷入困境的贫穷和弊病，他们记忆犹新。失去最基本的生命权，其他所有权利都是毫无价值，在这一点上中国人民和他们的政府持相同看法。

为了保存这份最为珍贵的生命礼物，中华民族总是能够勒紧腰带、忍受苦难，这是其他民族未能做到的。

最后，我将分享几位外国人士对中国以及中国人的看法，这些都摘自我收藏的数百本出版于 19 世纪和 20 世纪的藏书中。在了解几个世纪以来西方人对中国以及中国人的钦佩之情后，你一定会同我读到时一样感到惊讶。

如果能了解中国历代的精神，你也将了解这个世界人口最多的国家敢于正面解决和战胜这一流行病的原因和方式。

以下引文出自 19 和 20 世纪在中国生活的外国人之手。

麦肯齐·格里夫斯是一位英伦淑女，上世纪 20 年代生活在厦门。她写道：

> “在中国的第一年，我们异常激动……第一次踏上厦门的土地时，我就感受到巨大生命力带来的冲击。这种偶然发现不要理性分析，也不需要社会研究。那儿的生活充满生机、色彩斑斓，保留其一切原始冲动。这种生活不时还会发出惊人的能量。要在日复一日的苦难中生存下来，除了坚强别无选择。”

罗斯·塔尔曼（Rose Talman）从 1916 到 1930 年间在厦门传教。在其未公开的回忆录中，她写道：

> “在现实的生存环境下，中国人形成了自己的个性——节俭（在中国，没有一样东西被浪费）、忍耐、勤劳和幽默。这是中国人应对现实生活的一种达观的策略。也正是这些品质使得中国人坚韧不拔，富有与贫困抗争的意志。中国人鲜有追求奢侈的物质享受的，他们并非生活在一个物欲横流的社会。这个民族更加渴望和平与稳定——推崇劳作，而不是获得以享乐为目的的财富。东西方社会在心理上有着很大差别。”

接下来是一位曾就读于福建协和大学的中国人。他在 1926 年提到了对待生活的正确态度。他说：

> “福建教会了我如何去生活。在这个现实的世界里，物质的东西随处可取，但对待生活的态度只能在合适的环境中养成。福建给我提供了这样的一个环境。”

我也为福建养育我的方式感到自豪。

约翰·麦嘉湖（John Macgowan）是一位生活在厦门的苏格兰传教士，1907 年在他的一部谈论中国的重要作品中提到了中国人像东方斯巴达人。他说：

> “以对待痛苦为例，他们像圣人一般镇定、忍耐。他们身上没有轰轰烈烈的英雄气概，即使是正在承受着只有勇士才能担当的沉重苦难时……
>
> “……也正由于此，中国人富有耐心，能坚定地忍受各种痛苦。这种忍耐是彻头彻尾的斯巴达人式。一年中他们赖以生存的食物少得可怜，似乎完全不足以正常食用。他们任劳任怨，干着最辛苦的活儿，过着没有星期天的疲倦、单调的生活，大脑也没有时间得以休息片刻。但他们步伐坚定，面容神秘，且若有所思，不禁令人想起中国寺庙里常见的菩萨形象……中国人似乎有着无限的耐力。他们与生俱来的坚韧宽厚的心性正是力量的典范。”

同年，他还写道中国人强大的适应能力：

“中国人的长处在于他们拥有适应各种生存环境的能力。把他们丢在缺乏灼热阳光的北方，面对的是白雪皑皑、寒冰覆盖，但照样人丁兴旺，仿佛他们原就是住在冰天冻地的世界的远古居民。把他们丢到热带地区，头顶大火球般的太阳，呼吸着热得跟火山气体没有什么两样的空气，这时常人想的是找个清凉地躲避那令人无法容忍的热气，而中国人却能舒适闲散地四处走动，好像这酷热的天气正是他们的身体所需要的。

“中国人四海为家，天性如此。他们似乎不在意居住地方和环境的好坏。他们会去攀登冰雪常年覆盖的高耸山峰；他们也不介意在茅屋过夜，即使漫漫长夜被身带热病、嗡嗡作响的群蚊大快朵颐，依旧可以安然入睡，次日从茅草屋走出来时，还俨然一副胜利者的模样。他们深入暹罗闷热的锡矿劳作，到了晚上，头枕泥巴，睡在凹凸不平的硬地板上，但第二天起来时精神抖擞，就像前一晚睡在了羽绒床上。”

他还这样描述这些不受时间影响的中国人：

“不焦虑是中国人的优点。西方人做事急匆匆，竞争激烈，东方人并不为之所动。东方人冷静、从容，从不着急。英国人走路就很好辨认，即使没有别的标志，仅凭他们大步流星，双臂甩动急促，头部游移不定的动作就可以。这与他们周围那些面容平静的人大不相同，在后者看来，时间有的是，何必急匆匆。”

玛丽·甘威尔（Mary Gamewell）在1919年提到了这个未来的古老民族。她说：

“中国不像古埃及。尽管埃及依然存在，但她伟大的历史已经成为过去。中国是一个充满活力的国度，比起辉煌的过去，她的未来有更大的发展潜力。崭新的生命力正在这个国家的血管里奔流……”

1861年，也就是约160年前，苏格兰裔传教士麦利和（Maclay）在福州写道“中华文明经久不衰”：

“值得注意的是，在那些依靠洪水过后留下的充足水资源和肥沃土壤发迹的古代帝国中，中国是唯一续存至今的国家。亚述人、埃及人以及后来的希腊人都曾发展过相对高级的文明和修养，但只是盛极一时，文明的星星坠落在一片漆黑中。但是，中国从未遭受严重破坏，中华文明也未曾出现过倒退现象。这似乎有些反常，但中华文化确实已在至少3000年的时光里璀璨不已。在过去的数千年里，中国人一直在稳步延续最初的辉煌，将自身的社会、文学、政治等领域的重要特点保存至今，这些特点让中华文明在那个亚述人造着宏伟城市、埃及人创立灵魂转世的深奥理论、希腊人在特洛伊城门外叫置准备攻城略地的历史阶段展现出独特魅力。

“在这方面，颇值得关注的是中国社会风俗制度的持久生命力。一个意义重大而又惊人的事实是，从有正史记录以来，中原民族完好无损地保留了其国家治理方式和中华文明的所有重要特征、道德原则。来自北方的游牧民族持续不断地南下骚扰，也没能废除或根本性修改中原的风俗体制。马背上的游牧民族占领肥沃的平原后，在高度发展的中原文明前局促不安。因此，征服中原民族后，他们总会学习采纳中原的统治方式、法律制度、社会文明和语言体系。”

如果关于中国的以上观点不能让你感到自豪、充满自信，那就没什么可以做到了！爱拼才会赢！中国，加油！

潘维廉

2020年3月17日

Appendixes

附　录

Bill at the Seminar to Introduce the Publication of the *Stories of China Retold in English* Series, 2019

老潘在《用英语讲中国故事》丛书出版座谈会上（2019 年）

Bill at the Launch Ceremony for the First "Stories of China Retold in English" Event, 2020

老潘在首届"用英语讲中国故事"活动启动仪式上（2020 年）

扫一扫

看老潘读信视频

Speech at the Seminar to Introduce the Publication of the Stories of China Retold in English Series

April 21, 2019

I am delighted and honored today to share a few words about *Stories of China Retold In English* because this beautifully crafted collection of stories, which is certain to be an instant classic, serves two great purposes: 1) telling the world about China (Xi Jinping's desire for us all to 讲好中国故事); and 2) providing an exciting way to encourage foreigners to help Chinese master English!

Almost 20 years ago, when Xi Jinping was our Fujian governor, we discussed the problem that Chinese had learned much about the world but the world still knew far too little about China. So Xi Jinping said to me, "You've written about Xiamen, your second home; you should write about Quanzhou, your third home!" He suggested I start with Quanzhou because it was the start of the Maritime Silk Road – which gave Chairman Xi the idea for the modern Belt and Road Initiative.

I did write the Quanzhou book, and a dozen others, as well as develop English websites, and wrote and co-hosted over 400 TV episodes. Some Chinese say I am “Zhongguo Tong” (a China Hand), but I always reply that this is impossible. In a country this large, and changing so fast, not even a Chinese can be Zhongguo Tong! And, in fact, the more I learned about China, the more I realized how little I really knew. What really amazed me is that I discovered that China’s great accomplishments since I arrived in Xiamen University in 1988 were merely the latest of thousands of years of amazing accomplishments.

The ancient world witnessed the greatness of Rome, Egypt, Greece and China, but the only nation that has remained strong and vibrant for these thousands of years is China – and that is because Chinese have throughout history sought the Chinese Dream of peace and prosperity. Most importantly, as a former military man, is that China is the only great nation to have relied entirely on economic means to prosper. No war with distant nations, no colonialism, no nationalized opium sales and slavery – just pure economics and trade. So why are Chinese so different? CEO Hu Min’s books hold the answer to China’s success – past, present and future.

China has been great for thousands of years because it has had a solid Confucian educational and cultural foundation that has emphasized morality and responsibility to family and nation, and peaceful coexistence. Even the celebrated *Art of War* views war as the last resort. But though I’ve read many books about this great country, I’ve never seen so many fascinating stories, both ancient and modern, about the soul of China as I encountered while reading Prof. Hu Min’s

China Stories.

These masterfully selected stories cover everything from romance and love of family (the Cowherd and the Girl Weaver, for example) to love of country and patriotism – such as Yue Fei, a military hero who 1000 years ago, as a youth, had his mother tattoo on his back his lifelong motto, "Serve the country with supreme loyalty." There's also the story of "The Masterpiece of a Humiliated Master," about Sima Qian, who lived 2200 years ago, and the amazing story of Lin Zexu, who tried to end the West's opium trade. These stories also tell how paper, pen and ink and inkstick were invented.

As a former military person, I loved the story of how Mozi saved the State of Song by emphasizing "mutual love and restraint of strife," thus avoiding a war, and reinforcing Chinese love of peaceful coexistence. But other stories of ancient and modern martyrs show that the peace-loving Chinese are also heroic and fearless warriors when their nation is threatened.

I also liked the modern tales showing how Chinese braved the tundra to build the world's highest railway in Tibet, or worked the oil fields of N.E. China, developed hybrid rice to alleviate poverty, or worked around the clock to get their first manned rocket into space.

I also appreciated the story, "Running Like the Wind," about how Chinese lives have been changed by bullet trains – a miracle I've witnessed myself over the past few decades. In 1994, it took me 10 days to drive from Xiamen to Beijing. Today, you can take a train from Hong Kong clear across the country to Beijing in only about 9 hours!

The diversity of Prof. Hu Min's stories is astonishing. The way in which the stories have been selected, edited and organized is as much of a masterpiece as the tales they relate. It is impossible to read these stories and not marvel at the rich culture and character that have allowed China, of all ancient nations, to remain vibrant to this day. And China continues to this day to engage in historically unprecedented engineering feats to raise the living standard of people not just in China but in Africa and other areas of the world. I look forward to Prof. Hu Min's next collection of stories!

The second reason I love *Stories of China Retold in English* is that they are the perfect way to get foreigners to help you learn English!

One of the best ways to master English is to practice with native speakers, but it gets old hearing the same questions everyday from everyone: "Where are you from? Where do you work? How much do you earn? Do you like Chinese food?" I got so tired of these questions that I printed up cards to give my interrogators. On the cards were printed,

"Hi, I'm Bill Brown. I'm from the U.S. I teach at Xiamen University MBA Center. I earn enough money to pay taxes but not enough money to avoid taxes! Goodbye!"

But I suspect all foreigners in China are keen on learning more about this ancient and vast nation. If you can share some of China's history and culture in English to foreign visitors, you'll always have an enthusiastic audience. Therefore, English learners will no longer have to worry about a lack of materials to practise the language, and I will no longer be bothered by people wanting me to issue little cards for the same purpose.

On February 1st, I was astonished, and greatly honored, to receive a letter from Chairman Xi Jinping. Near the end of the letter, he wrote that he was confident that the best was yet ahead – that I'd write even better stories about China in the future. That was a great encouragement to me to continue my efforts to share China's Story. But my own China Stories are just those from one foreigner's perspective. CEO Hu Min's China Stories capture the heart and soul of China, ancient and modern, in a way that has never been done before. I cannot imagine a more rewarding way for Chinese to master English than by sharing with foreigners a collection that showcases thousands of years of Chinese culture and history.

And CEO Hu Min showed great foresight by producing China Stories in English for 3 stages of English learners, from elementary to intermediate to more advanced, with each level telling the stories from subtly different perspectives – many of which I'd never thought of before. And each story ends with an enlightening conclusion or insight about China and Chinese that helps us understand how the nation's rich past promises an even richer future – for both China and the world, thanks to the age-old Chinese Dream of prosperity and peaceful coexistence with neighbors near and far.

Thank you, CEO Hu Min, for an instant classic that I'm confident will kindle the imagination of the world – both Lǎowài and Lǎonèi. I hope the series will be used widely, both here in Chinese schools and overseas – especially in the hundreds of Confucian Institutes around the world that are helping to tell China's story well (讲好中国故事).

《用英语讲中国故事》丛书出版座谈会上的发言 *

2019 年 4 月 21 日

很高兴也很荣幸有此机会与大家分享《用英语讲中国故事》丛书。这套精心打磨的经典之作有两个目标：1. 向世界介绍中国（正如习近平总书记对我们的殷切期望）；2. 用有趣的方式鼓励外国人帮助中国人掌握英语。

大约在 20 年前，习近平总书记还在福建时，他就同我探讨过“中国十分了解世界，但世界对中国却不甚了解”的问题，而后他对我说道：“你已经写了你的第二故乡厦门，你也应该写写你的第三故乡泉州。”[①] 作为海上丝绸之路的起点，泉州也给习近平总书记提出“一带一路”倡议注入了灵感。

除了写泉州，我还写了十几本其它的书、搭建英语网站、参与编写 400 多集电视节目及参与主持活动。人们说我是“中国通”，但我却回答“这是不可能的”。在一个这么大的国家，即使土生土长的中国人都难以称之为“中国通”！事实上，当我愈加了解中国，我就愈加认识到我对它的了解之少。更令我震惊的是，1988 年我

① 此处引语为英译。

到厦门大学后亲见的中国伟大成就仅是这个国度几千年的宏伟篇章中最新的一个片段！

在古代，出现了罗马文明、埃及文明、希腊文明、中华文明，但数千年后，仅有中华文明依旧充满勃勃生机。这是因为中华民族历来追求和平发展的中国梦。作为一名退役军人，最令我惊奇的是中国是世界上唯一一个依靠经济方式走向繁荣的国家——没有发动远攻，没有对其他国家进行殖民主义，也未以国家的名义对外进行鸦片贸易和奴隶贩卖。中国为何如此不同呢？打开这套《用英语讲中国故事》丛书，你将找到中国一直以来繁荣的原因。

中国的富强延续了数千年，因为它有着坚实的儒家文化基石，强调对家国的道德和责任，以及和远邦近邻和平共处的理念，即使闻名于世的《孙子兵法》也认为战争是不得已而为之之举。尽管我读了许多有关这个伟大国家的书籍，但在《用英语讲中国故事》系列里我第一次读到如此多有趣的故事，它们从古至今有着宽广的时间跨度，向世界展示着最真实的中国。

这些精心挑选的故事题材广泛，从牛郎织女的浪漫爱情到精忠报国的岳飞，从成就史家之绝唱的司马迁到试图制止西方鸦片贸易的林则徐，还有笔墨纸砚的故事。

我十分喜爱墨子救宋的故事。墨子强调“兼爱非攻”，不主张发动武力，加深了中华民族对和平的热爱。但在古今烈士事迹中，热爱和平的中华儿女在民族生死攸关的时刻也是无畏的英雄。

我还喜欢阅读讲述现代发展的故事。中国人民攻克难关，在青藏高原的冻土上修建了世界上海拔最高的高铁线路；在中国东北开采了第一座油田；中国培育出的杂交水稻极大地解决了世界的粮食问题；它的科学家夜以继日地研发，成功发射了本国第一艘载人航天飞船。

我也很喜欢《像风一样的高铁》这则故事，它讲述了高铁对中国人民生活的巨大影响——这是一个我在过去几十年亲见的奇迹。1994年，从厦门到北京，我用了10天；今天，从香港出发一路北上抵达北京，只需大约9小时。

《用英语讲中国故事》这套丛书选材包罗万象，令人称赞。它的挑选、编辑和组织方式和故事本身一样，精益求精。当你读完这些故事，你会为其所展现的丰富文化，让中华文明永葆生机的品格而惊叹。今天，不仅在中国，在非洲以及世界其他地区，中国正史无前例地投入到当地工程建设中，大大改善了人们的生活水平。

我喜爱《用英语讲中国故事》丛书的第二个理由是，它们用完美的方式让外国人帮助中国朋友学习英语！

掌握英语的最好方式就是和以英语为母语的人进行交流、练习，但每天都是“你从哪儿来，你做什么工作，你赚多少，你喜爱中国食物吗”这类问题，也太无新意了，像我就不太爱回答这些问题。于是，我曾打印一些小卡片，每有“好奇者”我就递上一张，上面写着：“你好，我叫比尔·布朗，目前就职于厦门大学MBA中心，我的收入足够缴税，但未多到要避税！再见！”

但我相信，外国人其实非常渴望了解这个古老又宽广的国度。因此，如果能用英语向海外来访者分享中国的文化历史，你将收获大量听众。这样一来，英语学习者再也不用担心缺少练习英语的素材，我也不用在别人找我练习英语时发小卡片了。

今年2月1日，我收到了习近平总书记的来信，内心十分震惊，也深感荣幸。在信的结尾，他写道："我相信，你将会见证一个更加繁荣进步、幸福美好的中国，一个更多造福世界和人类的中国，你笔下的中国故事也一定会更精彩。"这是一份莫大的鼓励，鼓励我继续同世界分享中国故事。但我的中国故事仅是一个外国人的视角，胡敏教授贯穿古今的中国故事却用一种前所未有的方式抓住了中国故事的灵魂。通过英语向外国人讲述中国几千年的历史文化，这是我能想到的最好的英语学习方式。

胡敏教授为英语学习者从基础、提高、熟练三个级别编写了《用英语讲中国故事》，可谓极具远见。不同级别的故事有着不同的阐释角度，有许多角度甚至是我不曾想到的。故事结尾都配有令人启发的总结或对中华民族精神的深刻见解，这有助我们理解历久弥新的"繁荣与和平共处"的中国梦在现代中国和世界走向富强的过程中发挥的重要作用。

谢谢胡敏教授！我相信，这套丛书的出版将点燃世界的想象，不管你是老内还是老外！

期待这套丛书得到广泛应用，无论是在中国还是海外的学校，尤其是在遍布世界的几百所孔子学院。让我们一起"讲好中国故事"。

谢谢大家！

* 此为发言稿的修订版。

扫一扫

看老潘读信视频

Speech at the Launch Ceremony for the First "Stories of China Retold in English" Event

January 15, 2020

I am honored and delighted to speak a few words today – especially because I have been telling China's story in English since I moved to Mainland China in September, 1988.

From my first day in Xiamen, I realized that China was not at all like the country depicted by most Western media. I quickly found that Chinese were warm, hospitable people, and that they shared the same dream as people the world over: a peaceful, prosperous life for their children. So I immediately began writing letters to family and friends to help them see the real China, but in 1988 I would have never imagined that the world's most populous nation would actually achieve their China Dream.

In 1993, when China received the World Food Prize, former World Bank president Robert McNamara praised China's agricultural gains as "something of a miracle, a human development miracle that has gone largely unnoticed in the West."

The West may have ignored it but I did not. In 1994, my family and I drove 40,000 km around China, even into Mongolia and Tibet, to see China's changes first hand, and we were astonished at how China was fighting poverty in every corner of the country. But even so, I was skeptical when, in 2013, Xi Jinping said China could end absolute poverty by 2020! So in July, 2019, I again drove around China to see if such a goal was feasible by 2020. I was amazed to find that every corner of the country, from Mongolia in the North to Ningxia and Tibet in the West, was sharing in the China Dream.

In 1994, I was stranded 3 days even on a national highway after rains washed it out. Today, China has the world's most extensive highway and hi-speed train systems. Even in the remotest areas, farmers have concrete roads snaking through deep valleys to the very doorsteps of new homes the government helped them build. In the 90s, it cost me 450 USD and I waited 3 years for a telephone. Today, farmers in Tibet and Ningxia use cell phones for WeChat and to buy and sell online just like we do in the biggest cities.

I found that modern China, like ancient China, is great because it has both top-down farsighted leadership as well as bottom-up innovation and determination. In Mongolia, for example, I met a mother who earned enough from making traditional Mongolian snacks to send her daughter to my own Xiamen University. That is the China dream! Unfortunately, the rest of the world still does not understand that dream – which is why we need to tell China's stories in English.

In 2001, when Xi Jinping was governor of Fujian, he asked me to write more books to tell China's story to the world, so I've now written a dozen books. In January, 2019, I sent Xi Jinping my newest book, *Off the Wall*, which includes over 40 of my thousands of letters to friends and family. I never imagined that President Xi would write a letter in response! He said, "I believe you will witness even more flourishing progress, a happier and more beautiful China, a China that will make even greater contributions to the world and humanity, and your pen's China stories will certainly be even more wonderful."

I too am confident I will write more wonderful stories – but not because I'm a good writer, only because China's story is wonderful. But my stories aren't enough. For the world to understand China, you too must help tell China's Story – which is why I'm so excited about New Channel's *Stories of China Retold in English* series.

I was excited and honored when, two years ago, New Channel's CEO, Professor Hu Min, invited me to be one of the editors for his "Stories of China Retold in English" project. I immediately saw that this new series is very important for at least three reasons.

This series retells both classic and modern stories in a fresh light to reveal the ageless spirit and values of China that make it a vibrant and positive influence upon the world to this day. Confucius' ascent of Mount Tai, for example, exemplifies the unflagging determination that has made the China Dream possible. The story of the 1400-year-old Zhaozhou Bridge and the saga of the Hong Kong-Macao-Zhuhai Bridge reflect China's age-old creativity and resourcefulness. Su Wu's 19 years of tending sheep exemplifies Chinese age-old patriotism. The story of hybrid rice sheds light on how China has defeated poverty for 1/5 of the world's population. Each story is not only an adventure but also a window upon the soul of China!

What better way to improve English than sharing China's story in English with foreigners? I must confess that, as a foreigner myself, I sometimes get tired of Chinese using me as a target for English practice. I'm happy to help, but I get tired of the endless loop of identical questions. "Hello!" "How are you?" "Where are you from?" "Where do you work?" "How much do you earn?" In the early 90s, it so frustrated me that I finally started handing out cards to any bright-eyed English learner that zeroed in on me. The card read, "Hello, I'm Bill Brown. I'm from the U.S. I teach at Xiamen University. I earn enough money to pay taxes but not enough money to avoid taxes. Nice talking to you!"

But there is no doubt that any foreigner in China, including me, would be delighted to talk with Chinese who can share insights on this great nation's history, culture and modern life. Who could ever tire of such a conversation?

Finally, this series is not only helpful for Chinese learning English but also for foreigners learning Chinese. I am especially excited about the newer, bilingual classics such as *The Analects of Confucius* and *Sunzi: The Art of War*. Beautifully illustrated and bound, they have not only Chinese and English but also pinyin with tones, which I've found invaluable for foreigners seeking to master Chinese – like me! Learning Chinese, after all, was my initial goal in coming to China, and I still hope to master it someday – perhaps after I retire from teaching, though I hope to never retire from telling China's Story.

Although I was delighted to be asked to help edit this unique series, I was even more surprised, and honored, when I was asked to be the "Stories of China Retold in English" Ambassador. Professor Hu Min has shared their exciting plans for expanding this series, including new books with audio, interactive websites, forums, blogs, animated videos, contests and talent shows, and even cooperation with China Education Television.

I encourage you all to take advantage of these great opportunities to improve your English while at the same time sharing China's Story with the world. In my eyes, this is not only an opportunity and privilege but also a responsibility for all of us.

At the annual congress of 2019, Xi Jinping said he had Yuánfèn (fate) with Fujian, where he lived and worked for 17 and a half years. But in fact, you and I also have Yuánfèn with China! None of us chose where to be born, or when, and I could not imagine being alive in a more exciting period. What a privilege to witness China lift more people from poverty than any other nation in history – and through the Belt and Road Initiative, help dozens of other nations. Yet the fact remains that most of the world still does not really understand China. To open the world's eyes, we can't just rely upon the government and media. Each of us must do our part in telling China's Story. I am honored to be the Retelling China Stories in English Ambassador, but you are also Ambassadors – Ambassadors of China to the world.

So let's go into the world, and help the world to come to China.

Thank you!

首届“用英语讲中国故事”活动启动仪式上的致辞 *

2020 年 1 月 15 日

自 1988 年，我一直在用英语讲中国故事，因此，有此机会在此发言，我十分高兴，也倍感荣幸。

到厦门的第一天，我就发现中国根本不是大多西方媒体所描述的那样。不久后，我就被中国人民的热情好客所感染。正如其他国家的人们一样，中国人民也都怀有为子孙创造和平繁荣生活的梦想。所以，我迫不及待地写信告诉亲友，希望通过我的讲述，帮他们认识一个真实的中国。但在 1988 年，我不曾料到这个世界上人口最多的国家最终会实现它的中国梦。

1993 年中国收到了“世界粮食奖”，当时的世界银行行长罗伯特·麦克纳马拉（Robert McNamara）称赞中国的农业成就是“一项奇迹，一项被大多数西方国家忽视但推动了全人类发展的奇迹”。

西方世界对此也许并未重视，但我对此持截然相反的态度。1994 年，我和家人驱车 4 万公里环游中国，甚至到了中国边境的内蒙古和西藏，想亲眼一睹中国的变化。当时这片土地上的人们，为消除贫困所做的努力就深深地震撼着我。但即使如此，在 2013 年听到习主席提到中国将在 2020 年基本消除绝对贫困时，我仍有所怀疑。于是，2019 年 7 月我再次驾车环游中国，去看看这个目标在 2020 年是否能够实现。无论是在中国北部的内蒙古，还是从宁夏向西直抵西藏的路上，每一个角落都在向我展示着中国梦。

1994 年，我竟然在一条刚被大雨冲刷的国道上困了 3 天。而今天，中国拥有世界上最广阔的高速公路和高速铁路网，即使最偏远的山区也有了水泥马路，它们沿着深山峡谷曲折穿行，通到了政府为村民修建的新家门口。记得在上世纪 90 年代，我买一台电话机要花 450 美金并且得等上 3 年，但今天，即使新疆、宁夏等内陆西北省份的农民都能用手机聊微信、网购、做生意，他们享有的这份便利与身处大城市的我们并无二致。

无论现代中国还是古代中国，它的伟大不仅源自富有远见的上层领导，还源自民众的创新精神和坚韧决心。在内蒙古，我曾遇到一位靠着贩卖传统小吃供女儿到我所在的厦门大学求学的母亲！那就是中国梦！但还有许多其他国家的人们没有意识到这一点。这也正是我们需要用英语讲中国故事的原因。

2001 年，尚在福建任职的习近平主席鼓励我写更多向世界讲述中国故事的书籍；此后，我写了 10 余本书讲述中国的故事。2019 年 1 月，我给习主席寄去了我的新书《我不见外》，这是用我写给亲友的几千封信中的四十几封编撰而成。能收到日理万机的习主席的回复，真是令人喜出望外。他在信中说："我相信，你将会见证一个更加繁荣进步、幸福美好的中国，一个更多造福世界和人类的中国，你笔下的中国故事也一定会更精彩。"

我也相信我将会写出更多精彩的故事，但并非是我的文笔精彩，而是中国故事本就精彩！但我能讲的故事还是十分有限。要让世界更好地了解中国，诸位年轻的朋友，你们也将是重要的力量，也源于此，新航道国际教育集团“用英语讲中国故事”系列让我产生了强烈共鸣！

记得两年前，新航道国际教育集团董事长胡敏教授邀我加入“用英语讲中国故事”系列的编辑团队，当时我十分激动，也深觉荣幸。随后，我就领悟到这个新系列的重要性。我认为至少可以从以下三个方面去理解：

首先，它不仅包括许多经典传统故事，还不乏讲述现代中国飞速发展奇迹的故事，用全新的视角呈现出让中国立于世界民族之林，发挥强大、正面影响力背后的永恒精神价值。孔夫子登临泰山的故事体现了中国梦背后坚忍不拔的意志；1400 多年前修建赵州桥的故事和 21 世纪修建港珠澳大桥的壮举，展示了中华民族古已有之的创新精神和不竭才智；苏武风雪十九载身处苍凉北海之滨牧羊的故事，传递的是中华民族生生不息的爱国情怀；杂交水稻的故事，讲的是中华民族战胜贫困、解决世界 1/5 人口吃饭问题的伟大奇迹。它们是一个个开拓进取的故事，但更是向世界展示“中华之魂”的窗口。

第二，还有什么比用英语向外国人讲中国故事更能提高英语水平的方法呢？作为一名老外，我必须承认，对于别人仅将我作为练习英语的对象，我有时也深感烦恼。尽管我很乐意提供帮助，但对于诸如“你好，你过得怎么样，你从哪里来”这类无限循环的问题，也真心有些疲倦了。记得上世纪 90 年代初，我为此深感懊恼，于是，对任何闪烁着渴求的明亮眼神前来对我展开“集中攻势”的英语学习者，我开始分发自制的小卡片作回复。卡片上面写着：“你好，我叫比尔·布朗，来自美国。我在厦门大学执教，薪水足够支付税收，但还没多到要去逃税。很高兴能跟你说会儿话。”

事实上，包括我在内，所有待在中国的外国人，都非常乐意分享我们对这个伟大国家的历史文化和现代生活的看法。没有人会对这样的话题感到厌烦！

第三，双语系列不仅有助于中国人学习英语，对外国人学习汉语也大有帮助。像我本人对新航道的《论语》《孙子兵法》这类双语经典就非常感兴趣。它们有着精美的插画和装订，除了采用中英双语，还为经典原文配有带声调的拼音，这对像我这样致力精进汉语学习的外国人来说十分有益。学习汉语是我来中国的初衷，我仍希望将来能到达精通的水平。也许那时我已不再担任教学工作，但我希望能一直为“讲中国故事”贡献自己的力量。

比起应邀参加那套形式新颖的丛书的编辑工作，此次应邀成为“用英语讲中国故事”活动的形象大使，我除了兴奋，更多的是震撼和荣幸！因为我从胡敏教授口中得知，他们不仅将从制作音频书籍，搭建互动网站，运营论坛、微博，设计动画视频到才艺秀等方面对该系列进行打造，还会和中国教育电视台这类一流的媒体合作对它进行推广。

希望诸位青年朋友在向世界讲述中国故事的同时，也能提升自身的英语水平。在我看来，这不仅是一次令人深感荣幸的机会，更是一份催人奋进的责任。

在 2019 年的两会上，习近平主席谈到了他和福建的缘分，他在那里工作生活了 17 年。事实上，你我和中国也都有着无法割舍的缘分！我们无法选择出生的时间、地点，但我认为我正生活在一个最好的时代。在这里，我见证了历史上最大规模的扶贫计划得以实现，也见证了“一带一路”倡议让沿线数十个国家获得建设发展方面的帮助。能够亲历这些历史时刻，是多么荣耀的事情呀！然而，世界上大多数国家仍未真正了解中国。吸引世界的目光，不仅需要政府和媒体的力量，更需要我们每一个人尽力讲好中国故事。对于担任“用英语讲中国故事”活动形象大使一职，我深感荣幸，但这份荣幸更是属于诸位年轻的朋友——世界将从你们这儿听到最动人的中国故事。

让我们走向世界，也让世界走向中国吧！

谢谢！

* 此为发言稿的修订版。

后 记

2020 年初，新冠肺炎疫情暴发，在大量外国人士“逃离”中国时，老潘和妻子苏珊义无反顾地飞回中国，他们认为这是“世界上最安全的国家”。

老潘对中国的“信心”早在 33 年前刚来中国时就已经种下。那时，中国交通设施落后，即使在城市，常见的也不过是浩浩荡荡的自行车大军，冒着灰黑烟尘的公交车，甚至还有驮着货物的牲畜在街道上穿梭。但他耐心地等待，等待着隔山阻水的村子里有马路到门到户，色调单一的城市逐渐高楼林立、霓虹闪烁。

他两次环游中国，深入中国边远地区，亲自去看中国改革开放、脱贫攻坚等伟大举措带给普通百姓的改变；他关心中美教育，凭借自身跨文化生活、学习、教学的经历，对二者的利弊提出独到见解；他分析历史线索、客观依据，发现追求“和平繁荣”是文化差异巨大的中美两国人民共同的梦想。

正是源于对中国的这份信心和热爱，越来越多的中国故事从老潘笔下流淌而出，而这本书，也是其中一本。

写作的机缘是去年 2 月——中国新冠疫情的发展尚不明朗。彼时，老潘身在美国，对中国牵挂不已。他给好朋友胡敏教授发来邮件，向身处艰难时刻的中国朋友送上关心和慰问。他的文字情感真挚、逻辑清晰，字里行间传达出对“中国必胜”的信心，这感染了很多人。回到中国后，在胡敏教授的支持和鼓励下，老潘继续写作，聚焦中国青少年的成长，在新航道中国故事研究院的协助下整理出自己对于英语学习、中国故事、家庭教育、抗疫经验等话题的思考，以帮助中国青少年在后疫情时代更好地了解自己、了解中国、了解世界。

从新书编写到付梓出版，可以说，这本书也是对刚刚过去的2020年，这个充满魔幻和不确定年份的一种别样记录。回看书中文字，其中很多关于时局的判断和预测正得到验证，也展现出老潘作为一名学者的使命和担当。他将自己对中国的信心、对人类未来的期许都写进了这些信里，就如同一颗颗种子撒入青春的心灵，假以时日，定将长成参天大树，开出似锦繁花！

编者

2021年1月

图书在版编目（CIP）数据

老潘写给青少年的18封信：英汉对照 /（美）潘维廉著；李晶译．
—北京：外文出版社，2020.11
ISBN 978-7-119-12548-0

Ⅰ．①老…　Ⅱ．①潘…②李…　Ⅲ．①书信集—美国—现代
英、汉　Ⅳ．①I712.65

中国版本图书馆 CIP 数据核字（2020）第 247651 号

出版指导：胡开敏
责任编辑：于晓欧
特约编辑：张　灵　李　晶
装帧设计：李尘工作室
印制监制：秦　蒙

老潘写给青少年的18封信
潘维廉　著

出 版 人：胡开敏
出版发行：外文出版社有限责任公司
地　　址：中国北京西城区百万庄大街24号　　**邮政编码：**100037
网　　址：http://www.flp.com.cn　　**电子邮箱：**flp@cipg.org.cn
电　　话：008610-68320579（总编室）　008610-68996177（编辑部）
008610-68995852（发行部）　008610-68996183（投稿电话）
制　　版：北京汉风唐韵文化发展有限公司
印　　刷：荆州市翔羚印刷有限公司
经　　销：新华书店 / 外文书店
开　　本：889mm × 1194mm　1/32　**印　　张：**8.875　**字　　数：**207千字
装　　别：平装
版　　次：2021年8月第1版第2次印刷
书　　号：ISBN 978-7-119-12548-0
定　　价：38.00元